I0725215

TRICK OR TREAT

A September and Shadow Thriller, #9

by

AMY SHOJAI

Copyright

This is a work of fiction. Names, characters, places, and incidents either are the product of the author's imagination or are used fictitiously, and any resemblance to actual persons living or dead, business establishments, events, or locales is entirely coincidental.

FRIDAY,

October 25

Chapter One: KAI

Kai sniffed the hummock of dried manure, tail wagging as she relished the horsey aroma. Not fresh enough to indulge in a snack but well ripened for her next-favorite scent indulgence. She drove one shoulder to the ground, wriggling and grinding atop the mound. The dried dung fragmented as she writhed back and forth, all four paws to the sky, covering her short brown and white fur in delightful canine cologne.

Kai bounded to her feet and shook hard. Some moist portions stuck to fur on each cheek and shoulder, but the rest scattered in the hot breeze. She licked her lips and nose, to better collect the pungent remnants, as she enjoyed the indulgence. The horse paddock never failed to deliver delightful surprises.

Kai had slipped out of the fenced backyard early this morning, through the tiny excavation hidden by a wilting cascade of honeysuckle vines. Kai didn't know or care what people called the plants, only that bees loved the flowers, and buzzing kept people from discovering her escape route.

Not that the people in the house spent much time with her, besides filling her bowls. Sometimes, she played keep-away with the empty dish, just so the man would stay a bit longer, maybe touch Kai for just a moment. Sigh. A dog got lonely with nothing to do.

Kai tried barking, and sometimes even howling, hoping someone would spend time in the yard—if only to rest in one of the patio chairs while she sat nearby.

When nobody came, she began digging, and pocked the yard. That led to shrieks of *bad dog*, mostly from the woman. The woman liked the even green of the yard and the masses of flowers organized in regimented jumbles. Kai quickly learned what brought a person into the yard. Even yells of *bad dog* felt better than the emptiness of nobody there.

After spending much time in the fenced yard, Kai learned to silence her lonely cries, and that if she hid excavations behind the woman's flowers, holes got overlooked. Oh joy! The enticing adventures beyond the confines of the fence gave Kai the excitement her starved affections craved.

On the other side of the fence Kai met many other people. She visited horse friends in the paddock, and watched, enthralled, when people climbed atop the horses to ride around. She followed them, watching with curious excitement when they opened and closed fence gates, stacked straw bales, and sometimes traded horse rides for mounting noisy machines that mowed grassy fields.

Sometimes Lia, the girl with long yellow hair, spent time with Kai. Sometimes the people in the paddock shared lunches with Kai and taught her to do tricks for treats. They patted her brown rump or scratched her white chest. She'd wag so hard, she would nearly fall over. Kai wished one of the lunch-sharing people might stay with her all the time. She really liked what one of the men called *sammiches*. So Kai sneaked out as often as she could, yearning for the kind words and gentle touches.

Every time the tricks and sammich treats ended, though, people always led Kai back to the fenced yard. If the woman who lived there saw, she yelled *bad dog*, and the man who fed Kai made a sad face. That's how Kai understood she disappointed them. She whimpered at the thought. Kai wished she knew how to please them so they wouldn't call her *bad dog*. Kai wasn't sure what the words meant, only that the hurtful emotion behind the words made her tummy feel awful.

But for now, she forgot about shouted words that hurt her tummy. As the wonderful bouquet of horse poop enveloped her, Kai stood tall, ears pricked and tail gaily waving.

"Kai? Where is that dog? Bet it got out of the fence again."

The woman called again. Her voice made Kai's ears flatten to her head, and she tucked her tail, anticipating the bad-feeling words again. But without hesitation, Kai obeyed the summons.

She raced back to the corner of the fenced yard and dove into the hidden opening of the tunnel. Kai wriggled through and poked just her face out of the shielding greenery to better judge the woman's mood.

The woman walked across the stone patio, hands on hips,

glaring first one way then the other. White-blond hair crowned her head, and a long flowing silky robe swished around her thin body, brushing the grass. Her nose wrinkled when she saw disrupted dirt and an uprooted rosebush.

"Stupid dog! I try to be nice and adopt Lia's strays. Should have known better. Probably why your owner dumped you at her kennel and never came back. Dumb thing always digging my flowers, escaping to chase the horses, or…"

Kai knew better than to touch the flowers. Time after time Kai protected the flowers and chased away the over-sized pill-bug armadillo. But the creature still found a way to plow plants into ruins, and Kai got the blame.

If she came out now, the woman would scold and yell. She might even chuck something at Kai. Her aim never connected, but it made Kai feel even worse when she had to dodge objects.

Not like when Lia tossed toys for her to chase, not like that at all.

Kai yawned and stifled a concurrent whine of nerves. She decided to wait until the lady turned her back before creeping out. Sometimes Kai napped hidden away, so maybe the woman wouldn't figure out she'd left the yard. You could often fool people when they noticed only what they could see. Kai had learned people couldn't hear or smell all the details of the world around them. Sometimes she felt sorry for them.

The woman muttered, bending to gingerly retrieve the fallen rosebush. Quickly, Kai raced out of hiding, staying low to the ground. She whipped her tail side to side, smiled wide and licked her lips to show *no threat*. When Kai reached the lady's side, she threw herself on her back, baring her tummy to declare the woman's exalted status.

Kai's tainted fur rubbed against the woman's silky clothing.

The woman spun away, gasping in shock. "What an awful smell. What did you do? Get away from me, you nasty creature!" Her hands waved at Kai, the knuckles of one clipping Kai's jaw.

Yelping, Kai bounded upright, putting distance between herself and the windmill flailing. She looked around for escape.

The patio door stood ajar. Kai kicked up grass in her frantic race away. Paws galloped from the back yard, through the doorway, and into the coolness of the house. She'd been much younger the last time her paws touched indoor comfort—but they remembered and pelted down a narrow hallway to find a pale carpeted stairway.

Kai raced up to the second floor. Lia's scent lingered in the hallway. Kai followed to where Lia-scent smelled strongest, then she dove under the bed, shivering. She waited for whatever would happen next. Something horrible, probably.

A cat *meerowed*, startling her. Kai squinted and met the golden eyes of the creature sharing the crawl space. More than once, the housecat had slipped out into the backyard— the place that belonged to Kai—and she'd been happy to welcome the big gray and white feline until the woman came and carried Pippo the kitty away.

This place belonged to the cat, not to Kai, so she flinched away and averted her eyes. The harness Pippo wore smelled like the shrieking woman downstairs.

The creature stretched his neck, sniffing tentatively, and Kai's tail thumped with relief as she returned the nose-to-nose touch greeting. The cat rumbled with an odd sound, and moved closer, pushing against Kai's side in a comforting snuggle.

Downstairs, the woman yelled. "Dub Corazon, get rid of that dumb dog; get it out of my house, my yard, and my life, or I'll shoot the stinky thing myself!"

Kai loved car rides. She sat in the back seat of the worker's truck, poking her nose out the window as they drove away from the big house. She'd never had an adventure friend before. Kai's hackles rose; skin tingled with excited anticipation. What would happen? Maybe sammiches?

They slowed and turned off the smooth pavement, then bumped along a gravel drive. Kai barked, tail beating against the seat back. The driver pulled up next to a small wooden building and parked. He sighed, leaving the truck running, and turned halfway around in the seat. "Sorry, pup. But Mrs. Corazon wants you gone, and I already took in my limit of her unwanted critters."

The man climbed out of the driver's seat, and opened the rear door, leaving it wide as he grabbed the looped leash that encircled Kai's neck. "I ain't no dog killer, though, no matter what her majesty expects. This'll have to do."

He tugged on the leash. Kai didn't understand the words, but enjoyed the nice man's tone, free of angry emotion. Maybe he'd have a sammich? Kai happily leaped from the truck and sniffed the air. She detected water nearby, with an interesting scent of decay. Tail wags increased.

Gentle hands pulled off the leash. The man started to remove her collar, but Kai backed away to shake herself, hard. She waited, not sure what to do. Kai wanted to investigate the area but worried the man's nice tone might change to yells of *bad dog* if she moved.

"It's okay, pup. Hang out here for a couple hours until the kids and their folks show up to pick out their perfect Halloween pumpkin." He reached in a paper bag, took out a sammich and broke off a piece with stinky cheese, oh joy! "Find a big ol' pumpkin to sit beside. You already got a pretty little husky-looking face. So put on the cute, and betcha you'll find a great new home in no time. Okay?" He turned to close the rear door, then jumped back in surprise. "Where'd you come from? Oh crap, Pippo, not again!"

The gray and white cat hopped down, easily dodging the man's clutching hands and sped off across the field. Kai barked with excitement. She grabbed the rest of the sammich treat, swallowed it in two gulps, then ran after Pippo, eager for a new adventure.

Chapter Two: SEPTEMBER

September Day pulled into the gravel lot of the pumpkin patch. As she shoved the car into park, a large extended-cab truck kicked up gravel as it accelerated out, nearly clipping her bumper. She shut off the engine and twisted in her seat to watch it disappear, noting the motorcycle loaded haphazardly in the truck's bed.

"Yikes! How rude." She laughed as the big black German Shepherd muttered his own rude commentary from the back seat. Shadow couldn't contain his excitement.

The owners had already tricked out the field in full Halloween regalia, and September hoped all that noise wouldn't make her job harder. She had perhaps an hour before the place swarmed with youngsters and parents searching for their perfect pumpkin to carve into jack-o'-lantern magic—an hour to find Lia's missing cat, Pippo. That'd be a stretch, in all this open space.

She hated to disappoint Shadow, but this search belonged to another. From his carrier in the rear of the vehicle, Macy meowed his own comments. She'd trained the Maine Coon to track missing felines, since he had less chance of scaring the lost kitties into flight.

"Sorry, baby dog, you'll get another chance later."

Weird how Lia's missing cat ended up out here. The young woman spent Monday through Friday at the police training academy in Dallas. She kept her trained police dog, Magic, with her, and left Pippo with her grandparents. Now, Pippo had gone AWOL.

"Why'd it become my problem?" She asked the rhetorical question to the wind.

Mrs. Corazon called to ask for—no, to demand—help. September acquiesced, partly to give Macy the opportunity to track again; it had been months since he'd enjoyed the challenge of an outing. Shadow also needed something to stem his boredom, and he'd happily seek out the feline miscreant should Macy miss the mark.

Hopefully, the longhaired cat remained in this jumbled field. She saw pumpkins everywhere, bales of straw, cornfields nearby, and a veritable maze for a small cat to hide.

Mrs. Corazon blamed a worker for letting the gray and white kitty out. More likely, Cornelia herself left a door or window open and somehow the cat had hitched a ride in the worker's truck. Pippo routinely escaped, adept at opening doors and sneaking out. The worker admitted seeing Pippo dash away while out here to prep for the afternoon crowd.

To her credit, Cornelia's upset feelings went above and beyond disappointing her granddaughter; she was sincerely worried about Pippo. September smiled. Even sour dispositions sweetened when seduced by a loving feline friend. However, she feared the man would lose his job if Macy failed to find the missing cat. That must have been him, spinning gravel with his truck as she arrived. Leave it to Mrs. Corazon to blame others for dropping the ball. Or in this case, the cat.

She hadn't planned to spend Friday afternoon like this. But Lia was a friend. A dear friend, who'd saved her life— and vice versa. Mrs. Corazon wanted her to retrieve the missing cat and never reveal anything to Lia. But nothing Cornelia Corazon offered to persuade her would make her lie.

The Corazon spread numbered in the hundreds of acres, mostly dedicated to the champion cutting horses they raised. Over the years, they'd added cattle and, in a nod to Cornelia's ambition to play generous benefactor to the community, a pumpkin patch, hayride, massive Texas-shaped cornfield maze, and Halloween bonfire to the fall festivities. It culminated in an extravagant masquerade party at the estate house Halloween night. September had never attended and had no desire to mix with the social scene of Heartland, Texas. She'd had enough notoriety in her life.

September pulled her long dark hair into a ponytail, grabbed the small baby blanket Pippo used as a bed, and stepped out of the car. Shadow woofed with anticipation, his black ears perked forward with interest. "Need you to *wait*, baby dog. This is a job for Macy."

He yawned, whining noisily as his jaws cracked wide. September grinned, understanding his frustration. They'd had blissfully quiet weeks at the lake house with the Paladin team as they planned their future. While a lovely break for the humans, Shadow needed more to keep him engaged and happy. Stalking the banks of the lake after careless frogs only went so far.

The dry rustle of a spent cornfield bordered the area, and September guessed it made up a portion of the maze. The whole field, about three acres worth, contained hundreds of pumpkins in various shapes and sizes.

The broad leaves and vines had withered and died, leaving only the orange bounty scattered across the field. She scanned the area, taking in the rustic looking shed crouched at one corner of the property, with an artistically lettered sign inviting customers to weigh their pumpkin on the old-fashioned scale, and pay inside.

"We'll start there, Macy." September walked around to open the rear door and unzipped the cat carrier. September cradled the big cat close, snuggling her face into the coffee-colored fur that so closely matched her own hair. "What do you say, Macy? Want to play *seek*?"

In the backseat, Shadow's whine turned into an imploring yelp. He twisted to stare at September, his brown eyes meeting her green ones, willing her to change her mind. "Patience, baby dog. You may get your chance later." She owed him some one-on-one playtime. Maybe a game of his current favorite, hose tag.

Macy already wore his harness, so cradling the big eighteen-pound cat in one arm, September shut the hatchback and strode toward the outbuilding. That was the likeliest place for Pippo to take cover. If that proved unsuccessful, they'd check several other options in the field. Tipped over wooden wagons, and stacked bales of hay offered artistic displays of already-carved jack-o'-lanterns, ready and willing to provide inspiration to any who cared to look.

Cats liked hiding spots. They also liked high places. While Lia's cat had been around dogs, in this situation, Shadow's unexpected presence could easily spook Pippo, even though they'd briefly lived together. That was back when Lia called the kitten Gizmo, then somewhere along the line the Pippo nickname stuck. September didn't need the agile feline taking off across the pumpkin patch and disappearing into the ocean of corn.

September secured the leash on the cat's harness, then set Macy on the dusty ground and offered the blanket for a close-up sniff. The Maine Coon's tufted ears twitched, and he delicately examined the blanket, paying special attention to one area. He turned and padded directly toward the small building, keeping his head high and making no apparent effort to scent the ground the way a dog might. Thankfully, Pippo disappeared less than an hour ago, so the trail remained fresh.

She didn't bother calling the cat's name. First, Lia's pet only knew her in passing. September wasn't a trusted member of the family. But even if Lia had been here, chances were the cat wouldn't have answered her, either. When stressed, fight or flight took over. And with cats, the third part of that equation—freeze—meant once the cat found a likely spot, they'd go silent and remain hidden until or unless they felt safe enough to come out.

Chapter Three: SHADOW

Shadow watched Macy, pacing regally with plume tail held high, lead September toward the small outbuilding. He whined, then warbled deep in his throat, wanting to be a part of the excitement. He sniffed at the two-inch-wide opening of the window that allowed an intermittent breeze to gust through the car.

Reflexively he pawed the side of the window, trying to find that special place that made the clear glass scroll down, and let a good dog jump out. When it didn't work, he whirled and moved to the other side of the car, repeating the action, woofing under his breath with frustration.

Shadow returned his attention to September's progress, his brow furrowing with concern when she disappeared into the small building. One short sharp bark, and he again pawed at the window. He needed to be with her. That was his job.

They had spent nearly every hour together for the past several months, and Shadow relished the company. They trained together. He watched her perform odd exercises that sent her long stick whirling through the air. And together they learned and practiced all kinds of new skills. He learned even more words with the *show-me* game, not just scary words like *gun* and *knife*, and *fire*. (He really didn't like *fire*. That scared him deep inside…) She also taught him fun words like *hose*, and *phone*, and *keys*. He really liked *keys*, since they almost always meant a car ride. Like today.

September made sure he remembered everything about climbing ladders or digging up hidden treasures (a buried fetch-toy, oh joy!). Everywhere they went he kept September safe when she said *check it out*, making sure no danger lurked to cause her hurts. She needed Shadow to chase away the scary things that haunted her when she slept, and sometimes crept into the awake-world, too. Mostly these days, just pressing against her side thwarted the hauntings. And when they shared a pillow at night, and they cuddled together…bliss! His tail waved at the thought.

Yet with all the practice, the man they lived with didn't like September and Shadow going places alone. Either Combs, or one of the kids, always tagged along.

Shadow liked the kids well enough, but they took up too much of September's attention. So did the man. He knew Combs cared about September, but not the same way as Shadow.

Lately, car rides didn't include stops for a good dog to

sniff, or to enjoy an adventure with his person. Well, sometimes they got to play fetch by the lake house. After weeks with no new smells or experiences, a good dog yearned for something new, something fresh.

So today, Shadow eagerly hopped in the back seat when September mentioned the *hide and seek* game. He loved searching for lost dogs. September always called him "good dog, what a smart baby dog" when he found the missing. The *seek* game meant new places to sniff and explore with his best friend, September, by his side.

But instead, she ignored his concern when she should have trusted a good dog. Nerves made his fur itch. He didn't like this place. Not at all. Even with the windows barely open he could smell bad things, dead things, as the wind shifted.

And gunfire. He growled. That potent scent he'd never forget.

Shadow's person and cat friend were out there alone, without a good dog to warn and protect them.

He blew out his breath and wagged with relief when September reappeared, still following Macy as the cat tugged her around the outside of the little building. Shadow's head tipped one way, then the other, trying to make sense of the situation and what he should do next. Boredom forgotten, he savored the challenge. Experience had shown him a good dog must always be ready to defend his person. But being locked in a car frustrated that imperative.

He watched Macy hesitate at the corner of the building, sniff a place nose height on the wooden siding, then tug September around the back of the structure. Out of sight.

Shadow stuck his nose through the window crack, inhaling deeply, and whiffering it back out. Something smelled very wrong. Coppery. Pungent.

Footfalls thumped closer and closer…

Thud!

With a snarl, Shadow whirled to face the other door. His ears pinned back, nostrils flared, and snarls bubbled deep in his chest.

A pair of bloody hands smeared the glass. One stretched through the two-inch gap at the top of the window, reaching for a good dog's face.

Chapter Four: LIA

Lia Corazon yanked open the truck door, slid behind the wheel, then slammed the door as hard as she could. She gritted her teeth, watching her fellow police academy cadets leave the area. At least, they'd let the class out an hour early, a nice change for a Friday.

Up until this week, she had loved the training and the time spent with like-minded men and women eager to make a difference in the world. Never much of a fashionista, she even loved the clothes cadets wore: navy blue polo shirt, coyote-color 5.11 trousers—a police version of cargo pants— with polished black boots and matching belt. The white gimme hat with Police Training Academy emblazoned on the front helped keep her frizzy blond hair contained and tamed.

They'd already cycled through the academy basic instructors (BIs) and now progressed to advance instructors (AIs). They were all experts in their discipline and cut no slack, but she welcomed the challenge. Every couple of weeks, a new instructor rotated through the class. She'd learned a lot from all of them. But this week's AI was a real piece of work.

One of the few other young women in the training class paused near Lia's car, motioning her to lower her window. "Cool logo. You really run a kennel? What breed?"

The door of the old truck sported a now-faded dog and cat cartoon logo, surrounded by her business name, Corazon Kennels. "Boarding dogs mostly, sometimes cats. Police work's steadier." Lia spoke shortly, not in the mood to chitchat, and pulled off her white hat to fan herself.

"Cool. Listen, a bunch of us are heading over to Chico's for drinks. You coming?" She quirked a grin. "Drown yer sorrows?"

Lia shook her head. She ought to make the effort, knew relationships born and nourished during training would last the rest of her career. "Another time. Gotta get my dog."

"Bring 'em along! We'll sit out on the patio."

She smiled, tempted, but then shook her head. "We're visiting kids at the hospital." Lia picked up the rainbow-hued fright wig and red clown nose resting in the passenger seat, and beeped the nose, making a silly expression. "The kids love Magic."

"Okay, sounds good." The young woman leaned closer, speaking quietly. "Don't let Drummond knock you off your stride. You've been rocking it, and he's a known hard ass.

Thinks it's his job to make us miserable." She grinned and jogged away to join the cadets jostling each other and laughing loudly. After a week of intense study and training, everyone needed the weekend off.

Lia rolled up the window and switched on the AC. The last week of October in Texas still meant uncomfortably warm temps. She fumbled in the glove box for her phone. She left it in the car to avoid distractions during class. Now she wished she had a way to document the hazing, not that Drummond would tolerate anyone filming him. Hazing remained part of the culture in many ways, especially for female cops, and those who complained clearly didn't fit in. Anyone she might confide in, like Grandfather or, God forbid, Jeffrey Combs, would just tell her to suck it up.

She quickly checked messages as the AC did its job. Mostly spam, plus a phone message from Grammy. She made a face. "Give it up, already."

Cornelia Corazon always got her way and couldn't, no, refused to, understand why Lia repeatedly declined the invite to Thursday's Halloween bash. Grammy wanted to turn it into Lia's birthday celebration. Twenty-two years old…not like it was some kind of benchmark or anything. She kept hinting at a *wonderful birthday surprise.* "Like that would change everything."

At least they were talking, after nearly a year of chilly silence between them. She'd been surprised when Grammy offered to look after her cat while Lia spent weekdays in Dallas at the academy. She figured the hired help scooped Pippo's litter pan, not her impeccably dressed grandmother. Lia laughed out loud at the notion.

Grammy had been surprisingly tolerant of the gray and white food thief. She couldn't seem to remember Gizmo's name, either, and instead called him Pippo so often (probably referring to his potbelly thievery) that she'd stopped correcting Grammy. The cat frequently opened cabinets to fish out treat bags and particularly enjoyed stealing from the bread box. He even dared raid the dog's food bowl from time to time. Lia kept a cover on her coffee cup or Pippo would stick his white paws inside. Grammy wouldn't tolerate such antics.

She'd never seen the woman with a hair out of place. Cornelia always dressed to impress. Underneath that pleasant veneer lived a cruel, calculating person, a reality Cornelia Corazon had kept hidden from everyone. Until last summer.

Another text caught her attention. From September.

>Call me. About Pippo.

September might be the one person to understand about Detective Kincaid Drummond. Maybe she could help Lia parse out what sort of game he played. Why was September concerned about her cat? She mentally shrugged. After September's crazy reveal about her inheritance, nothing she did surprised Lia.

Lia shoved the truck in gear and began the tricky drive back to the hotel to pick up Magic. An earlier AI had invited her to bring the Rottie/Shepherd cross to class for a demo. He'd impressed everyone. With September's mentorship, she'd already trained Magic in a variety of skills, from tracking and protection to bomb detection. He'd make an ideal K9 partner once she graduated.

She dialed September's number as she pulled onto the highway. It took several rings before September answered. "What's up with Pippo?"

"Yeah, about that. Your grandmother didn't want me to tell you, but there's always a chance these searches don't turn out well." September paused, then slowly spoke. "I'm out in the pumpkin patch with Macy, doing a search. Mrs. Corazon said somebody let Pippo out. You know how he loves hitching rides in cars, and the last sighting was out here."

Lia cursed under her breath. "Grammy promised to keep him safe. I shoulda known better." Blinking furiously to keep tears at bay, Lia slowed the vehicle. She'd given Grammy a chance, and it could end up with Pippo losing his life. "Can you find him?"

Lia hadn't been out to the old pumpkin patch in years, probably not since high school. She remembered an old shack where the pumpkins were weighed, hundreds of the big orange globes glistening in the field. Fields of maize one year, winter rye another, and who knows what now surrounded the whole area. No fences—not that any fence could contain Pippo—and plenty of places for a cat to get lost or eaten by wildlife. Red tail hawks, coyotes, bobcats, owls and more patrolled North Texas land and sky. The territory belonged to them more than human usurpers.

"I'll do my best. Macy has the scent. We're in the middle of the search now. Just finished checking the little outbuilding. He's leading me across the field. I'll keep you posted." She hesitated. "So sorry, Lia. Been meaning to call and get together for your birthday. Or are you going to the party your grandmother has planned? She's telling everyone you'll be there for a big ol' surprise."

"You'll find Pippo, I know you will. And no, I've no plans to attend the Halloween bash. I can't leave Pippo there anymore, either." Lia made a turn and stopped to wait at the light.

"Take the cat with you to the hotel. He gets along okay with Magic, doesn't he?"

"Yes of course, they grew up together, but —"

"I'm not using the presidential suite, Lia. I changed the pet policy, and the staff knows you're authorized to hang out as long as you want; you, Magic, and Pippo might as well use it until you finish the academy. There's no reason to trek back and forth to Heartland, and your clientele will show up if and when you decide to reopen Corazon Kennels." September chuckled. "Lots of cops have second jobs, you know. I guess you're loving the academy."

Lia loved the kennel. She'd turned it into a great success with equal parts stubborn determination and blind faith things would work out. While Grandfather and Grammy set their hearts on her joining their championship horse breeding business, she'd dedicated her life to training dogs. Working Magic, and before that his police dog mother, made her believe her future lay in law enforcement. But now…

She started to share her concerns about AI Drummond's treatment. He stared at her, said odd things with weird hidden meanings she couldn't fathom, and belittled her every effort.

But now wasn't the time. She tightened her jaw, shook her head, and pulled up in front of the Grand Chisholm. September, also known as Sorokin Glass, had inherited the luxury hotel, and a zillion dollars. Something like that, Lia hadn't asked. "Academy is everything I've dreamed of, with all the expected challenges." She couldn't keep the tartness from spilling into the words.

September laughed again. "Let me get back to tracking. I can't keep Macy standing still much longer, or he'll totally lose interest. Don't you worry, we'll find your cat for you. Now go play with Magic. Do something to take your mind off things. And I'll call you later."

Lia nodded, although September couldn't see. "Magic and

I have a date with the kids at Heartland Hospital. I could swing by your place to pick up Pippo once we're done." *Think positive, Lia.* "Unless you tell me otherwise." She laughed without humor. "Magic is dressing up as the cowardly lion, complete with shaggy mane, and I've got a clown wig and rubber nose ready to roll. The kids get a kick out of Magic. We do this drill where they say, *Timmy's down the well, send help,* and he runs to fetch a nurse or doctor." She laughed. "One time Magic fetched a biker guy waiting for a friend in the ER."

She had to put on a good face for the kids. The visit lifted the spirits of Lia and the staff as much as the children. What started as a lark turned into something more. Magic had decided he loved kids. Not only could he sniff out bombs, capture and hold the bad guy, but he could lick away tears, and coax laughter from children going through the worst they could imagine.

Compared to a lost house kitty trying to dodge coyotes, and innocent kids navigating scary hospital procedures, her own angst over AI Kincaid Drummond counted as next to nothing.

Chapter Five: SEPTEMBER

September pocketed the phone and prayed she'd soon have good news for Lia. The long lead connected to the back of Macy's harness stretched taut. September's footfalls increased, trying to keep pace with the big cat's accelerating stride. She kept her eyes on her feet, trying to navigate the uneven ground and clods of dirt between the furrows in the field, as Macy weaved between the jumble of pumpkins. September didn't want to slow the cat's pace, but now and then she had to gently guide him away from ducking beneath dried vines and stems that would tangle the tether.

She shifted the straps of the portable cat carrier on her

back. If successful, she had a secure place to contain the missing feline.

The small building had been a bust. She'd encouraged Macy to check out all of the cubbyholes at ground level, and he'd conducted due diligence emerging with whiskers coated in spiderwebs and dust, but no sign of Pippo. Without urging, Macy had leaped on top of the stacked square bales, to investigate potential scent there as well.

September wondered, not for the first time, if Macy might be more interested in sniffing out vermin, never mind that the cat ate well and had no need for mousy sustenance. Hunger didn't trigger the feline hunting urge, and there were no guarantees he wouldn't become distracted. From time to time, he brought her a gift—lizard, bird, mouse. He rarely ate them.

She'd been hopeful when Macy spent an inordinate amount of time in one area. Upon further examination, she could see the scooped-out place in the straw looked like a cat-size bed, complete with a few telltale wisps of gray and white fur. Likely the cat—or a cat—had been here not long ago. Something had spooked the cat from this comfortable retreat, possibly September's own vehicle. So when Macy immediately hopped down and tugged September to the back exit of the wooden structure, she felt encouraged they followed the right track.

September expected Macy to head to the old-fashioned wagon halfway across the field. When he instead took a sudden turn toward the tank on the other side of the field, September worried. Had the feline taken flight from something more threatening than her car's arrival? You'd expect a fearful feline to go to ground. Striking out across the field felt more like a run for his life.

Almost as if summoned, a single coyote voice sang out, quickly followed by a half-dozen others, creating a spooky lament. September wrinkled her nose and debated cutting short the search. She couldn't risk Macy. With coyotes so near, she feared the worst had already happened to Pippo. Carried away in the jaws of the hunter—she shivered.

Behind her, Shadow raised his voice to join the howling sing-along. That surprised her. He rarely reacted to coyotes, and he sounded much more upset than he should. She smothered a half smile. His frustration over being left behind must have tipped him over the edge.

By the sound of the snarls and yipping cacophony, the coyotes had found their dinner. The sound faded into the distance as the group raced away.

Keeping a wary eye out and her ears pricked for their return, September proceeded but cut the distance between herself and Macy in half. She pulled her 9mm semiautomatic pistol from the holster beneath her sleeveless red blouse. She now carried her weapon everywhere. In Texas, you needed no license for open carry, as long as you met the other restrictions, but Combs wanted her to go the extra steps for a license to carry a concealed weapon. With her history, she needed every precaution available to protect herself, and those she loved. September would defend Macy without hesitation. Sure, coyotes had a right to live, and they were ubiquitous in this part of the country. As long as they kept their distance, she'd do the same.

Macy increased his pace, leaping and bounding ahead. September broke into half trot, as they drew closer to the cattle tank, little more than a glorified manmade pond. She supposed the hot afternoon prompted Pippo to seek water. If hungry, he could ambush other critters there, too. Tall grass and towering reeds surrounded the perimeter of the shallow basin of water.

On one side of the tank, the spraddling bois d'arc tree held court, its thorny branches holding dozens of long-legged snow-white birds. Below, an equal number of egrets lay prostrate on the ground, several floating dead in shallow water like rose petals shattered by a storm.

With a gasp, September stopped in her tracks. Macy meowed and looked back over his shoulder, clearly questioning why she refused to move. She gathered up the slack in the lead and scooped him into her arms. Slowly she walked closer to the tank, taking in the heartbreaking scene.

Not only cattle egrets, but also several sick or dying ducks floundered in the shallow water. Ducks started migrating in late August, but it sometimes lasted through October. These birds must've been stragglers of the flock, perhaps weaker or younger. But September saw egrets year-round. Something bad had happened to the birds.

From across the pond, a flash of motion caught her attention. A large coyote, pelt thick and shining with health, boldly gazed at her with one of the dead egrets clamped in its mouth.

"Go on! Get out of here." Macy struggled a bit, and she tightened her grip, fingers hooked in his harness, fearful to risk waving an arm to speed the creature away.

It stared back, locking eyes with her for another fifteen seconds, not even an ear flick acknowledging any concern, before calmly turning and bounding into the field of shriveled corn. September shuddered. Pippo might have been attracted by the bounty of birds and carried away by marauding predators taking advantage.

September turned to go. She wouldn't risk further exposing Macy to whatever had killed these birds. Shadow's barks, sounding more and more harried, continued from the car. "Let's go, Macy, we can't always make things turn out the way we want." She hugged the Maine Coon.

A meow sounded, higher pitched and more plaintive than Macy had ever sounded. It came from the direction of the witchy bois d'arc tree.

September knelt on the ground to set Macy on the grass, making sure to press her knee hard atop of the lead to keep the cat in place. She shrugged off the portable cat carrier and rummaged inside to pull out a stake and small hammer; she jammed the stake into the dry ground until only the eye hook remained visible. Then she secured Macy to the tether so that he would not be tempted to follow her. "*Chill*, Macy-cat, stay here. Paws crossed I can collect Pippo and we'll go home."

She searched inside the bag again and found a paper plate, along with a tube of Macy's favorite soft treat. September smeared a healthy sample onto the plate. Bribes were legal in recovering lost cats. And Macy had payment due.

"Good job, Macy. You tracked 'em down." She left the plate with him, and he immediately hunkered down to lap up every bit.

September trotted toward the bois d'arc, glad she'd worn high top boots and heavy jeans despite the warm weather. She took care not to turn an ankle on the dozens of horse apples littering the ground beneath the tree. She remembered harvesting springy sapling branches, as kids, and sticking small rotting horse apples on the end to fling far away. Once, her brother Mark caught one in the face and nursed a black eye for a week. The memory made her wonder where Mark was, and hoped he was doing well….

The missing cat clung to the crotch of the tree's lowest branch, just above a large hollowed out space in the trunk. Pippo wore a tattered harness that was entangled in the thorns of a smaller branch. She guessed the cat had dashed up the tree and got caught.

At least Pippo couldn't run away. She smeared more of the Churu treat on a new paper plate to offer the cat. Churu tempted even the most discriminating feline palate. September hoped that it might calm him long enough for her to unhook him from the tree and get loaded into the carrier. Lia better get Pippo checked by the vet after the exposure to these dead animals.

September would have to notify the Corazons about the bird die off, too. Fortunately, they kept their horses and cattle pastured elsewhere. The birds must have been attracted to the water. Sick birds did strange things.

September took slow, quiet steps, pointedly keeping eyes averted. Eye contact and hard stares escalated fear, which easily transformed into aggression. She didn't want Pippo any more frightened, nor did she want to get bitten. She gave a quick glance back at Macy. He'd finished his treat, and now concentrated on spiffing himself up, licking debris away from nose to tail.

The ground squelched beneath her shoes. The soil was soggy several feet from the tank itself—probably why the tree survived despite the hollow trunk and broken-down limbs.

"Here you are Pippo, let's get you home." She murmured softly, in a high-pitched baby talk cadence cats responded to best. She held the paper plate closer, and the frightened cat sniffed but turned away. Fear trumped appetite even from a favorite. September's brow furrowed when she saw the cat's white front paws stained red. A possible injury?

A low, guttural yowl came from behind her. Macy! She whirled.

The big Maine Coon paced with herky-jerky gait at the length of the tether. His mouth opened in shallow panting breaths. Macy fell over.

"Damn! Hold on Macy." *His heart.* But he'd been doing so well, he loved these outings…Had she just killed her boy?

Quickly, September grabbed Pippo's harness, grateful he froze. She yanked and tugged to break free the thorny limb that trapped the animal, slicing her fingers on the thorns in the process.

She'd cut the strap; then she'd rush both cats to see Doc Eugene. No time to waste. She stooped to reach the knife sheathed at her ankle, bringing her face level with the opening in the trunk of the tree.

A dead man's face, battered and bloodied, stared back.

Chapter Six: SHADOW

The boy's fingers clawed at the window leaving bloody smears on the glass. Shadow snarled and redoubled his barking, then subsided when he recognized the boy's fear. The child meant him no harm. He tentatively stretched his neck to sniff the bloodied hand.

"Help! Anybody? Aw, there's nobody there." He craned to look over his shoulder, fingers still reaching through the small opening in the window.

Slashes on the palm of the hand bled freely, and so did the boy's other forearm. He held one fisted hand hard against his middle, as if a deep hurt burned inside.

Shadow recognized the plea for help. The boy smelled of blood and rotten water, pee and terror. Shadow whined deep in his throat, licked his lips, and nose-touched the child's fingers. He wished September was here.

"He's coming, he's coming, said he'll get me, too." He panted in deep guttural gasps. The small hand pressed farther through the window's opening to drop something inside. "Keep that safe, okay, dog? It's important… Oh gosh, where's Uncle Ricky's truck? Gotta hide!"

Shadow understood little of the boy's mumbling and cocked his head as if that would clarify the meaning. The child stepped away from the window, then staggered away from the car, bent nearly double, both fists pressed to his middle. Shadow tracked the boy's progress as he limped toward the outbuilding, his concern and warbling whines escalating when the figure fell hard against the building's entrance, clutched the opening with one hand before disappearing inside.

Barking again to alert September, Shadow then paced back and forth on the backseat, anxious for her return. She'd know what to do.

At last he saw her slim silhouette jogging toward him. The fur prickled on the back of his neck, escalating his tension when he recognized the urgency in her actions. She held Macy in her arms. Something was wrong.

Dogs understood how to read the air for danger, and to alert their people. But over time, he and September had become so attuned to each other, that sometimes she knew as much as a good dog, even without his sniffing and hearing gifts. She was smart that way.

The knapsack strapped to her shoulders shifted with extra weight. She cradled Macy under one arm and pressed the phone to her ear with the other hand. Even from a distance, he read the concern, anger, and horror coloring her tone.

"That's what I said. A body at the foot of a bois d'arc, looks like he tried to hide inside. Yes, I checked, there's no sign of life. I left the scene, didn't want to contaminate any trace."

She came abreast of the car, and Shadow slicked his ears down while his tail churned the air with semaphore shouts. She'd know what to do. Together they fixed everything. He waited for her to see the blood on the window, to open the door, so he could lead her to the boy needing help.

But she ignored Shadow to continue talking on the phone. "Yes, I'm in the parking lot." She hurried to the back of the vehicle, and opened the rear door to deposit Macy in his safe place. She shrugged off the backpack while juggling the phone, and Shadow's ears twitched at the stranger's small meow. She slammed the door and returned to the front of the vehicle next to the driver's door. "No, as far as I can see, no one else is here, though a big truck left as I arrived. I didn't see the driver." Again she paused. "Yes, of course I'll give a statement." She pocketed the phone.

Finally, September turned her attention to Shadow. "Sorry, you need to stay in the car, baby dog. We're going to get enough questions when the police arrive. They'll want to know why we're here." She threw up her hands. "Why me? Just tracking a cat and I find a body?"

His whine morphed into a yelp, and he paw-thumped the door, making it as plain as he could that he wanted—no, he needed—to get out, out, out. Right now! The blood smears were on the other side of the car. And people had to see things before they believed what was as plain as the smell of bacon.

Blood. And blood never meant anything good.

Shadow whirled in the seat and crossed to the other side of the car. He again paw-thumped the door, scratching the side panel. When she didn't immediately respond, he clawed and dug on the glass itself. He looked over his shoulder, barked twice with great deliberation, then turned back to again paw thump the door.

"Okay Shadow, I get it. What's got you so upset?" She hurried around to the other side of the car, and gasped at the bloody smears against the glass. "How'd you cut your paws?"

Quickly, she opened the car door and reached for him. Shadow gave her a quick slurp across the face, then ducked beneath her embrace, and leaped from the car.

"Shadow, *wait*. We can't run around with the police on the way. *Wait*."

He hesitated, flinched at the word. Of all the commands he knew, he disliked *wait* the most. Shadow glanced over his shoulder, acknowledging the command. But sometimes good dogs knew better than people.

So he deliberately turned away and bounded toward the shelter, not needing to put nose to ground to track the blood trail the boy had spilled in his wake. September followed him without further argument. She understood, finally. Even without a leash, Shadow felt the trust that traveled from both directions through that invisible bond they shared.

He pawed open the door and entered the small building, scanning one way then the other, before moving unerringly to the rear. Shadow hopped up on the platform where stacks of hay bales formed an artistic display. The dry straw felt stiff and prickly beneath his pads. He traversed the elevation carefully. A paw step out of place could spill him into an undignified heap.

"Good dog, Shadow. *Seek.*" He heard her retrieve the gun from the holster and understood she feared for their safety. So he glanced back to make eye contact, his happy grin and low tail wags showing no danger threatened.

When he reached the wooden ladder at one corner of the platform, he paused, sniffing to make sure. It led to the high loft above, where his nose said the boy hid.

"Whoever's up there, come on out. I see blood on the ladder. I know you're hurt. Let me help you. Come on out. The police are on their way…"

Shadow put one paw on the bottom rung, hesitated, then began to climb. He didn't wait for September to tell him and would've ignored her order to stop. The terrified boy needed a good dog. Shadow saw that as clearly as September's love.

He heard her holster the gun, and vault onto the platform to follow him. He climbed steadily, remembering the ladder lessons learned months ago and refreshed with routine drills. As he cleared the loft floor, he saw the boy slumped in the far corner.

The child—not much older than Willie—blinked tears from frightened eyes. He made mewling sounds Shadow couldn't understand. So Shadow treated him like he would a terrified dog, signaling *no threat* with silent posturing plain even to human pups.

With head lowered, ears slicked back, and tail wagging low and slow, Shadow approached the boy. The final few feet he lowered himself to his belly and crawled, smearing the blood spill on the wooden floor with his own fur. He lowered his chin to rest on the boy's thigh, and whimpered, still sweeping his tail to and fro against the wooden flooring.

With a sob the boy leaned forward. He buried his face in the black fur of Shadow's neck.

"That man hurt Uncle Ricky. Why did he do that? Why? He said he'd get me, too."

Chapter Seven: SEPTEMBER

Two ambulances, four police cars, and one unmarked vehicle crowded the pumpkin patch parking lot. Authorities had cordoned off the area, turning away disappointed parents and kids intent on choosing the perfect jack-o'-lantern prospect.

September had given her statement to the first responding officer, and now waited impatiently next to her car for the detective to release her from the site. Shadow hadn't wanted to leave the boy—Peter, he said—and she'd had to calm him down before the EMTs could approach. Peter had suffered multiple knife wounds, mostly superficial defensive injuries to hands and arms, but she worried about his painful tummy. It was a miracle he'd made it to her car. He must've run the perimeter of the field, taking shelter in the cornfield to evade his attacker.

Confined again on the back seat, Shadow jittered impatiently. She wanted him beside her, pressing hard against her side; she needed that contact to help calm her own distress. But September understood the necessities of keeping as few people tramping through the area as possible. *Deep breaths. Ten, nine, eight…* she continued the calming litany. Macy appeared to have recovered, but September needed Doc Eugene to weigh in. Pippo slept the sleep of the righteous (or exhausted) inside the spare carrier.

A cluster of uniformed men and women worked around the old, gnarled tree. The sparsely leafed branches clawed the air, mimicking the anguish the dead man must've suffered. September shuddered. She reached for her phone and texted Combs. He called her within 30 seconds.

"I'm still at the lake house." Combs had fully embraced transforming her recently acquired property into a high-tech headquarters for the Paladin Group, which was so new they had yet to clearly nail down their mission. Righting wrongs, championing the innocent, thwarting bad guys. *Like the graphic novels Willie favored.* That seemed to be her life. "How'd you get caught up in another murder?" Combs didn't hide the disapproval.

She sighed. "Lucky, I guess."

They'd had a conversation about Cornelia Corazon bullying her into searching for Pippo. "Found Lia's cat and the victim in the same spot." She hesitated. "I told Willie I'd pick him up, but there's no way I'm gonna make it."

Willie spent as much time as possible at the community

theater. He'd walked over after school to help paint sets, since his most recent audition failed to secure a role. She felt proud he didn't grumble, and he seemed happy to be a part of the group.

"I can't leave yet. Teddy's downloading new software. We can't stop in the middle or we'll have to start over."

Teddy Williams, a dear friend and invaluable member of the Paladin Group, now lived at the lake house as caretaker. While Combs's legs had mostly healed from the wedding bombing, he worried his bum leg would give out or slip off the car pedals at the wrong time. Oh, he could drive when he had to, and especially felt worried about driving the kids. And he stubbornly refused any accommodation. Most days, he relied on September or Teddy for transport.

"I'll call Melinda. She's cheering tonight and going with a group to get a snack at Whataburger after. Yes, Delaney's going, too." After meeting the older boy, Combs grudgingly agreed Melinda could attend group gatherings that included Delaney.

She laughed. "Good luck with that." No teenage girl wanted a tagalong little brother on a group date or any other outing.

"She'll get over it. I'll tell her it's part of a Paladin operation." He chuckled. "She and Willie still want to be part of things."

She wrinkled her nose and shook her head. "You're joking, right? We don't know what happened here, that's for the local PD to take on. We only know a man's dead, and a young boy injured." She wasn't ready for another roller-coaster chase-the-bad-guys adventure. Leave it to the professionals, the police could figure this out. "No need to involve Paladin…"

"Slow your horses, September. Gallows humor. I agree."

She imagined him cracking his knuckles with frustration. Sometimes she took things too seriously. She took a deep breath. "The injured witness says somebody attacked his uncle. The man must have tried to escape by sheltering inside the tree trunk." She shivered. "This place already feels Halloween spooky. It's such a weird place to die." She glanced around, shivering as the air cooled with the dropping of the sun. She caught a glimpse of the detective winding her way between scattered pumpkins. "Gotta run. The detective wants to chat."

Detective Paige Brummitt, promoted to the position after Combs resigned, had served on the Heartland police force for six years. After losing both Combs and his partner Gonzales, the local PD had no choice but to quickly promote from within. Brummitt deserved the position, but September's history with the police made her cautious.

"Detective." September nodded, without offering her hand. Shadow stuck his nose through the opening of the car window, snuffling loudly. In the rear, Macy meerowed repeatedly, acting normal again, probably because his dinner time had come and gone. Pippo remained silent.

"September Day. Or is it Sorokin Glass?" Brummitt held out her phone, recording without asking permission. "Which do you prefer, ma'am?" She raised one pencil-thin eyebrow, but her expression was bland and September could detect no sarcasm.

"For the record, I prefer September Day." The pseudonym she'd been forced to choose still rankled. It tied her irrevocably to her father Henry Wong's criminal dynasty. She spelled both names when prompted.

"How did you happen to find the body? And the boy,

Peter. Please start at the beginning and walk me through everything."

She obliged. Surprisingly, Brummitt didn't blink at the notion of a cat tracking a missing pet. September figured her reputation preceded her. Most of the Heartland police knew her from past encounters. She had met Combs during his mother's murder investigation.

One of the ambulances moved, bubble lights blinking, and the siren wailed, taking the living victim to the hospital. The deceased wouldn't need warnings.

"An officer said you spoke to the boy? He lost consciousness before I got here. Anything you can tell me will help connect the dots." Brummitt's shoulder-cut chestnut hair matched her eyes. The plain scrubbed face with a scattering of freckles dropped years from her age.

September felt older than her actual years (in dog years she should be dead), but she'd celebrated her 30th birthday last month. She and Brummitt must be near the same age.

"His name is Peter. He identified the tree victim as his Uncle Ricky. Peter tagged along to some kind of business interview."

"Weird place for a job interview." Brummitt played with the gold pendant on the chain hanging about her neck. "How did they get out here? Long way to hike, without a car."

September had had the same thought. "I arrived about an hour before opening, and a big extended-cab truck nearly clipped me as it left the parking lot. Had a motorcycle in the back." She quickly described what she could remember of the color, and model.

"Whoever killed Uncle Ricky maybe stole his truck to prevent the boy's escape. You said Peter believed the killer threatened to come after him?"

"That sounds right. I don't know what happened. Something went sideways during the interview; the uncle tried to get away and got nailed. I never saw Peter, but I was focused on Macy's tracking." *I should have had enough situational awareness to heed Shadow's alert.* In hindsight, his barking pointed out what she missed. "That's a long way to crawl, especially if you're bleeding."

She led Brummitt to the other side of the car and pointed out the bloody handprints Peter smeared on the window. "I got clear across the field before I found Uncle Ricky. Meanwhile, Peter made his way to my car, looking for help. He pounded the windows to get someone's attention." She stuck her hand through, stroking Shadow's muzzle. "Only my dog saw that. So with no one to help, he ran to hide in the little shack." She smiled when Shadow's tail thumped against the rear seat. "Shadow led me to the boy up in the loft."

"Oh yes, the hero dog. Heard a lot about Shadow." Brummitt smiled, and then immediately regained her serious expression, as if she couldn't risk any break in protocol. "My team already took your shoe imprint, correct?"

September nodded. They wanted to identify or eliminate prints from her, the victims, or potential attackers. She doubted they'd have much success. The ground baked hard in the fall sun, plus hundreds traipsed through the pumpkin patch this time of year. The soft soil around the bois d'arc tree might offer clues if they could sift through the bird carcasses.

"You're free to go Ms. Day. Please stay accessible, in case we have more questions. Oh, and just a friendly word of advice. Leave this investigation to the professionals this time, will you? I know you and Combs got some new pie-in-the-sky PI organization planned. But I will not look kindly on anyone stepping into my jurisdiction. Got it?"

September felt her face flush at the admonishment. She had no intention of sticking her foot into this mess but resented the dismissive way Brummitt characterized her past accomplishments.

She never asked to become the target of an international crime family, or to inherit the reins. Just imagine what she and the Paladin Group could accomplish with a plan, once they actually launched.

But she gritted her teeth, nodded without saying a word. September hurried back to the driver's side door. The sooner she got away from here, the better.

September rolled out of the parking lot when the police waved her through the ribboned off area. In the rear of the car, Macy restarted his yowling commentary and Pippo joined the chorus.

"Yes, I hear you guys. Time to make an appointment with Doc Eugene and get you both checked out." The clinic closed an hour ago. She'd have to call for an appointment in the morning.

Shadow whined and woofed under his breath, recognizing the man's name. "Yes, Shadow, we'll go visit Doc Eugene soon. I'll call Lia later tonight."

She felt sorry for Peter and what happened to his Uncle Ricky, but that had nothing to do with her.

Chapter Eight: SHELLY

Shelly sat in the hospital's emergency room lobby, holding an ice bag to one side of his head. Smoke and mirrors. Give 'em what they expected, and people believed what you wanted them to see. He had no injury, other than the thin line he'd drawn with his favorite blade to aid the masquerade. The blood stained his long blond hair and dripped onto the shoulders of his work shirt. Paint spattered jeans and steel-toed boots, soles still shedding mud from his latest adventure, completed the outfit.

From his position, Shelly watched for the arrival of the kid. Cop chatter on the radio meant the kid was enroute and his best guess, they'd wheel him through here. The boy must've been born under a lucky star the way he dodged that final knife thrust. It should have ended him. Earlier slices, somewhat thwarted when the kid took refuge behind the old tree, bloodied the boy but allowed him to scurry away while Shelly took care of the more important adult target.

Ricky Molingo, a nobody, a wannabe hero, reached above his station. Someone put him up to it, though. Next step, he'd ferret them out and deliver similar justice. He couldn't allow buried secrets to claw their way out of the grave.

Shelly needed to touch base with the other players he'd recruited all those years ago. Molingo must have reached out to the others, probably talked to at least one of 'em. Probably Walford gave up his name or Molingo wouldn't have invited him to that little interview to spill his gut. *How'd that work out for ya, Mr. Reporter?* Time to silence them all…permanently. Never mind the dragon lady couldn't reach him from six-feet under—others still pulled strings in the organization, strings that could easily hang him. His day job provided excellent cover, a day job that would eventually give him access to neutralize Robin Gillette—but destroying the cockroaches would help seal her lips. Then, and only then, could he safely retire, and turn his knives to more pleasurable targets.

Weird that the ER waiting room wasn't busier on a Friday night. A couple of old ladies, sobbing into disintegrating tissues, sat at the far end but remained wrapped up in their own trauma. When they stood, and the receptionist crossed the room to help them out, he had a brief window to multitask. He dialed. Kinkaid Drummond answered on the first ring.

"I'm not buying whatever you're selling."

"Hang up, and you die."

"Who is this?" You could tell Drummond got what he wanted by blustering his way through life. Typical wannabe king. He hadn't changed. Shelly remembered the drill sergeant demeanor, one that made him itch to carve the smarmy grin off the man's face.

"If you want to stay vertical and breathing, you will do exactly what I say. You know who I am. And what we did together. Percolate on my voice from the past."

A soft gasp acknowledged recognition, the seriousness of the call.

"That's right Detective Drummond; that job you ran seems to have gone sideways."

"But that was… What, 15 years ago? Or more." The man's voice rose. Must be alone, nobody within earshot. Good.

Shelly smiled. It didn't surprise him. Drummond wasn't a people person, another reason to recruit him. That cleared the way for what might have to happen next. He waited, letting the silence increase the man's paranoia.

"This is about *her*, isn't it? I recognized trouble soon as she showed up on the roster."

Shelly raised his pale eyebrows. "You always had great instincts." Feed the man's ego and see where it led. "Sorokin Glass?"

"Oh, you mean September Day? Yeah, heard she'd taken on a new name. Come to think of it, she's probably connected; she and the Corazon bitch are as thick as ticks on a hound dog."

Corazon… Ricky Molingo blubbered the same name, the person who hired him.

"Just a reminder you remain under a binding agreement. Sharing any information about that operation burns you and everyone you care about."

"Oh, I've never…"

"Give me everything you've got on Corazon, crib notes version, text me in the next 60 seconds. After that this phone number disappears. Next time you hear from me, you won't see me coming." He lowered his voice, turning the words into fists. "No amount of professional training will save you. Got it?" He disconnected before Drummond could answer.

Within 30 seconds, the phone ding-ding-dinged with several incoming texts, and a few photographs. Corazon looked like a kid. Pretty blond in a girl-next-door kinda way. Slight build, corn colored frizzy hair tied up in a messy ponytail, and an expression of extreme concentration.

The first photo had been taken surreptitiously while she aimed a gun. Looked like a 9mm semiautomatic. She wore a police academy cadet uniform. He smiled, understanding. That's how Drummond knew the woman.

She's probably one of those altruistic do-gooders. Oh, it'd be fun to take her down. Slowly, with attention to detail. He stemmed the urge to unsheathe his knife. Shelly licked his lips.

Before he could read the rest, the automatic ER door whooshed open. He looked up and immediately replaced the fake ice bag on his forehead, shielding his face as the receptionist returned and took her place behind the desk.

"Only one doctor on call, sorry for the wait. We have an ambulance two minutes out with a possible severe trauma. But I can put you in one of the rooms for the nurses to …"

"Thanks, I'll wait. Hope the ambulance person's okay." Finally, the kid. With luck the boy wouldn't make it. The limited resources of the hospital played into his plan.

A large black dog, tail waving with excitement, strode through the door. The Rottweiler wore a lion's mane around his massive shoulders and pranced with pride in the ridiculous costume. Behind him, at the end of the leash, trailed a slight young woman wearing an outlandish rainbow-colored wig, bright red rubber nose, and fuchsia-colored painted lips that extended nearly to her ears.

"Trick-or-treat!" She fairly danced across the linoleum, one of those blithe spirits that seem to bubble with energy and delight.

The receptionist looked up and laughed out loud. "No parking out front again, I suppose? Go on up, Lia, the kids are expecting you. Or should I say, they're anxious to see your magical dog."

The young woman grinned. She blew an air-kiss to the big dog, and he leaped high in the air to catch the invisible smooch. The pair disappeared down a long hallway.

The receptionist met Shelly's eyes and shrugged. "No, you're not seeing things. Lia's got permission, had to jump through major hoops to make it happen."

"Thought I was seeing things, and my head injury was worse than I thought." He grinned, playing along.

She laughed. "The Corazons have a way of cutting through red tape."

His eyes widened. Hadn't recognized her with the costume. She'd made it easy for him.

He made a call.

Chapter Nine: LIA

Lia flexed her shoulders as she exited back into the ER waiting room. She pulled the bulbous red clown nose off and shoved it into her pocket. No longer empty, the area was crowded with police. She'd had to cut short the visit this evening almost as soon as it started, when the children's ward turned frenetic with a new admission accompanied by Heartland police officers. Lia recognized most of them and Magic recognized the activity, his long tail waving in short hard arcs, painting exclamations in the air.

Detective Paige Brummitt spoke softly to the uniforms in the room. A few years Lia's senior, Brummitt made detective earlier than expected based on the bad luck of others, and Lia kind of felt sorry for her, with everyone waiting for a misstep. While Brummitt had the qualifications, she had yet to prove herself. That could mean some head-butting along the way.

Suddenly self-conscious, Lia pulled off the cheap clown wig and shook out her hair. It was one thing to goof off with the kids, another in front of peers. When Brummitt made eye contact, Lia nodded cordially, then turned away and dropped the wig in the trash. She refrained from asking questions, as a cadet had no standing in an ongoing investigation. The rubber nose fell from her pocket, and Magic picked it up, biting hard to make the honking sound.

One glance from her and Magic stopped, ears lowered sheepishly. They didn't need more attention focused on them. She turned to leave. Magic pressed against her thigh, needing no voice command to follow her lead.

"Hey, Corazon. Hold up."

Lia waited at the door, her brow furrowing as Brummitt strode across the room. "Yes, detective?"

"Can you stick around a while?" Brummitt played with the pendant at her neck then glanced back at the activity across the room. "You're friends with September Day, right?"

Her shoulders tensed. Magic responded with a low growl, the rumble nearly silent but felt. He dropped the clown nose, and it rolled across the floor. She placed one hand on the dog's domed head, and immediately the growl subsided.

"I know her, yes. We've worked together." Lia waited, her shoulders hunched. Not everyone liked September, especially not the police. More than once Lia had heard officers speculate the woman attracted trouble by interfering in police matters or—worse—getting too close to the bad guys.

"Relax, just wanted some insight, that's all. I've heard lots about her but just met September for the first time. She's the one who found that injured kid." Brummitt nodded toward the cubicle surrounded by medical personnel.

Injured kid? "At the pumpkin patch? What happened?" She bit her lip.

"Walk with me." Brummitt strode down the hallway, shoes shedding red clay Lia recognized from the pumpkin field. "Boy sustained defensive knife wounds on both palms, and at least one stab wound in his stomach. He's conscious but won't talk to us. And I got a call from a Dallas Detective on his way to debrief the boy. Says the attack on his uncle has connections to an old investigation he's revisiting. Oh, and he may want to talk with you, too."

"Me? Why?" She blinked.

Brummitt shrugged. "He didn't share that with me." And she wasn't happy about it. "Detective Savatch has a rep for getting things done, and I'd rather avoid putting the kid through an interrogation with him." She avoided looking at Lia before finally making her request clear. "I saw you with the other kids. Maybe he'll talk to you. You and your K9 partner, I mean. September said the boy responded well to her dog. That big black shepherd didn't want to leave him."

She had a point. Comfort dogs helped kids and adults open up. "I can try, but no promises. Good to know he likes dogs, but sometimes people like shepherds but get scared of Rotties like Magic." She scratched her head, where the wig left her scalp itching. "What about his folks?"

"September called him Peter." Brummitt's jaw worked. She seemed to weigh her words before continuing. "We need his last name before we can look for his family. Besides, the medical team already knows and trusts you and your dog. I'm trying to save time."

In other words, the doctors wouldn't let Brummitt or anyone else talk with the boy; Lia and her dog were the workaround. She stroked Magic's floppy ears, thinking. Brummitt held something back. Nothing new, investigators often held things close to the vest. Right now, Lia was just a handy bystander with a costumed dog that might help Brummitt's investigation.

"Okay, sure. Happy to help." Never a bad idea to make points with the new detective. "Let's see what Magic can do." She turned, still holding the loose lead that attached to his harness, and reentered the treatment area. Lia crossed to the duty nurse, leaning in to speak quietly to her. "The boy, Peter, with the stab wounds, just admitted?"

"Now Lia, you know I can't tell you anything about that."

"I understand, and don't want you to do anything against policy. But Detective Brummitt says he doesn't want to talk, and you can't find his family without a last name. The detective thinks Magic might persuade him…"

"Oh honey, I don't know. Magic's the best, but it's not up to me. I can ask the doctor, but the poor child's been through something horrible. He's shut down, not saying a word to anyone."

She held up a hand, silencing any argument Lia might offer. She hurried across the room to speak to the doctor in charge. He glanced up from making notes, cocking his head to one side as he listened to the nurse. She gestured with her hands and pointed back at Lia.

Lia gave a hand signal. Magic planted his tail on the floor, and sat up, waving one paw toward the doctor with a wide grinning expression on his face.

The doctor's solemn expression cracked into a fleeting smile. He shrugged and gave a short affirmative nod to the nurse before hurrying away.

When she beckoned, Lia hurried across to join her, then followed the nurse to the boy's room. Brummitt started to follow but stopped when the nurse crossed her arms and scowled.

"Get his name, so we can find his parents. And what the hell happened to him, in that order, so I can satisfy Detective Savatch when he gets here." She crossed her own arms, clearly frustrated at the exclusion.

The nurse grasped Lia's arm but let go when Magic softly growled. "He's woozy from the pain meds. You have five minutes. Ask about his name and parents, nothing more. Understand?"

Lia nodded. "Thanks." She turned to the big dog and bent, setting her cheek next to his. She closed her eyes, using the warmth to settle herself. It did the same for him. "Magic, this boy needs help. You know what to do."

Magic licked her face, then turned to stare into the room. He padded softly toward the bed.

Peter's pinched face matched the sheets. His eyes clenched tight. One bandaged hand above the covers grasped and twisted the fabric as though to make sense of some internal nightmare. The other hand, less injured perhaps, pressed against his middle.

Lia knocked on the door and took a step inside, not wanting to startle the boy. He blinked.

His eyes widened, taking in Magic's broad muzzle and lolling tongue. Lia stayed alert, ready to call the dog away should the boy act frightened. He struggled to sit up, wincing. His eyes welled.

"Is he yours?" He reached his hand across the bed, and offered a tremulous smile when Magic slurped his fingers.

"Dog saliva helps heal cuts and stuff." He showed her the crisscross knife wounds on his palm. "That's what Uncle Ricky always says." He scrubbed away the tears with his other fist.

She didn't think the doctors would agree. But she smiled and drew closer to the bed, leery of spooking the boy back into self-imposed silence. "My name's Lia and this is Magical-Dog. What's your name?"

"Peter Molingo." He patted the bed, and after a glance at Lia and her nod of encouragement, Magic did a paws-up on the mattress beside the boy. The dog's black nose worked, muzzle wrinkling as he read the boy's emotional state, as well as the trauma he suffered. Antiseptics didn't clean away the blood smell from a dog's acute nose.

Magic gave a huge sigh, and settled his broad chin on the mattress, allowing the boy to stroke his brow. "Rottweiler? I thought they had short tails?"

"Very good, Peter. Magic's mom is a Rottweiler police dog in Chicago. And his daddy's a German Shepherd who lives right here in Heartland. I think you met Shadow out at the pumpkin patch. He got that beautiful tail from his daddy. He needs that long tail for proper dog communication." Shadow sired her beautiful Magical-Dog, a miraculous story for another day. "Can I call your parents, Peter?"

"My parents died, so me and my brother live with Uncle Ricky. And now he's murdered! I saw it, I saw what he did. And he saw me." His breath quickened, hands again clutching and twisting the sheet. "He chased me, he cut me, and I got away… but he's after me." The tears finally spilled down his face, teeth chattering with emotion.

"I'm sorry, Peter. You're safe here now." Her stomach churned at the child's deep distress.

"No, no, no! I saw… saw him here, he's after me, here at the hospital. He's going to kill me because I took the proof. Uncle Ricky said run and hide it, so I took it, and he knows. He knows! He followed me here; I saw him when I came in! Oh no, no, no, he's going to kill me, too…" His voice hiccupped to a stop. "Magical Dog, I don't want to die, too."

Magic's voice joined the child's wail in his own dog-song of sorrow.

Chapter Ten: SEPTEMBER

September pulled the large car into the garage and barely had it in park before rolling out of the driver's seat. Combs had started parking his car in the driveway, just in case he had to drive himself. It also left room for him to enter September's car. His injured leg still lacked flexibility, and space in the cramped carriage house garage remained the bane of his existence.

Shadow warbled and agitated in the backseat. "Shush, baby dog, settle." She heard Kinsler's answering yaps from the back of the house. That either meant Willie had yet to return home, or Combs banished the terrier to the fenced garden to burn off some energy. Probably just as well. She didn't need the high energy dog trying to get sniffs of Lia's cat before she had Pippo settled.

She pocketed her keys and opened the rear car door to release Shadow. Even though Combs had installed state-of-the-art security, she knew from experience that nothing was totally secure. She trusted Shadow's nose and instincts far more than electronics. "Shadow, *check it out.*" She made a sweeping gesture with one hand, and the dog leaped away.

While she waited for him to return and signal his all clear, she glanced around the property and took deep breaths to settle her own unease. The big green gate at the front of the circle drive had automatically closed and locked. A tall fence surrounded the several acres to create a fortress around the old Victorian she'd renovated. Not even a tornado managed to destroy her dream home, and the rebuild made the property even more secure. She felt a fondness for this grand old house, a building that had taken years of abuse and neglect, and remained standing, mirroring her own evolution.

September moved to open the rear of the car to collect the cats. "Macy, kitty-boy, what am I gonna do with you?" For now, Macy seemed recovered from his fainting spell, but although necessary, the questioning by Brummitt had delayed getting the cat prompt vet attention.

Cats with hypertrophic cardiomyopathy had a limited lifespan. He'd already beaten the odds of many cats with his diagnosis. She couldn't bear to consider Macy's luck might run out. She and the big Maine Coon had been family longer than anyone else in her circle of friends. Macy got her through the worst moments of her life.

She'd call the vet clinic tonight, at least leave a message, and be on the doorstep early tomorrow—as a longtime client and friend, Doc Eugene would do his best to work Macy in. Pippo also needed evaluation. All those dead birds around the tank suggested a horrible situation.

Shadow raced back to her, happily panting and tail waving with accomplishment. He skidded to a stop before her, sat, and barked once, his signal he'd found nothing of import. She smiled, stroking his cheeks. "Good dog, Shadow, good *check it out*." She hadn't expected he'd find anything, but the worst surprises came when you let your guard down.

Floodlights shined from the rear of the house, illuminating the brick sidewalk leading from the garage to the rear kitchen entrance. Combs called, "Need any help? I'll send Willie."

She raised her eyebrows. September gave a thumbs-up to the monitoring camera mounted near the ceiling of the garage. So Willie beat her home after all. "Thanks, I could use a hand."

She heard the pelting steps of the youngster, grateful for his sunny disposition and puppy-like eagerness to help.

"You found Lia's cat? Macy tracked him down? Totally fire. So is Lia coming over?" He ducked his head without meeting her eyes.

September hid a smile. She suspected Willie had a crush on Lia, despite the woman's fifteen years on him. "Yep. Pippo's in the spare cat carrier in the back, and still pretty stressed out. So handle carefully and wait for me to release him. I haven't had a chance to call Lia yet, and it's late for her to head this way. Let's set him up in the laundry room at least for the night." Willie's slight frame wasn't strong enough to heft Macy's solid weight.

She watched him gently cradle the carrier in his thin arms, murmuring softly to Pippo as he returned to the kitchen door. The boy had matured over the summer, especially after his August adventures at the Celtic Festival. Of course, kids grew by leaps and pounces anyway, you blinked and they gained inches. But surviving mayhem had a way of changing people, for better or worse.

She grabbed Macy's carrier, slung the strap over her shoulder, and closed the rear car door. "Doc Eugene will figure things out. For I wish it to be so." She blinked hard, quelling the hollow feeling in the pit of her stomach. She wouldn't make a big deal of this with Combs. He understood and accepted her bond with the animals, but for him and many others, that connection paled in comparison to human victims. Oh and she agreed.

But *they* were strangers. *Macy* was family. Macy held her heart.

"Yes, you're family too, Shadow." He bounded by her side, making happy chortling noises at being free of the car, and back in their familiar place. "I suppose everybody's ready for treats?"

Macy meerowed and echoed Shadow's bark of acknowledgment. Shadow got two meals a day and intermittent treats, while Macy received five to eight mouse-size meals daily. Both were well past due.

September reached the rear kitchen door, where Shadow waited for her nod before rushing through as Combs held it wide for them both. Once inside, he shoved the door closed, banging it with his good hip out of habit, from when the door used to stick.

September set Macy's carrier on the kitchen island and zippered open the front. She spoke as she worked, crossing to the drawer that contained Macy's medication, and retrieving the proper dosage. "Glad Melinda's friends fetched Willie. Hope it didn't cause too many fireworks." Combs's daughter had a firecracker temper to match her red hair, and though she was a good kid at heart, she resented playing babysitter to her little brother.

He nodded. "I had to bribe her. Instead of Whataburger, she's out with her friends at a movie." September raised one eyebrow, questioning. "Yes, Delaney is part of the group, he's driving. But it's not a date. I made that clear with them both." He shrugged at her smirk. "One of the other kids' parents promised to chaperone, like it or not."

Melinda wanted to grow up too fast, while September wanted to slow the years down. She might be only thirty, but on days like today she felt three times that old.

She returned to the kitchen island with Macy's medication, and the treat chaser. Shadow sat and pawed her leg, licking his lips. "Combs, why don't you give Shadow his food."

Combs leaned against the door and didn't move. "You know he won't eat anything in that bowl unless he sees you put it there. That may be a problem."

She nodded. A new behavior for the big dog. She supposed it makes sense to him. As her PTSD service dog, they were never apart, unless something bad separated them. It had felt devastating the few times it happened, and had left a mark on Shadow as well, particularly since she had no way to explain to him.

"Macy, pill time." The cat sat on the counter, huge fluffy tail curled around and over front paws. He obediently tipped up his face with mouth slightly open. September gently grasped his chin to hold it steady and popped the pill into his mouth with the fingers of her other hand. As a reward, he got some more of the Churu paste.

Shadow watched avidly. Now and then, she offered him cats treats, but he always tried to take the whole tube in his mouth, leaving nothing for Macy. Adding insult to injury, the cat must endure dog spit by licking the tube after Shadow's turn.

"Combs, would you please shut both of the kitchen gates? I'd like to keep Macy here for the night. Need an appointment with Doc Eugene asap." She didn't want Macy running around the big house, passing out in a closet somewhere, and having a hard time finding him.

He obligingly latched first one and then the second metal pet gates for keeping the animals in the kitchen. "That won't keep Macy in, though. He's hopped over this from a standing jump."

Her lips tightened. She spooned a dollop of wet cat food into Macy's bowl and set it atop the refrigerator, his preferred perch. She watched when Macy poised to make the leap then gave up with a soft mew. She moved the bowl down to the lower level on a cat tree next to the wall. "I think his heart issues will keep him grounded."

"Oh babe, sorry. That why the vet check?" Combs crossed to her, his stiff leg making his gait awkward, and took her in his arms. "But he found Lia's missing cat."

She nodded, hugged him back, then hurried to scoop Shadow's food into his bowl. He whined, knowing she still felt upset, ignoring the meal until she pointed at his bowl.

"I got Pippo all set in the laundry room. He wasn't antsy or anything, purring and pushing against the carrier, so I let him out. That okay? Cuz I gotta go study." Willie talked nonstop, a habit when he got excited about anything. He stopped a moment to loop thin boy arms around her waist for a quick hug. "Can we go pick out my pumpkin tomorrow? I gotta work on my costume and the jack-o'-lantern design contest. I wanna go as something nefarious."

That was his new favorite word. "Maybe a vampire. Kinsler can be a werewolf."

"Don't forget to bring Kinsler inside, once Shadow and Macy finish eating." She preferred feeding them separately, just in case one of them got protective of their bowl.

Willie nodded, opened the refrigerator and grabbed an apple. He munched a bite and kept talking with a mouthful as he left the room. "Double, double toil and trouble; Fire burn and caldron bubble…" He had to memorize a certain number of lines from Shakespeare to pass his next level of Thespian membership. Of course, he chose one appropriate to the Halloween season.

Combs waited until he heard Willie ascend the stairs. "Another murder, seriously? We agreed to a hiatus, at least until we get the Paladin Group squared away."

"We did. We are. I didn't go looking for this."

"Funny, how Lia's missing cat just happened to—"

"Lia didn't even know about Pippo. Her grandmother asked me."

He blew out his breath in exasperation. "And I warned you she's always trouble. You shouldn't have even taken her call."

"Combs, nobody could anticipate what happened. And for heaven sakes, it's Lia's cat. If Macy went missing, Lia'd go the extra mile for me." At her tone, Shadow abandoned his bowl to lean against her thigh. His big brown eyes stared up at her, and he whined softly under his breath. She felt her pulse slow, and she took big even breaths to further stem the rising stress.

She wasn't a fan of the woman, either. Cornelia Corazon liked to play lady of the manor and had the wealth and the clout to get her way on almost everything in the county. "I need to update both Cornelia and Lia. But Doc Eugene should check out Pippo too. Dead birds littered the entire area; looked like a bomb went off." She immediately regretted her choice of words.

He crossed to her, and caught up her left hand, his thumb tracing the green jewel of the engagement ring she still wore. "Just so we agree. We're not ready to take on clients." His jaw tightened. "Teddy and I heard about it on the police scanner. Is the boy okay?"

She leaned into him, liking the solid feel of his strong shoulder. "They took him to the hospital. He had knife wounds on his hands and arms. Maybe in his gut. Peter was covered in blood and scared to death. And just so you know, yes, I agree. No clients, not yet. We're not ready. I'm not ready." She laughed ruefully. "Not that anyone'll ask for help, especially not Detective Brummitt. She even warned us away. She's lead on the case. Grilled me up one side and down the other before letting me leave the scene."

He grinned. "She'll be good at her job. Catching a crazy case like this only a few months in has her revved into overdrive. Be good for her rep to catch a case she can solve quick." He hesitated. "Guess the victims didn't have ID?"

She sighed. "Only know the boy's first name, Peter." She stroked Shadow's brow then pointed him once more toward his bowl. As he began to munch in earnest, she added, "The boy mentioned his Uncle Ricky. But the kid was pretty raw, as you can imagine, all wrung out on adrenaline and pain. They shipped him out pretty quickly, already had an IV hooked up and Brummitt said he was unconscious when they left the pumpkin patch." She hoped he survived his injuries. Some of the blood might have been from the other victim.

The distinctive chime announced someone at the driveway

gate. Combs limped to the intercom and keyed the video to eyeball the entryway. His brow furrowed. "It's Melinda. She's back early." He waited until she made a face into the video to confirm her identity, then watched as she hopped out of an unfamiliar car. He pressed the button to open the gate and make sure she slipped inside. Combs waved at the driver, thanking her before switching the gate back into place.

September walked to the kitchen door, thumbed the lock open and pulled it ajar in preparation for the girl's arrival. Huffing angrily from her race up the drive, Melinda banged into the door, a curly haired tornado with all the angst and energy of a thwarted teenager.

"September, thanks so much for ruining everything." Her sarcasm cut deep.

September sighed. The on again off again relationship with the girl kept her walking a tight rope. "What did I do this time?"

Melinda flounced across the room, opening the pet gate and leaving it swinging wide as she crossed into the living room. September followed, shutting the gate behind her. "Melinda, tell me. What's wrong?"

The girl's eyes overflowed, and she impatiently scrubbed tears away, smearing carefully applied eye makeup. "I waited weeks to go out with Delaney. I mean with the group. And now it's all spoiled. Why do you always have to find trouble?"

A bad feeling grew in the pit of September's stomach. "I need a little bit more…"

"Delaney got an emergency call just as the movie started. You found his Uncle Ricky out at the pumpkin patch. Now Delaney's at the hospital taking care of his little brother, Peter."

"Oh honey, I'm so sorry…" September tried to take the girl in her arms.

Melinda backed away. She breathed heavily. "Why do you have to spoil everything? When does the Paladin Group start solving the crime?"

Chapter Eleven: LIA

The boy is scared to death. And rightly so." Lia spoke softly in one of the small treatment rooms with Brummitt, grateful for the empty space. On a Friday night, prime time for emergencies, she appreciated the lucky break, especially considering what the boy shared. "Peter insists he saw the killer here at the hospital; in the ER waiting room."

"Paranoia kicking in. Understandable after what he's gone through." Brummitt had already dispatched officers to track down Peter's remaining family. "He's got an older brother, high school age, I think, who's on the way here. Also an aunt, but she's out of state. Take a while to get here."

Magic had calmed Peter, and at least the brothers would have each other. "Do you have anyone to stay with them?" Lia hoped someone would stay with the two boys.

Brummitt shrugged. "We'll call social services. Did you get an address for the uncle? Need to go through his residence, see if we can find what might've put a target on him."

Lia rattled off the Molingo's address, which Peter had given her. Lia ran her hands through her frizzy blond hair, the wig had done a number on it. "The boys' parents died sometime last year, and ever since they been living with their uncle. I don't know any further details. Oh, the perp stole Ricky's truck, means he'll know the address too."

"Did Peter say what they were doing out there? The place didn't open until after school. Your buddy September made that point."

Lia shook her head. That was the burning question. "The nurse chased me out before I could get any more information." Somebody knew they'd be out there, and when, to kill Molingo. If it was a random attack, that worried her more.

That reminded Lia, she hadn't heard from September. The horrible day could get even worse once she knew the fate of Pippo. At least this time, there was no way anyone could connect the mayhem to her friend.

She heard the automatic door into the emergency waiting room whoosh open. They stepped back into the area in time to see a tall thin young man, long hair hanging in his wild eyes, dash through them. He stopped dead to stare all around, the very picture of *deer in the headlights*. His eyes focused on the receptionist.

"They said my brother's here. Where's Peter? Is he okay?"

Brummitt stepped forward before the receptionist could answer and guided the young man to a chair. "I'm Detective Brummitt. Peter will be fine, a few minor cuts and a little shook up, but now he's resting. Let's you and me have a little talk, then you can go see him, okay?"

More than minor cuts. But it wasn't her place to correct Brummitt. Lia took that as her cue to leave. "Magic, let's go."

It felt like years since she'd arrived at the hospital. The happy feeling from raising kids' spirits faded, leaving a deep unease. She had the creepy feeling of being watched and glanced around as they left through the emergency doors. Lia saw no one. And Magic would have alerted had danger been nearby. The dog's short fur above his hackles bristled briefly, but that had as much to do with her own emotional state as anything he sensed.

She took out her phone from one of the many pockets in her regulation slacks, checking quickly for messages. Then Lia dialed, grateful when September answered on the first ring.

"Before you say anything, September, I know why you haven't called. I'm at the hospital and just spoke to the boy you rescued." She hesitated before rushing on. "It's been a crappiocca day, to borrow your word, so if you have bad news give it to me straight. Then me and Magic will go howl at the moon for a while."

Shelly stubbed out his cigarette when he saw Lia exit. He watched from behind a dumpster on the other side of the street as she crossed the parking lot with her big dog.

The cops and medical team made it impossible to get close to the boy. Nearly had a disaster when the kid recognized him and had a meltdown on his way in. He'd take care of that stray thread later. The boy knew next to nothing, but Molingo had given the kid something Shelly must recover. Kids were easy to convince to do the right thing. He grinned.

For now, Shelly wanted to learn more about this Corazon woman. Ricky Molingo got wound up and turned loose to dig into the past. He was tipped off by someone with insider information, and she fit the bill. This little girl had signed her own death warrant, and he'd take care of her right after he eliminated the big furry protector.

At the thought, Shelly pulled the red rubber ball from his pocket and squeezed it to make the beeping sound. He clenched the rainbow clown wig rescued from the ER trash in the other hand. At just under five-ten and a slight build, a change of clothes with the nominal disguise offered more than enough of a match. Anyone making life miserable for Shelly deserved what they got.

"Trick-or-treat, bitch."

SATURDAY,

October 26

Chapter Twelve: SEPTEMBER

Shadow paced on the back seat, whining and muttering under his breath, as September pulled into the vet clinic parking lot. She appreciated them working her in. "Just chill, Shadow. You like Doc Eugene. Nikki works Saturday, too."

At the young girl's name, Shadow offered one sharp bark of acknowledgment, and his tail beat against the leather upholstery.

In the rear of the car, Macy added his meowing commentary, but Pippo in the other carrier stayed silent. She'd arranged to meet Lia here. September climbed out of the car and waited for an elderly woman exiting the clinic to reach her own car. The lady pressed a disintegrating Kleenex to her red eyes, trying to stifle her weeping. September hesitated before asking, "I'm so sorry. Can I do anything for you?"

The woman shook her head. "Pray for my Itty-Bitty. She is the sweetest ever, and she's so sick." She scrubbed her eyes with the heel of both palms. "I'm always so careful with her, had her since she was tiny. Well, she's still tiny. Loves to chase the butterflies, and the hens in the backyard. She can't catch them, but it's great fun for her." The woman leaned against her car, sighing and dabbing her nose. "She was playing, then just stopped and fell over. I rushed her in quick as I could." Her lower lip trembled. "Doc Eugene said he'd do what he could." She climbed into her car and slowly drove away.

September shook her head and reached for the rear door to let Shadow out. She'd always adored animals, and prior to dedicating herself to music in her youth, briefly considered veterinary medicine. But she couldn't bear the thought of failing someone's beloved cat or dog. They called it the *practice* of medicine for a reason. Sometimes life-and-death decisions had no good outcome.

But the woman's comment about her pet fainting gave September a chill. A vague symptom, perhaps, but one shared with Macy. The big Maine Coon had always been very active, and she believed quality of life trumped longevity. As long as Macy enjoyed his tracking games, she refused to limit his fun.

"Shadow, let's get Macy-cat so Doc Eugene can help him feel better. Sound like a plan?"

He danced around, dragging the short leash attached to his harness. The vet clinic had a *no exceptions* policy that all animals be leashed, or in carriers. Even a well-trained service dog like Shadow must follow the rules. Rule breakers gave everyone a bad name.

As she moved to the rear of her car and keyed open the hatch, Lia's truck pulled into the crowded lot. September slung the strap of Macy's carrier over her shoulder and grabbed the handle on the second one containing Pippo. She waited for the younger woman to join her then handed her Pippo's carrier without a word.

Shadow glanced at September for approval before heading quickly to Lia's truck. He placed paws up against the side of the vehicle. From inside, Magic nose-touched Shadow through the half-open window. The two dogs' tails created semaphore signals in the pleasant October morning.

"I'd better leave Magic in the car. He loves other dogs, but other dogs don't always love him back." Lia lifted the cat carrier to eye height and peered inside.

"Did you stay out at the Corazon Ranch last night?" September silently signaled Shadow, and he came away from the car to glue himself to her side. She stooped to grasp his leash and led the way to the clinic entrance.

Lia scowled, her nostrils flaring with emotion. "Heck no. Not after Grammy lost Pippo. We stayed over at the kennels, and Magic got to sniff out all the bunnies and squirrels." She doubled her stride to keep up with September's longer legs. "Besides, Grammy just wants to arm twist me to attend her party."

Laughing, September waited for the younger girl to open the clinic door with her free hand. "Your birthday, too, right? Melinda can't stop talking about it."

"The police still had the pumpkin patch blocked when I came by. I feel bad for the kids. Did you know Peter thinks he's next on the killer's list? Poor scared kid." She cocked her head. "You and Paladin taking the case?"

Why did people keep asking that? "No way. Don't even think that." She pretended to shiver. "Melinda's already pressuring us to butt in; but even if I wanted to—and I don't—Detective Brummitt warned us off."

She and Combs both wanted a clear separation between what law enforcement handled and what the Paladin Group focused on. Cold cases made the best sense. She specifically wanted to address the horrors perpetuated by the Wong family, and right those wrongs. Nobody had the bandwidth to focus on every random murder that happened. You couldn't take everything personally, or you might as well hide in a closet in a fetal position.

Just the thought echoed the feeling of spiraling out of control in one of her PTSD episodes. No…no-no-no… Shadow bumped her hip, and September centered herself.

September crossed the waiting room to the check in. Shadow followed, performing another paws-up on the counter.

"Shadow! How's my favorite doggy?" A girl with white-blond hair leaned forward and giggled when he aimed a slurping kiss across her nose. Nikki turned to the two women. "I already pulled Macy's chart. Hi Lia. I couldn't find a record for your Pippo. Has he been here before?"

Lia shook her head, and her face flushed. "My bad. He's one of the kittens that Magic's mother adopted during that police investigation last year in Oklahoma. Used to call him Gizmo."

September remembered Karma nursed the kittens alongside her pups, and Lia kept the pale orange and white one. Not only his name, but the fur color had changed, maybe due to better nutrition.

"I had to spend some time in the hospital shortly after and just got covered up, never got around to following up. My bad, not a good excuse, I know." Lia shrugged. "Grammy's been calling him Pippo. He actually answers to that name better. Cats choose their names." She took the clipboard and questionnaire Nikki handed her to fill out and took a seat on one of the padded benches.

"You mean over at the Corazon's? That's where the hayride and Halloween party is, right?" Nikki grinned, fairly dancing back and forth with excitement. "I'm going to the hayride and maybe the bonfire after." She made a face. "Mom said the party's for grownups. Says it's got adult beverages."

Macy yowled. September juggled the carrier. "Do you have a room for us? He wants out."

"Oh yeah, sure. Take Macy down to room one. Doc Eugene's just finishing up with another cat. Really sick one, poor little thing. He says it's the third one this week showing the same signs."

September thought of the weepy woman she'd met on the way in. "Shadow, let's go." He led the way down the short narrow hallway and slipped into the small examining room. She latched the door behind her before setting the cat carrier on the small metal tabletop, gratified to see the slick aluminum surface had been covered with a soft padded towel. Cats never appreciated the cold slick metal. In the past several months, the clinic had made changes to bring the practice in line with the new Fear Free movement. They'd set up a bird feeder outside the window, and a water fountain splish-splashed in the corner beside a cat tree, all designed to reduce feline stress.

Doc Eugene bustled into the small room. "I was

concerned to get your call. His signs escalated?" He held out a finger to the cat and smiled when Macy first nose-touched then stroked his cheek against it. "Let's take a listen, big guy." He placed the stethoscope against the cat's side.

She waited to answer until he'd had a chance to hear the cat's heart. "Macy eats well, and I've monitored gum color. He doesn't seem to tire during play, either. But we were tracking a lost cat yesterday…"

The veterinarian nodded. "Lia's missing Pippo. I heard about all of that." He made a motion with one hand, taking in all *of that*.

"Macy fainted. First time in forever, since we first got his diagnosis. I understand that can happen with HCM, but it scared me. He's done so well with the daily oral meds."

Doc Eugene nodded. "One in seven cats develop hypertrophic cardiomyopathy at some point in their lives. Most show no symptoms at all, until they die."

She felt her face drain of color.

He shrugged. "Macy's lucky he showed signs so we could try treatment."

He'd educated her about the disease, and she knew it could progress with or without treatment. Just like people, a cat's heart had four chambers. When the left ventricle excessively thickened, it narrowed the inner chamber preventing it from filling properly or working efficiently. To compensate, the heart beats faster than normal, and needs more oxygen. Lack of oxygen caused fainting spells or worse—death of heart muscle cells, resulting in HCM.

"September, you've known from the get-go, there's no cure. The beta blocker he's on may not be enough to keep his heart rate under control as he ages."

Shadow pressed hard against her thigh, recognizing her

emotional state. "Guess I thought—hoped anyway—it pointed to something more treatable."

He sighed. "I'll run another echo and check for changes. There's also a new HCM experimental treatment…"

"Do it! Whatever it is, get Macy on the trial if it'll help him." She scrubbed her face. "I can't lose him, Doc. Please, help my cat."

Macy leaped from the table, and reflexively September caught him and buried her face in his long dark fur.

SUNDAY,

October 27

Chapter Thirteen: DOLORES

Dolores trotted around the house, switching on lamps throughout the formal living room, and the more informal family room. She loved this tidy little place, a luxury she never imagined they could afford on Clarence's retirement, but she never questioned providence. Or Clarence. She knew better.

Sunday was supposed to be a day of rest, but it was the one time of the week she knew Clarence stayed out of the house. He and his buddies played cards, or puttered on their cars, went fishing, or any of half a dozen pastimes they'd taken up since early retirement. She didn't begrudge him the time away. It gave her a break from fixing three meals, since he indulged in multiple beers and snacks with the guys. She only had to fix dinner when he returned.

So after church on Sunday mornings—Clarence didn't attend, wasn't a believer no matter how hard she tried—she rolled up her sleeves and made the house sparkle: vacuumed the rugs, dusted every surface, polished the glass tabletop, and oiled both Clarence's mahogany desk and her antique sewing cabinet. The whole house smelled of furniture polish, a clean lemony odor that made her feel virtuous.

He'd returned home an hour ago and taken no notice of how nice the place looked. No matter, Dolores knew. Besides, he'd eaten the Sunday pot roast, two helpings, a high compliment. The evening was shaping up nicely, the best in many weeks, with no manufactured arguments.

Clarence belched loudly, scratched his large stomach, and pushed back from the table. "House looks nice. Smells fresh." Without waiting for her response, he headed for the family room to prop up his feet and watch his favorite Sunday shows.

Dolores's mouth dropped open and she blushed with pleasure. But she knew better than to make any kind of comment. Instead, she hurried to clear the table and start the dishwasher so she could join him. Sometimes Clarence fell asleep and she could switch channels to watch one of her preferred shows. After two large portions of pot roast, she figured chances were high.

"Did you turn on the outside lights yet? Sheesh, gotta do everything myself."

"No, you just sit down, let me do that. I meant to do it earlier, sorry." Drat! Now she'd gone and maybe spoiled the pleasant evening.

Dolores hurried through the formal living room, reflexively straightening a lampshade as she passed by. At the front door, she switched on the outside lights, illuminating the yard in front of the house to reveal the ornate jack-o'-lantern display she'd put together.

They lived on a cul-de-sac, with no house closer than three lots away. Clarence liked it that way, treasured his privacy. He'd purchased the lots on both sides for that reason, but Dolores kept hoping he'd sell at least one of the lots to a young couple, preferably with lots of kids. Their own kids, now grown, had moved away the first chance they got. She wished they'd make the effort to bring the grandkids for trick-or-treating. But she understood travel took time and expense. Next month she'd hug their necks during Thanksgiving visits.

Movement at the end of the road caught her attention. She squinted and took off her glasses. Since cataract surgery, her far vision had improved, and she saw better without them. "Clarence? What day is Halloween?"

He grunted. "31st."

She rolled her eyes. She knew the date. "I mean, *when* is it? I thought trick-or-treaters don't come until that night? I don't have enough candy yet."

"Thursday. But the HOA moved trick-or-treating till Friday night, so the kiddos have the next day to recover. Not that anyone follows their stupid rules, though."

As the figure passed under a streetlight, she could see their bright neon rainbow flyaway wig, a bulbous crimson nose, and wide magenta lips; with the baggy tan cargo pants and blue crewneck shirt it looked like a box of crayons had melted. Walking with a distinct limp, the clown made a beeline for their front door—probably because they had all the Halloween decor.

She blew out a breath. Drat. This poor child got the wrong weekend, but that was no reason to disappoint. Idly, she wondered where the parents might be. In years past, carloads had driven into the subdivision, dropping off groups of kids and picking them up later in the evening.

"We've got an early trick-or-treater. Could you please answer the door? Stall for a minute while I scrounge up some candy."

Clarence grumbled and groaned as he climbed out of his La-Z-Boy chair. He loved Halloween, and got a kick out of all the costumes, though he'd never dress up himself.

She scurried into the kitchen and pulled a hidden bag of chocolates from a cupboard. Clarence also loved Halloween for the candy, so she had to protect the stash until after the kids got their share. She poured the sweet foil-wrapped treats into a basket as the doorbell chimed, and hurried to return. At the last minute, she grabbed up her phone. Dolores loved taking pictures and sometimes video of the best outfits among their visitors.

"Here we are. Now smile for the camera." She juggled the phone in one hand, pressing record as she entered the foyer.

The clown's foot booted the door as it swung open, catching Clarence on one shoulder and knocking him off balance. Dolores's eyes widened when the pink gloved clown hands shoved a bouquet of fresh flowers against Clarence's chest. A muffled thump sound made her husband's mouth drop open with a gasp. He dropped to the floor, eyes blinking rapidly, and clutched the flowers to his chest. Crimson blossomed beneath spasming fingers and spilled down his chest to pool on the spic-n-span entryway floor.

That's going to make a mess.

Dolores, still recording, dropped the candy basket, and backed away from the clown's pointing gun. She turned quickly, slippered feet sliding on the marble entry, and grabbed for the table to keep from falling.

She never heard the second thump from the clown's gun.

Carefully stepping around the growing crimson puddle, the clown stooped to collect the phone. It continued to record until poking the red button stopped the operation. He had to pull off one glove to replay the video. It gave a clear view of the last few seconds, from the top of the rainbow wig to the black regulation shoes. It also revealed bloodshot eyes that itched and burned with each eye blink.

His finger hovered over the delete button, clearly the best choice. But an alternative might simplify the job. The clown smiled, stretching painted purple lips wide at the thought. A quick action and the phone sent the video via text to the perfect patsy. Only then did the killer delete the video, polish the phone with the pink gloves, and set it on the table.

He grabbed a handful of the chocolates on the way out. Treats for a job well done.

After carefully closing the door, the clown retraced his steps, making sure anyone watching would note and easily describe the limping gait and clown regalia. The operation had taken less than three minutes.

MONDAY,

October 28

Chapter Fourteen: SEPTEMBER

Willie, for the last time, get downstairs and finish your breakfast. Melinda, stop picking at your food. Eat it or leave it. We head out in three minutes." September took another long chug from her coffee mug, then set it on the stained-glass table. Monday mornings always proved challenging.

Combs took the last bite of his breakfast burrito while scrolling through his cell phone. "They can take the bus, September." He didn't look up.

She shook her head. The bus rarely stopped any more since they'd been ferrying the kids to their school drop-off points all term. Despite no known overt threats, she wouldn't risk the kid's safety. Truth be told, being the new head of Wong Enterprises, hidden danger remained. After decades of villainous dealings, and layer upon layer of criminal enterprises, it would take many months—probably years—before she felt safe enough to let her guard down. She hated carrying weapons but accepted that as part of her life.

Willie thundered down the stairs, his dog at his heels.

"Willie, take Kinsler out for a break before we leave. You don't want to be cleaning up messes when you come back." The boy finished tying his second shoe before leading Kinsler out the kitchen door.

She glanced up at the refrigerator, empty, since Macy remained with Doc Eugene to finish tests. Funny how the cat's absence left such an enormous hole in the ambiance of the house. Shadow whined and nudged her hand.

Melinda pushed her cereal bowl aside. She let out a sigh that reached clear to her toes. "Can't I stay home? I feel horrible."

Combs looked up. "I'd be more concerned if you didn't feel bad. I'm sorry about what happened to Delaney and Peter. But there's nothing you can do except offer support. Maybe after school we can arrange a visit."

September shook her head. "Lia told me Detective Brummitt has the boys in protective custody. So no visiting, or knowing where they are."

He raised his eyebrows, started to say something then thought better of it. He shrugged. "Detective Brummitt knows best."

"But I'm no threat. I wouldn't tell anyone where they are." Melinda pushed back from the table and walked a couple of steps. At a sharp look from September, she grabbed her cereal bowl and placed in the sink. "The Paladin Group fights for the innocent. Delaney and Peter didn't do anything wrong, did they? What happened to championing them?" She crossed her arms, bottom lip pouting with frustration. "Delaney said we'd go to the hayride. There's a cool bonfire after. Everyone's going. I can't go alone. How cringe."

"With that attitude, you won't go at all." The sharp words deflated the girl's defiance.

She crumbled. "I'm just so worried about him, that's all."

The kitchen door swung open, and Kinsler trotted inside with Willie in his wake. "He did all of his stuff. We're good to go."

Combs stood, wobbled for a moment while grasping the chair back with one hand. Once steady, he walked slowly to the door. "Load up."

Shadow sat in the middle of the back seat, while the kids took the window seats. September waited for Combs to lever his stiff leg into the foot well before starting the car. She knew it frustrated him, but he'd shot down her suggestion to purchase a vehicle with hand operations. Point of honor, she supposed. He continued rehab, determined to regain full use of his leg.

Still sulking, Melinda stormed out of the car at her school, but as soon as she saw one of her friends, her expression transformed. She rushed to spill the latest tea. The girls' heads bent as gasps and giggles were stifled.

September drove the several blocks to reach Willie's drop-off point. As he unhooked his seatbelt, Willie also sighed, a hilarious mimic of his older sister's expression.

"What's the problem? You sound like a balloon with a slow leak." She smiled, trying to get a giggle out of him.

"It's just that… I'm sad about Peter, too. But that means

the pumpkin patch is closed and we didn't get to find one over the weekend. I still need one for the contest, they moved it to Friday. Too many other parties the night before. The winning team gets to pick the next one act play." He sighed again. "On top of that, my vampire costume flamed out. Somebody else already got dibs on that. Any other ideas for nefarious characters?"

"Why not a hero?" She glanced sideways at Combs.

Willie shook his head. "Heroes are boring. Playing bad ass guys is more fun." He grinned.

"Language, mister!" Combs hid a smile.

Shadow barked, always happy to add commentary to happy conversations.

Halloween fell on Thursday this year, but most of the kid-age parties happened Friday night. Most of North Texas had decided on the switch. That gave kids, teachers, and parents a day to recover from sugar highs.

Combs cracked his knuckles. "I don't know how long they'll keep the pumpkin patch closed. That's a big area to search."

Willie looked deflated.

"There're other places that sell pumpkins. I saw some at the grocery store, too. How about after school, we stop for you to pick out your pumpkin," September said.

He grinned, instantly transformed. "Fire! We'll make it a perfect pumpkin patch pick. Say that fast five times." He laughed, the sound making her heart swell.

"You got it, kiddo." She watched him lope away to join other youngsters. He'd really blossomed since finding his tribe on the stage. They chattered as they entered the school.

"About Melinda and the Halloween party…" September glanced again at Combs.

"Not gonna happen. She's too young to date. And the Corazons charge a month's salary for tickets to that shindig." Combs crossed his arms and stared out the passenger window as they pulled away from the school.

"Oh I agree. Maybe the hayride? With a bunch of girlfriends." Besides, if forbidden, Melinda had been known to sneak out. Better to give a little than risk full rebellion.

He snorted. "She's fourteen, going on forty. So much like her mother."

September smiled sadly. "Yes, her mother was a beauty, and you had a beautiful daughter."

She suspected he kept a tight rein on Melinda partly because he hadn't been able to protect his wife, or rather ex-wife, who died far too early.

That was Combs, always the protector. And look what it got him. A bum leg. And trapped in a relationship with her that could never move forward.

The beautiful fall day burnished the water on the small lake to a patent leather shine as they pulled into the lake house drive next to Teddy's RV. September used the remote to open the garage door, and as soon as they cleared, it automatically began to close. Teddy and Combs had retrofitted the old house with an abundance of security devices, including motion-activated cameras. September still got creeped out by the constant surveillance.

Combs accessed the hidden security panel on the interior door. He waited for it to scan the unique eye signature of his iris. As the door unlocked, he also announced himself on the intercom.

"Combs here, with September. And Shadow, of course." He paused before stepping through the door. "Let's keep this latest tragedy under wraps. You know how Teddy acts around a puzzle."

She nodded. The older man dearly loved a challenge. She followed Combs into the kitchen, then waited for him to securely latch and lock the door.

Teddy waited at the foot of a small single-passenger elevator he'd installed. His old-fashioned wire rim glasses sat askew, and he wore tan cargo shorts and a gold and green Aloha shirt.

He'd fit in on a beach somewhere but was more at home behind a keyboard, and all his computer equipment now lived in the tower room of the third floor. The original spiral staircase remained mostly a playground for Teddy's orange and white Maine Coon cat, Meriwether.

"Paladin has its first client?" He took off and polished his spectacles then replaced them on his nose. He stepped inside the elevator. "Follow me." It silently whooshed him upward, and once he disembarked, he sent it back down for Combs.

"What are you talking about?" September didn't wait; she trotted up the circular stairs. Shadow slowly climbed after her.

Teddy grinned, his expression saying he'd already bought into a new adventure. "A young man named Peter, and his cute-handsome brother Delaney. And a certain young woman who doesn't want her Halloween spoiled."

Melinda had stirred the pot.

TUESDAY,

October 29

Chapter Fifteen: SEPTEMBER

September pushed her chair away from the small table in the tower room, standing to stretch the kinks out of her back and knees. She crossed to peer over the banister, taking in the view of Shadow and Meriwether. The big dog had tucked in lanky legs to fit into the window seat, and the cat snuggled on top of his back. The setting sun shined a spotlight on the pair.

She smiled, always enjoyed seeing how well Shadow interacted with other creatures. It must offer him a respite from constant stress of looking after her. She worried he might burn out, something not everyone recognized in service animals. She'd not had a meltdown in a long time, thanks to Shadow, and was grateful for his sacrifice. But she doubted he'd categorize it as sacrifice, if he had that notion at all.

She turned back to the two men huddled over the laptop. With Melinda and Willie tied up with after school commitments, they'd taken advantage of the chance to work late. Teddy had wanted to run a preliminary investigation into the dead victim she'd found. Going through the motions wouldn't step on Brummitt's toes but would give a nod to Melinda so she'd stop pestering. September didn't want the girl poking around on her own. Too easy to wake up sleeping goblins and get in trouble.

"Ricky Molingo didn't tell his editor about the assignment?" She rubbed her eyes. "We just read the newspaper online now. I don't remember his byline." She missed the days of sitting with a cup of coffee, the newspaper pages rustling, and arguing with Macy for access. The cat loved to spread out on top of the funny section. Did they even have comics anymore?

"Investigative journalists are funny about sharing. Worried about others scooping their story." Teddy squinted through smeared glasses. "Molingo's old-school. His editor said he'd been working on something hush-hush for weeks." Teddy took off his wire rim spectacles and cleaned them on the hem of his parrot shirt before replacing them. "The folks at the paper won't say anything, probably on advice of their lawyers with the tragedy, but I get the feeling they don't know much. Bet they want to reserve juicy bits for their exclusive story, plus cover their butts against potential litigation. Damn vultures."

He'd called the newspaper directly, and met with "no

comment" until he pressed to speak with higher ups, finally speaking with the guy in charge. "The boss guy's pissed Molingo didn't clue him in. He's up to his Gutenberg with unanswered questions from the police. News organizations hate being the cover story. They've got detectives sniffing all around his organization. Molingo, he says, is one of the good guys, but we know how that goes."

Whatever the tale, Ricky Molingo's investigation got him killed. "Who else did he interview?" He must have poked a major goblin to get that response, but September worried what else got awakened in the process. "Other interview subjects could tell us at least the topic." That'd make points for them when they shared intel with Brummitt. Let the police do their job and leave Paladin out of it. This had nothing to do with them.

"I got stonewalled, too." Combs leaned back in his chair, and September worried he'd tip over backward as he balanced. "I called Brummitt. She won't give anything away, not that I expect her to. Well, she did find Molingo's truck, but shared nothing else. Told her to call if she needs help." He grinned. "Guess how well that went over."

Teddy chuckled. "The editor said Molingo kept meticulous notes. He recorded interviews and notes on his phone. Also, he said the newspaper pays for the phone, and he wants it back." He wiggled white eyebrows that reminded September of fancy caterpillars dancing above his glasses. "Love to take a gander at those notes. Did they find his phone?"

"Nope. Still canvasing the pumpkin patch. Brummitt asked if September found it. Apparently, Peter hid it but won't say where." Combs shrugged. "He's scared."

September paced the narrow bird's nest of an office space. The renovation expanded the original shelving lining the walls of the tower room and added built in computer monitors and other technical equipment. They also replaced and upgraded the large floor-to-ceiling window with bulletproof glass.

She stared at the gorgeous view, enjoying the smooth glassy lake surface that reflected the lowering sun. "There's a whole lot of places in the pumpkin patch to hide something. The little outbuilding alone could take ages to comb through. It's got stacks of straw to make hidden tunnels in the hay loft, not to mention the ground floor level."

Teddy growled agreement. "They have the field shut down. Why not use dogs? They sniff out termites and bedbugs these days, why not cell phones? Heck, Lia could bring Magic, since he's already a certified police dog." He winked at September and shrugged. "No offense to Shadow."

Downstairs, the dog roused at the sound of his name and gave a quick sharp bark of inquiry.

Quickly, September strode back to the overlook. "Hey baby dog. Chill. Everything's okay." He sat in front of the elevator, tilting his head one way and then the other as she spoke. He could manage the circular stairs but preferred the easy way up.

She smiled and nodded. Shadow jumped up to paw-punch the appropriate button. The elevator door opened for him, closed almost catching his tail, and began to ascend.

Combs's eyes widened. "When did you teach him that?"

"I didn't. He generalized from dealing with other elevators." When the elevator opened, she knelt on the floor and opened her arms. "Smart boy, aren't you a good dog." He rolled onto his back, tail sweeping the floor and forepaws waving as she stroked his chest.

"Too bad you and that ferocious dog can't interview Peter.

Shadow would lick the kid's face until he gave up the hiding spot." Combs laughed at Shadow's antics.

"Lia and Magic already got as much as they could." September rejoined the two men at the table. Shadow followed, plopping down at her feet with a sigh of contentment. "Teddy, anything you could suss out with your special skill set?"

Deep furrows mapped Teddy's brow. "You mean, break into the police database and steal information? Or the newspaper? But that's against the law." He opened his eyes wide, blinking in faux innocence. "Sure, we can resort to hacking if or when the circumstances warrant. But you've already got an insider who can get the information with a lot less grief or risk."

She wrinkled her nose. *An insider?*

"Absolutely not." Combs's chair landed back on all four legs with a solid thump. "Melinda's already too vested. I don't want to encourage her any further."

Aha. "If I know your daughter, Combs, she is still texting with Delaney no matter what you or I, or the police say." She looked at Teddy for back up. "Asking her to relay a few questions won't put her in danger."

Combs tightened his lips, considering.

She didn't want further involvement, either. "It'll make her *feel* involved, like she's helping her friends. That makes it less likely she'll go off on her own."

"And do something dumb." He finished the thought. His frown had etched permanent creases at the corners of his mouth. That, and premature gray at his temples, aged Combs a decade over the past few months. Protecting his family remained his highest priority, especially when they'd all come so close to losing each other more than once.

He blew out his breath, and rubbed his eyes, as if seeking a clearer picture of how to handle his daughter. "Okay. But let me deal with her. I don't want her arguing later that September agreed to *this*, or Uncle Teddy said she could do *that*." He pulled out his phone and dialed.

September glanced at her own phone to check the time. Willie still had another hour at the theater before someone needed to pick him up. Juggling the kids' activities kept them all busy. It felt normal. She hugged herself, enjoying the feeling. She'd wanted *normal* for a very long time.

Combs placed his phone on the tabletop with the speaker activated. Usually they communicated with texts, so Melinda would know a call meant something serious.

"Daddy, it's the middle of cheer practice." September could almost see the girl tossing her red curls.

"I'm here with September and your Uncle Teddy. I understand you messaged him?" He waited.

She paused, formulating her answer. "Well, you seemed really busy. And I thought with everything going on I didn't want to bother you. So I just made a teeny tiny suggestion that maybe if he thought he could help…" Her voice trailed off.

Combs ran his hand through short, cropped hair. "Yes, I'm sure you didn't want to bother us. But as it happens, because you asked so darned nicely"—his voice dripped with sarcasm—"Paladin Group agreed to do a little digging, just to set our own minds at ease."

She squealed.

He cut her off. "Let's be clear. As agreed, we'll keep you informed of projects for your safety. But you are *not* a part of the organization, nor will you have *any part* in investigating this situation or any other in the future, until or unless you hear otherwise from me. Do you understand?"

He waited a beat. "Melinda?"

Small voice. "Yes Daddy."

Combs rocked back in his chair. "Now it so happens that you may be able to help. Are you still texting Delaney?"

"Well… You see, I…"

"You're not in trouble for that. In fact, is there anything Delaney shared with you that might help? Does he know why his uncle was out there?"

"He worked for the newspaper. A reporter. Delaney said he'd been researching some story that was gonna win all kinds of prizes. Maybe a Pulitzer. Said 'big pay day' coming."

Teddy whistled under his breath. He grabbed a Post-It note, scribbled and passed it to Combs.

Combs read, nodded tersely, and continued. "We talked to his boss at the paper, so that scans. But does Delaney know any details about the story? Who'd he meet? What was he investigating? I understand he kept audio notes on his phone?"

"Delaney didn't know details. Peter didn't either, except that they were out there for an interview. He thought it might be Lia? Have you talked to her?" In the background, they could hear the rest of the cheer squad chanting in unison.

Wait. September's jaw dropped. Molingo couldn't have met Lia. That made no sense. She couldn't be in class in Dallas and in Heartland at the same time.

"Delaney said Peter got majorly upset over losing his uncle's notes." She hesitated, and September waited for the girl to go on, biting her lip to keep from asking her own questions.

September scribbled it on a Post-It and handed it to Combs. He glanced at the paper but ignored her prompt to continue his own line of questions.

"Did Peter leave the phone somewhere specific? Like in that little outbuilding? Or inside a particular jack-o'-lantern? The police need the phone to get Mr. Molingo justice."

September understood. He didn't want Melinda to know that possession of the phone put the brothers at high risk.

"Dad, see that's what doesn't make sense. Delaney doesn't get it either. But Peter says he hid the phone, and then it *went away*. He swears it's not at the pumpkin patch anymore. It's gone."

September flashed back on the big truck leaving the parking lot just as she arrived. Had Peter stashed the phone in that truck? She scribbled another question on the paper and handed it to Combs. He looked at it and nodded.

"What kind of car did his uncle drive?" He looked at the first question September had scribbled, and added, "Why'd he want to interview Lia?"

In the background, they could hear the coach calling for Melinda to return to practice. "Daddy, I gotta go. And I don't know about the car, but I can ask Delaney." She started to hang up.

September couldn't help herself. "Melinda, what does this have to do with Lia?"

"I have no idea. But Peter said his Uncle Ricky told him to get the notes to that Corazon woman."

Chapter Sixteen: LIA

Very conscious of the eyes drilling into her back, Lia kept her posture military straight as she strode away from the police academy training facility. She had nearly sweated through the blue polo shirt, saved only by the standard issue white undershirt. The cargo pants suddenly felt too tight.

Nobody came to her defense, nor did she expect them to. As Drummond's whipping girl, Lia must prove she could take it. Other AIs, in earlier weeks, had singled out other cadets for the traditional look-the-other-way hazing. Only one cadet had packed up and left.

She wouldn't flinch. She owed it to the other female officers-in-training to stand strong. Lia pulled off the cap to mop her brow. When she reached her truck and climbed inside, Lia still refused to look back at where the rest of her class slowly left the area.

A big meal, a hot shower, and some mindless video games would clear her mind, would relieve the knots in her shoulders, as would playing with Magic and cuddling with Pippo. Tonight, she refused to crack her books or run drills the way she had every night since beginning the program. After what Drummond put her through today, and all of last week, she needed a reprieve if she was to make it through the rest of the week. She just had to last three more days.

Lia took a slight detour to swing by the Whataburger drive-through, ordering an extra sandwich for Magic. The only good news she'd had was Doc Eugene giving her cat a clean bill of health. Pippo had been AWOL less than half a day, limiting exposure to dangerous germs. Most cats kept indoors all their lives had no clue how to hunt. But eating vermin could transfer all kinds of bad illnesses. But in Pippo's case, he missed out on receiving his mother's protective colostrum, since he'd been nursed by a dog. She wasn't a vet, but figured that it had to influence his protection. Now with a full coterie of vaccinations, and parasite protections, she expected Pippo to hide or sleep for hours. Based on how much he scarfed from his bowl, Pippo had been more fearful of getting eaten while adventuring, than scrounging up anything dangerous to eat.

Lia munched the hot, salty French fries as she drove. Half the time Lia preferred French fries to Whataburger's signature sandwich. She knew Magic and Pippo would help eat any leftovers.

She pulled into September's parking slot at the front of the hotel. Along with the presidential suite, September insisted Lia use her reserved parking. That way, she didn't need to run Magic up and down extra stairs to reach the dog relief station. Although September owned the hotel and changed pet policy, guests and some staff still sniffed at the dog's presence.

Lia sat for twenty minutes, finishing the fries, then licking the grease and salt from her fingers. She gathered her belongings, grabbed the bag of burgers, locked the truck and left.

The glass doors whooshed open as she approached, letting her into the lobby proper. She nodded and smiled at the uniformed young woman staffing the desk. Lia always felt under-dressed in this fancy place, and plain-Jane ugly compared to the women with perfect makeup and glittering nails. After the day she'd had, she smelled bad, too. Not that she dressed girly anyway, despite what Grammy tried to drill into her throughout her adolescence.

Lia was gratified the elevator door opened almost immediately when she scanned her key card. This elevator climbed to the top floors, including her suite and the private workout rooms, business offices, and specialty accommodations. Other elevators serviced the lower floors, as well going directly to the restaurant on the roof. September had instituted that security measure shortly after gaining control of the building. A second elevator on this floor provided service to the top floor's restaurant.

Lia reflexively checked both directions as she stepped out of the elevator car, before hurrying to her suite at the end of the hall.

"Magical dog, it's me." She always announced her presence, although sure his acute senses knew well before his ears recognized her footsteps or voice.

She swiped her key card, and opened the door just enough to allow Magic's exit, and toss the Whataburger bag onto the nearby table. Best to give him a potty break before they got settled in for the night.

He wagged and pushed hard against her thigh as they headed back to the elevator. She quickly retraced her path, and this time noticed the hotel lobby staff smiling in recognition of the handsome dog. He'd won most of the staff over, although the housekeeping staff remained leery.

"Need to take-a-break, honey-boy? I brought your tug toy, too." After staying cooped up all day in the small room, Magic would need the exercise. It would do them both good.

Nearly an hour later, Magic had taken care of business several times, what Grammy referred to as "three little ones and one big one." Lia had tossed his tug toy back and forth the length of the parking garage dozens of times, stopping now and then to allow cars to roll past.

"I'm hungry. Bet you are, too." Lia picked up the tug toy one final time, gave Magic the hand signal for one more leg-lifting opportunity, and then together they headed back into the hotel. The lobby, relatively empty at this time of the week, meant her shoulders could relax. She always felt on alert with others present, part of her training.

They had to wait for the elevator, unusual since they were the only ones using the presidential level. Others could use the same elevator, of course, but without the right keycard, it wouldn't stop at her floor, only bypass and head up to the restaurant.

At the thought, she noticed the elevator headed on up to the restaurant level as soon as they stepped out on her floor. Magic voiced a low growl and hurried to sniff at the double doors. Lia cocked her head in puzzlement.

"Magic, chill." She swiped her key card for the room access but also pulled out her service weapon. She bet Pippo had done something that got him upset. The Whataburger…dang, she should have thought of that.

Still, she took security seriously. Most of the cadets used the standard issue Sig P226R, but she and a couple of the women instead carried the Sig P239. It fit her smaller hands better. She banged open the door, quickly scanning the interior. Something had him on alert. Maybe the staff had visited while they were gone. She hadn't left the "do not disturb" sign on as was her habit.

The large room offered no hiding places. Lia noticed the bag of food had been knocked off the table. She crossed the room in half a dozen long strides, nudged open the bedroom door with one foot, and determined it, too, was clear.

Behind her, Magic stood foursquare, facing the suite's open double doors. It should have automatically swung shut. But a man's boot propped it open. The door plate had been taped, preventing it from latching.

"Drop your gun. Kick it over here."

Drummond. She did so. What the hell? Pulling a gun on her? Training kicked in. She stayed silent, swallowed hard, waiting for she didn't know what.

Magic continued to rumble. He kept his solid form between her and the man.

Her AI stepped fully inside the room, letting the door latch behind him. Drummond leaned against the door, swaying a bit. "Call off your dog, or I'll take it out right now."

She didn't say a word, didn't have to. Magic whirled and planted himself by her side, pressing his muzzle hard against her knee. She rested one hand on the Rottweiler's broad brow, steadying herself with the confidence he felt. She'd protect him at all costs, just as he would protect her.

"How'd you get up here? And what d'you want?"

"I'm a cop, remember? Front desk gave me the elevator key, with just a little persuasion."

Had he been drinking? What else would explain him showing up here. She kept her voice low pitched, calm and steady, just as she'd been trained. Something had set Drummond off. If she could figure out the reason for his animosity, she stood a chance of living through the next few moments.

"Now, here's what's going to happen. You're going to quit the academy." He breathed heavily, bracing himself against the wall. "I've given you every opportunity, but you won't take the hint." His words slurred despite himself. "There's no place for you wearing the badge. Not the daughter of a murderer." He smiled when she flinched at his words. "I know who you are, and I know what you're doing. You're not getting away with it. Nobody would believe you anyway."

The gun wobbled as he fumbled to pull out his phone. "I know what you did." He spoke through gritted teeth, spittle spraying. A whiskey cloud filled the air. "And I won't be next."

She kept her voice calm, although her emotions screamed. "Sir, I'm not clear on what you think I did." Lia couldn't see the phone screen, only that a video played.

He screamed, "You think I'm a fool? I've been a cop twice as long as you've been alive. You're not gonna bury me that easily."

He took half a step toward her, and Magic snarled in response. "Tomorrow morning. Your resignation. Or I send this video to the Captain, and you spend the rest of your life alongside your daddy. He shoulda got a lethal injection, and saved taxpayers the money."

He pocketed his phone before swiveling toward the door. Drummond staggered, grappling at the door lever to keep his balance.

Magic would have attacked, had she given silent permission. But that would only make matters worse. She hadn't a clue what was going on and only wanted him out of the room.

With a banshee screech, Pippo streaked across the room and launched himself onto Drummond's back, digging claws for purchase. Blood soaked through.

Drummond yelled, grabbing at the cat with his free hand. The door swung open. His gun went off.

Magic snarled and leaped forward, unable to restrain himself any longer. He grabbed Drummond's ankle in his massive jaws, snarling and shaking his head in a ferocious display.

"*Release!* Magic, *release.*" Lia shouted the command, all the while thinking: *I'm so screwed.*

The cat fled to the end of the room, clawing his way up the drapes to perch high above and watch the unfolding drama. Magic reluctantly gave up his grip. He returned to Lia's side, grumbling the entire time.

Drummond fell through the open door. Lia ran to push it closed behind him, making sure it locked. She backed away to stand beneath the hissing cat.

Drummond continued yelling through the door. "Your resignation tomorrow morning. I'm filing charges on that stupid mutt. I'll have its head sent to the state for rabies testing. See if I don't."

Chapter Seventeen: DRUMMOND

Drummond limped away from the hotel suite, tempted to call and have the girl's mutt impounded this very night. He flexed his injured ankle, cursing silently as he staggered to the elevator. He punched the button and when it didn't open immediately punched it again. He didn't like to admit it, but the video the bitch sent gave him chills.

He suspected it was artificial intelligence designed simply to taunt him about a past that should've stayed dead and buried. Now, all the sweet benefits he'd accrued from that major indiscretion tasted sour.

He had a reputation, and Lia Corazon could take him down with just a word—if she truly had evidence.

The elevator finally slid open, and Drummond lurched inside. He grabbed the polished wooden safety bar lining the small booth and avoided looking in the mirror. His back stung from the cat's claws; his shirt was likely ruined from blood, but at least the suit jacket covered the injury. Usually smartly dressed, always respecting his position as a detective, tonight his loosened tie, scuffed shoes, and flushed face betrayed the number of drinks he'd already downed in the upstairs restaurant's bar. Of course, he'd started in the car on the way here, with a flask he'd stashed in the glove box.

"Not enough. Not nearly enough." He blinked blearily and poked the button for the restaurant on the floor above. It had a bar.

When the elevator opened on the rooftop floor, Drummond steadied himself against the wall as he crossed to the escalator leading up to the restaurant proper. He could hear a crowd talking and laughing, clinking cutlery, and general sounds of merriment, which seemed odd for a Tuesday night. He'd expected to find the place nearly deserted so he could enjoy perching on a bar seat by himself. He had major things to consider.

Drummond clutched the handrail and stumbled onto the escalator. The movement made him dizzy, and he nearly fell at the top when it dumped him off. He caught himself, wiping his face with one hand, and tried to straighten his tie. The front of the restaurant had many small tables, all empty, while the rear of the place was jam-packed with partygoers, most in elaborate costumes. Aha, that made a weird kinda sense. Some losers hosting an early Halloween party.

With disgust, he flexed his shoulders as though to shed

discomfort, averting his eyes from the party goers. His luck, he'd see a clown costume and go punch 'em out—or shoot 'em, even better. That damn freaky video remained cued up on his phone. He'd nearly deleted it, but thought better of it, and now congratulated himself on using it as leverage to get rid of the Corazon girl.

He weaved carefully between the empty tables to reach the fancy bar. He'd have some privacy after all.

It took two tries to get his butt up onto the barstool. Why did people make the seats so tall, and uncomfortable? No place to rest your feet. Unless you were seven feet tall, it left you swinging your shoes like a middle school brat. Probably some jerk designer said it looked peachy-keen or exuded the right ambiance or some such stupid-ass idea.

His stomach didn't want to fit, and he had to climb off the stool, adjust, and climb back on, pissing him off all over again. Sure, he'd put on some girth over the years, but he still had what it took. And respect! That's what mattered. The badge demanded respect, and those that failed to understand that got what they deserved.

"Yes sir?" The barkeep looked too young to serve. But Drummond didn't care, as long as she kept the glass filled. He ordered, and she started to say something—probably because he slurred his words and had to repeat himself—but showing his badge silenced any questions. She brought three glasses and set them before him: one straight rum, one ice, and the other Coke. And not diet, either, the good stuff.

Thing was, that video looked like Walford. He hadn't seen the man in the years since they'd both been caught up in that little business. Walford took early retirement shortly after, built a little dream house for him and the missus, then sorta fell off the map.

Of course Walford'd been on the take for years, working from the Grand Chisholm that housed plenty of high-roller bad guys. If questions arose, he'd been the first to get a closer look.

The money had been so good, they really had no choice. Do the job, take the payment, or suffer the consequences. And everything had been fine for fifteen freaking years. Then out of the blue, Lia Corazon surfaces. He knew the connection immediately, suspected something hinky as soon as she showed up on the academy rolls.

Drummond took half a swallow of the Coke, grimaced, and topped it off with a shot of straight rum. He took another swallow without mixing and smiled. Better.

Back then, Lia Corazon'd been too young to ask questions—or know who her daddy was, but not anymore. Questions rang alarms with people you didn't want to awaken. It went lots higher than Clarence Walford, or Detective Kincaid Drummond. Once you lit that match, the fire burned far beyond this little burg.

Never mind the puppet master couldn't come back from the grave, or that her successor pretended to be squeaky clean. Drummond had no illusions about the consequences of upsetting this carefully orchestrated plot. The people who cared still had teeth, and the reach to destroy.

He took another swallow of his drink, sloshed rum back into the diluted Coke, stirring with his index finger and licking off the wet. He knew two other names but didn't know the men personally. All of them, Drummond included, came out of the deal with a nice juicy windfall. But unlike Walford, they managed the payoff with more care. Any suspicion meant blow-back on them, and those they cared about. They all understood, no details needed.

He should've killed the Corazon girl tonight. He would've been justified when her dog attacked. The booze clouded his judgment; he wouldn't get a better opportunity.

And what was up with that cat? Nasty creatures.

He missed his opportunity, but probably for the best. This place had a butt-load of security now. Cameras were everywhere, in the lobby, hallways, even the friggin' elevator. No matter if her dog attacked, they'd want to know why he followed a cadet to her hotel room. They always had it in for cops, and twisted stuff the wrong way.

He took another slug directly from the glass of rum. It burned all the way down, exactly what he needed. His eyes watered, and he fisted away the wet. He blinked, and the room faded in and out of focus.

Drummond's phone buzzed. It took him a while to fumble it out of his pocket and set it on the surface of the bar. Nobody called him, not when he was off duty, unless an emergency happened. He didn't recognize the number and almost ignored the call. "Drummond here."

"This Detective Kincaid Drummond?" The other voice spoke barely above a whisper. Drummond propped his elbow on the bar and cupped his forehead. "What you want? Who's this?"

"Clarence Walford's dead! I got a video. You get one?"

His elbow slipped, and his head nearly hit the bar surface. Drummond levered himself upright. "Who this? Yeah, I got it. Somebody playing games."

Heavy breathing. "It's true, all over the news. Him and his wife both." The voice growled. "Don't play dumb. You know what this is about. Walford, you, Stan Frisco, and me. It's happening, just like she said, pulling strings from the grave. What are you gonna do about it?"

This must be James Mann. He still practiced somewhere in Dallas, but Stanford Frisco retired five years after Walford. "Don't put this on me. What can I do that a prosecutor can't?"

"You're still a cop, you still have juice. You gotta know who's dredging this business up again. It got all settled years ago. This will ruin my career, my reputation."

"Yeah, but we'll all be dead, so your precious rep won't matter." Drummond lurched to his feet, grunting with the effort, the sound more like a sob. Oh, he knew how to stop this, but it would mean sacrificing himself to save the others. Why should he be the one? "I know who's coming after us. Already put them on notice, told 'em to back off. Give me some time."

Drummond had to silence Lia Corazon without implicating himself. Hell, they'd managed the same operation 15 years ago. It could be done again. Kind of, what you call it, poetic justice. Yeah, poetic justice. He liked that.

"What are you going to do?"

Drummond snorted. "You don't want to know. Just keep your mouth shut and your head down. And don't call me ever again, or you'll have me coming for you, too."

He disconnected. The call sobered him up. He tried to pocket his phone but missed. Okay, maybe not sober enough. He finally got it back into his jacket pocket and slammed back the remainder of the straight rum.

He'd take care of the Corazon bitch tomorrow at cop school. There'd be a little accident. Tragic, but accidents happen when newbies made mistakes. *Lia Corazon, died so young, such a tragedy…* He smiled blearily, and left a folded twenty on the bar.

"Can I call you a cab?" The girl bartender was back.

He hesitated then nodded tersely. Wouldn't do to get a DUI at this point in his career. He needed to sleep it off, then put the finishing touches on his plan.

Drummond staggered back to the escalator, holding on to the banister with both hands. He made it to the elevator by bracing one hand on the wall and waited impatiently for it to open. Stepping inside, he punched the lobby button.

"Hold the door."

Drummond blinked blearily. His mouth dropped open, and he frantically punched the *close* button over and over. He stumbled backward, bracing his back against the mirrored wall.

The grinning clown stepped inside, bloodshot eyes an echo from the past.

Chapter Eighteen: LIA

Lia returned from the massive marble-covered bathroom with a handful of wet paper towels in one hand, the other hand clutching an equal number of dry ones. Magic, still revved up, danced around when she knelt to mopped up the blood from Drummond's bite wound, then swiped it dry.

Magic shook himself, and crimson-tinged saliva hit the wall.

"Did that really happen, what am I gonna do, oh geez Louise, wake up Lia, wake up…" Lia muttered. This had to be some kind of nightmare.

Magic crossed to the paper bag on the table and nosed it. The now cold burgers switched on his drool. She half barked a laugh. Nothing killed the big dog's appetite.

Not the same for her. The thought of eating anything made her want to throw up.

Mind spinning in a dozen directions, Lia forced herself to grab the paper bag. She unwrapped and dismantled the first sandwich, then fed the hamburger patty to Magic and Pippo bite by bite. Nothing frightened Lia more than uncertainty and loss of control, so she focused on mundane actions to avoid thinking about what just happened. She was on the precipice of a bottomless pit, one unwary step away from plummeting to her death. Of her career, anyway.

Her phone rang. Lia half-screamed. Damn, Drummond had really done a number on her. She wiped greasy fingers on a wad of paper napkins and pulled the phone out.

Just what she needed. Grammy.

Lia wanted to ignore the call, but she'd already declined four calls this week. The woman never gave up, and grew more insistent when ignored. If Lia didn't take her call now, Grammy might show up during class tomorrow and demand an audience.

"Hello, Grammy. This is sort of a bad time. I'll call later." As she spoke, Lia filled the food bag with the scraps of vegetables and bun, gathered soiled paper towels, and carried the whole mess to the wastebasket in the bathroom. She set the waste can atop the commode to keep Magic from rummaging inside. Go figure, her highly trained police dog loved trash picking.

"How can it be a bad time? It's a Tuesday evening, what could you possibly be doing? Don't tell me that police school has you working nights?" She tsk-tsked, adding, "I've left messages, but you never returned my call."

Lia straightened her posture at the tone. The petite woman on the other end of the line held even more clout than her AIs. Fine boned with high cheekbones, ice blue eyes, and blond hair styled into a shellacked helmet, Cornelia Corazon always looked perfectly put together, like a high couture drill sergeant.

She'd grown up under the woman's critical eye, aching to be accepted, but finally gave up trying to meet impossible standards. Lia *going to the dogs* rather than into the family's equine business was seen as a personal affront. Even worse, Lia wanted a career in law enforcement, a blue-collar aspiration that didn't fit Grammy's idea of the Corazons' social position.

Disappointment worked both ways. Cornelia's manipulation cost Lia any relationship with her father. They'd come to a minor truce but that bitter reality remained a wedge between them.

"What do you want, Grammy?"

"You don't have to be snippy. I just wanted to remind you about your birthday on Thursday. Your grandfather and I have something very special planned. I promise, you'll be most delighted." She waited a beat. "I won't take no for an answer."

Lia shut her eyes and counted silently to ten. "I have already told you I can't do anything during the week. I have school the next morning." It was a great excuse, but she wouldn't have gone even if they moved the annual event to the weekend. Besides, she was in no mood to play dress up for a bunch of high society wannabes in Heartland, Texas. That was Grammy's jam, not hers.

"I know you're busy, Lia. Truly, I don't want to infringe.

But this is very important. I…" Unexpectedly, the woman's voice broke before she regained her composure. "I've arranged a very special birthday surprise. You won't want to miss it. I hope it'll make up for… a lot."

Lia's phone buzzed again with an incoming call. September.

"I've got another call Grammy, gotta take this." She disconnected without making any further commitment. Knowing Grammy, the birthday present would be some kind of sparkly jewelry that she had no intention of ever wearing. Or a horse.

Well, a horse would be nice. Her childhood mount, now in his twenties, they'd retired to ramble as he wished in one of the family's massive pastures. She missed those carefree days on her pony Sebastian's back.

Lia took September's call. "Listen I'm having a horrible week, capped off by a terrible day. My Academy Instructor just—oh, you don't want to know. Can we talk later?" No way would she share anything with September about Drummond, and have it get back to Combs. Combs might be out of the force now, but the cop ties remained. She didn't need any more rumors going on around her.

"Sorry about your day. But we need to have a conversation, preferably in person."

How much more could she take? "Really I'm not in the mood—"

"You need to hear this, Lia. And figure out what to say when the police come asking you questions. Because they will."

Lia crossed to the big, overstuffed sofa, and slowly sank into the cushions. She leaned forward, resting her forehead in her hand.

Magic's head suddenly came up, neck arched, alert to her swiftly changing mood. Then his solid form leaned hard against her thigh. She felt her heart slow to beat in tandem with his.

"What are you talking about?" She pulled her hand away from her forehead, to drape it across the big dog's neck. His short black fur felt sticky. Wet.

September sighed. "Peter, the boy you saw at the hospital? He says *you* hired his Uncle Ricky to investigate something, and it got him killed. So, what was he after?"

Lia pulled her hand away from Magic's neck and stared at the crimson stain.

Lia lay on the king-size bed, staring at the ceiling. Magic lay curled hard against her side, a makeshift bandage covering the bullet wound creasing his neck and shoulder. His fur, still damp from the tub, smelled not unpleasantly of dog.

She'd used the shower head to clean the bloody injury as best she could. Always stoic, Magic put up with the painful first aid, barely quivering under the stream of water, but he'd need more than her meager help to prevent infection. She wasn't a vet but knew bullet wounds were notoriously dirty. Drummond's wild shot had left a divot in Magic's hide that almost looked like a burn.

Pippo nestled on the small mound of her belly, purring and grooming his fur. The pair anchored her in place, transforming the bed covers into a straitjacket.

She turned her head slightly to take in the green glow of the digital alarm clock: 3:15 AM. She hadn't slept at all.

Around and around her mind circled, analyzing the scene

with Drummond, the words spoken, the what-ifs and maybes. Magic attacked her supervisor. Would her superiors understand he'd tried to protect Lia? Drummond would use that to punish her and maybe hurt her dog.

Yet she hadn't a clue what he'd raved on about. Had he mistaken her for someone else? She never saw the video he threatened her with, so that made no sense. And his demand that she resign and drop out of the police training academy—or else? Or else what? He'd share the mysterious video? Drummond acted like he had the juice to force her out.

Usually someone trying to coerce Lia made her dig in her heels. Grandfather and Grammy would testify to that. She snorted at the thought.

But she couldn't risk Magic's life. Like any K-9 officer, he had all his vaccinations. The threat of using rabid behavior to destroy him rang false but the mere threat could sideline him. By law, bites must be reported. Sometimes, pets with current vaccinations still were quarantined.

At that thought, she stiffened. Pippo stirred and mewed in response. He'd just received first shots, putting Pippo at much higher risk for forcible removal and rabies testing. Lia shuddered. She didn't think the cat had bitten Drummond, only scratched him deeply.

"Got what he deserved, the creep." What was he thinking, forcing his way into her room? She stroked the cat, needing the cuddles as much as Pippo did.

If he truly believed he had some devastating leverage against her, why threaten? As a law enforcement professional, Drummond should turn her in for whatever the infraction might be. He must have had a compelling reason to threaten but hold back.

In less than three hours, she had to get up and prepare for

class. And face Drummond, pretend like nothing happened. Or would he call her out in front of the other cadets? God, what to do…

She couldn't complain to any of the other students. They all had their own issues. Maybe this was Drummond upping the hazing? Surely not. He'd held a gun on her. Shot Magic! She could press charges—yet it'd be her word against his.

No, she'd suck it up and grit her teeth the next three days.

September's call just added more confusion to the situation. What did this have to do with Molingo's murder? Lia didn't believe in coincidence. Why the hell had Peter dragged her name into his tragedy?

WEDNESDAY,

October 30

Chapter Nineteen: SHELLY

The clown staggered away from the body. Drummond had been easy to take out, so drunk he thought himself caught in a waking dream. They'd sat in a stairwell, drinking and reminiscing. It all began in the Grand Chisholm fifteen years ago… a full circle moment, planning how to get rid of their mutual problem. Too late, Drummond realized what Shelly planned.

As they staggered together into the parking garage, Shelly giggled. "Beware clowns bearing gifts." He quickly squelched it down, as laughing made the growing headache worse.

One pink gloved hand wiped his runny nose before pulling out his knife.

He left Drummond's body propped against one of the cement pillars in the garage, chin on chest with blood draining from the neck. Until the light of day, passersby would think him a homeless person taking a much-needed rest.

Shelly wanted the body found, though. One of the man's hands now held the rubber clown nose. With a bit of luck, the police would find the girl's prints on it. Incriminating Lia should derail, discredit, and delay any information she'd uncovered in her partnership with Molingo.

Shelly checked to ensure the rest of his costume remained intact. Wouldn't do for the cameras to catch a glimpse and betray the masquerade. He doubled over as a coughing fit shook him, echoing in the space. First time for everything. Never before had illness struck in the middle of an important campaign. No time to be sick. His hit list wouldn't wait. Three down, and at least two more to go, not counting the Corazon girl.

Misery. Head spinning migraine. Clutching the wall, Shelly struggled to stay upright. Over there, his motorcycle… He needed somewhere safe and out of sight to shed the costume. Hole up for a day, maybe two. See what shook out before taking next steps.

The motorcycle roared to life, and Shelly nearly screamed with the corresponding pain throbbing between his ears. Stomach clinching, the retching brought acid up with the small amount of liquor he'd faked drinking with Drummond. On the way out, he spat to clear the nasty taste.

Without conscious thought, hands steered the zooming cycle through deserted Dallas streets. Shelly stopped appropriately at traffic lights, followed the speed limit, and otherwise played the role of perfect citizen. He looked forward to locking the door on the budget hotel room booked two weeks ago when he returned from a much glitzier vacation. Shelly couldn't afford to have his clown campaign associated with his regular place. Once he cleaned up the loose ends, he could retire for good. He was this close to putting a deposit down on the condo of his dreams…

Traffic increased closer to the motel. Late-night revelers—on a Tuesday, actually Wednesday now—loitered on street corners. He showed his teeth, more snarl than smile at the perfect opportunity. Sticking strictly to the hit list would draw too direct a line for those who knew the right questions to ask and connected the dots. But a random victim, using the same weapon while wearing the Corazon clown get up, would take the heat down by several degrees.

He waited until only one person remained visible within a two-block space. Shelly slowed the cycle to come abreast of the flamboyantly dressed woman. Probably a hooker. Shelly knew how to play that game, too.

"Wanna party?" She leered suggestively, dropping one hand to rest on her cocked hip.

One short sharp nod set Shelly's head throbbing in a double-time rhythm. He hooked a thumb over one shoulder, and gunned the motorcycle once she was astride. He counted on video cameras recording them. More confusion to keep the boys in blue scrambling gave him more time to eliminate the real targets. Shelly knew just what buttons to push to keep the cops running circles.

Forty minutes later, Shelly left her body in a culvert, gaudy clothes cut away, with bruises and random cuts stippling her bare flesh. She hadn't acted surprised when the knife appeared. In fact, she offered her soft neck willingly, ready for the pain to end, even whispered "thank you" as the blade cut short her life.

Shelly left the rainbow wig clutched in the woman's fist. And smiled. The headache abated to a dull roar.

Chapter Twenty: SEPTEMBER

The incessant dinging of her phone receiving texts roused September from a deep sleep. She groaned, rolling over to check the time: 4:42 AM?

"It'll be there when we get up." Combs punched the pillow on his side of the bed and turned his back to her.

"It's Jack." Her uncle wouldn't reach out at this ungodly hour unless it was an emergency. Something to do with the hotel…and her alter ego, Sorokin Glass. "I'll take care of it." She sent a quick text:

<be with you in five.

As soon as she slipped from under the covers, Shadow

hopped off the foot of the bed and pressed close against her bare legs. She grabbed a thin robe from the master bathroom door.

Without a word, the pair padded softly down the stairs, taking care not to rouse the kids. September had no desire to hear Melinda complain should her beauty sleep get cut short. Willie, on the other hand, would want in on the excitement.

Before dealing with Jack, September needed coffee. No chance she'd get back to sleep after this, no matter how short the conversation, and being fully caffeinated would help her face whatever he had to say.

Conversations with Jackson Glass elevated stress with even the most innocuous topics. After their last adventure, she preferred keeping her birth mother's strange and intense brother at a distance, for her own emotional health. Jack had moved his headquarters into the Grand Chisholm. Neither she nor Combs wanted him as an official member of the Paladin Group, but Jack's skill set and insight into Wong Enterprises had proved invaluable. She couldn't afford to ignore him.

While the coffee brewed, September pulled a chair up beside the stained-glass table. Shadow clung close, resting his chin on her lap. Idly, she stroked his brow and gently tugged his silk slick ears while she read the text thread.

>Situation here. We need to talk.

Tiny hairs rose on the back of her neck. This couldn't be good. Ten minutes later:

>Bloody body in parking garage. Hotel staff going nuts. Guests called 911.

She snuck a cup of coffee but set the mug down too hard when her phone dinged again. She retrieved a roll of paper towels to mop up the coffee.

>Sorokin, you there??? Vic's a cop! Police swarming

>It's Detective Kinkaid Drummond. Call me ASAP.

"Oh my dear God in heaven." She whispered, but in the big kitchen it echoed like a shout. Why did that name sound familiar? Wasn't that the name of Lia's academy instructor? So much for not bothering Combs.

Shadow whined. He pushed the front half of his body into her lap. He knew she needed the grounding weight of his warm presence. She opened her arms to encircle him and pushed her face into the thick black fur of his neck. "It's Jack, Shadow. Big trouble, maybe for us."

He wagged, as if he recognized the name.

Using her birth name, *Sorokin,* underlined the seriousness. No matter how hard she and Uncle Jack strove to root out the old influences, and prove everything was legit, something always reached out to drag her back into the festering pot of crime.

Double, double toil and trouble; Fire burn and caldron bubble...

She would call back but only with Combs there for backup. She rose, dropped her phone into the robe pocket, and filled a cup with coffee for Combs. Grabbing both cups, she trotted to the stairs, but Shadow galloped ahead in a thundering burst of noisy energy. She winced, sure thumping paws would rouse the kids. Neither Melinda nor Willie needed to know anything about this.

Shadow zoomed into the bedroom and leaped onto the bed, making happy murmuring sounds when he rolled onto his back, squirming and waving all four paws at the ceiling. Mornings, they often snuggled like that, her rubbing his chest while he did his best to wash her face.

But usually, they indulged the snuggles only after Combs got up for his shower. Now the dog's pistoning rear paws punched into Combs's bum leg.

"Son of a—" he hissed and struggled to sit up in bed. "What the hell September?"

She bumped the bedroom door closed with one hip and elbowed the light switch.

He squinted, blinking until his eyes adjusted. "I take it Jack has unhappy news?"

She handed him his coffee, which he cupped in both hands, jaw tight as he waited for her explanation.

"Shadow, move." She climbed back into the bed when the dog shifted position. September leaned against the headboard then pulled out her phone, queued up the text messages, and handed it to Combs.

After a long minute, he handed the phone back to her. "Did you call yet?" He sipped the coffee, wrinkling his nose at the bitter taste. In her hurry, she'd neglected to add sugar.

"Wanted to talk with you first."

He sighed and handed her his mug so he could use both hands to maneuver his sore leg from beneath the covers and get out of bed. "Jack's your security man at the hotel. You two agreed. He gets paid to handle it."

"Yes, but…" Jack didn't always play nicely with the law. He'd skirted the rules since long before she'd known him. Never mind that he had good reason.

Combs ran a hand through his short hair, pacing in a lurching limp the length of the room and back. It took him a while to get his leg limbered up in the morning. "The Dallas PD has jurisdiction. They'll handle that investigation, especially if it's one of their detectives. Yes, you're the owner of the hotel, so they may have questions about security— again, something Jack can best answer. You were seventy miles away, with another cop…okay, a retired cop, when the man died." He yawned deeply and reached out to take the coffee mug once again.

He was right. She took a slug from her own mug, swallowed, and toyed with the blankets. Shadow tried to grab her hand as it moved under the covers, growling with delight at the game.

"The police know Wong Enterprises owns the hotel. Having a detective killed in the garage will surely raise eyebrows, if not worse." She must inform the board of directors, if they didn't already know. She groaned. September wouldn't put it past one of them to have a hand in this—but she wouldn't dare say that out loud.

Combs took two more swallows from the mug. "Just because it happened at that particular hotel…" He shrugged. "When you hear hoof beats, think horses not zebras."

She knew the saying, but it was still quite a coincidence. She found a body in Heartland, and days later another was found in her hotel. "I get it. Can't have anything to do with us. The victim, Detective Drummond? You know him?"

He nodded. "Kincaid Drummond had a reputation. Been coasting for the past several years, one of those guys nobody wants on their team. Suspicion floated about him for years, but nobody could pin anything specific on him."

"What kind of suspicion?"

He smiled. "I wouldn't want to smear a fellow cop." Combs drained the coffee cup. "But I'd bet money some of his hinky dealings caught up with him. That's no reason to involve Paladin."

"Oh, believe me, I want no part of that." She rubbed Shadow's ears. "Besides, Dallas PD don't take kindly to outsiders sticking their noses where they don't belong."

"Especially from podunk Heartland. He's one of theirs.

Let 'em clean up their own mess."

She squeezed shut her eyes. Shadow registered the change in her attitude, and crawled closer, pushing half his body into her lap. She raised her coffee mug to keep from spilling it on the dog. "We've also got Lia somehow linked to Molingo."

"Oh for the love of… September, what the holy hell does that have to do with Drummond? You're looking for connections that don't exist."

She blew out a shaky breath. "It's not just that. Combs, I think Lia's in serious trouble." She drained her coffee cup in one last long swallow. "When I spoke with her yesterday, she sounded all shook up. Her academy instructor showed up at the hotel and threatened her… and now he's dead."

"Drummond was her academy instructor?"

"Yeah. Dead in the hotel garage basement. She's staying in the hotel's presidential suite."

Chapter Twenty-One: LIA

Lia finished braiding her hair, twirled it into a knot at the base of her neck, and wrapped it securely with a bright orange hair tie. She knew once it dried her hair would frizz with more unmanageable curls, but it kept her from having to deal with the mess during class and exercises.

She wiped the steam from the mirror and peered blearily at her reflection: eyes red from no sleep and face pale from the stress. She dressed in a fresh pair of 5.11s and blue polo, then pulled on the white cap. She loaded standard gear into the appropriate cargo pockets, so everything would be where she expected it to be in an emergency.

Today, Lia would keep her phone with her, silent but handy for documentation if needed. Her jaw tightened with grim resolve. Drummond would not chase her away. Before heading out, she'd take Magic for his potty duty, and maybe some playtime. He didn't have the luxury of a litter box, like the cat did.

The thought of him squatting in a tiny box made her giggle. Magic whirled, ears pricked forward and tail waving, not from reading her mind at the silly image but from knowing a bathroom break was imminent. Magic kept track of time and routine better than any watch.

His injury looked raw and seeping. A trip to Doc Eugene would set him right, but that had to wait until after class. No way would Drummond give her time off for her dog.

During the class demo, Magic searched the classroom and found the hidden cache of weapons planted in one of the student's gear. But Drummond had taken one look at the Corazon Kennel logo on her truck, made it clear he had no time for demos, and made fun of K-9 partnerships as a weak-ass girly option. Lia sniffed at the characterization. *Bet he didn't feel that way after meeting Magic's teeth.*

The female cadets worked twice as hard as their male counterparts. Granted, most of the men were good guys, but a couple used every opportunity to put them down or sabotage training drills.

This wasn't a competition. There were plenty of open slots on the Dallas PD or other North Texas forces. She'd prefer working closer to Heartland, but newbies had little choice and she'd consider any offer. Lia just wanted to get through the training, earn her credentials, and work hard for the next few years with Magic by her side. Was that too much to ask?

In the bedroom, the fierce animal lounged on the bed

playing footsie with the cat. As if he heard her speak, Magic paused and looked directly at her, tipping his broad head from side to side with wet tongue lolling and a happy doggy grin.

Her phone buzzed on the nightstand. Lia frowned, in no hurry to answer. Grammy had left a new message thirty minutes ago. Did the woman ever sleep? Grandfather also left a text—she figured Grammy put him up to it. She'd read everything later.

After the brief phone conversation last night with September, Lia dreaded hearing back from her most of all. Why had Molingo implicated her? Thinking about the conversation made her head hurt. She unplugged and stashed the phone without opening it.

Before leaving the room, Lia grabbed half a handful of cat kibble, stored inside the mini-fridge to keep Magic's nose at bay. She filled Pippo's bowl that sat atop the tallest cabinet in the room. The dog's bathroom break gave Pippo a chance to eat undisturbed. When they returned to the room, she'd feed the dog his ration.

She'd removed Magic's collar so it wouldn't irritate his wound. His harness, complete with K9 badge attached and a short lead, gave a nod to propriety. They made it to the elevator before another ping announced a text. She sighed and dug out the phone.

>Classes canceled rest of the week.

The news stopped her cold. Had class ever been canceled before? What in the world... Quickly, she punched the elevator button, grateful for the reprieve. She wouldn't have to rush Magic to do his duty. And she'd be able to get him seen by Doc Eugene.

Halfway down to the ground floor, the elevator paused to

let on other guests. They gave her and Magic a wide berth but didn't seem too dismayed by the big dog's presence.

"Hold the elevator!" a voice called just before the door closed.

Lia hit the open button and a couple jogged inside, moving to the far side of the car but undismayed by the big dog's presence.

"Is he searching for the killer?" the woman asked with breathless curiosity.

Her companion touched her arm. "Just let the police do their job." He turned to Lia, not hiding the admiration in his eyes for both her and her K9 partner. "We appreciate you keeping us safe. When do you think they'll let us leave the hotel?"

Confused, but sure she shouldn't show it, Lia shrugged. "Above my pay grade." *Killer?* "What were you told?"

"They won't let us into the parking garage. Said they're collecting evidence, and to go back to our rooms until notified. They want to question everybody in the hotel. Can you imagine?" She whispered, as though leery of saying the words too loud. "Somebody died. Murdered."

"Now we don't know that for sure." He corrected her as though used to clarifying everything she said. "Somebody died, yes. Must have happened late last night. Hotel security doesn't want anyone getting in the way. There's gotta be five or six patrol cars, an ambulance, and even the fire department."

"Like a massacre!" She raised an eyebrow at her companion. "If it's only one body, why do they need all those people?" She turned back to Lia. "You would know more than anyone else. Is it true what the hotel staff said? Was a detective killed?"

Pippo leaped to reach the high countertop and explored the food bowl. He sniffed delicately, disappointed in the dry ration, always preferring the wet stinky offerings provided at night. He ignored the closing door, confident Lia and Magic would return shortly. They always did.

The past few days had yielded more adventure than he'd experienced in many months. And now he got to tease Magic. The big dog couldn't pounce or leap to keep up with Pippo. He smelled funny, too, so Pippo spent much time rubbing against Magic's black fur and licking him to share good-smelling cat scent.

Pippo also liked snuggling in bed with people. Now that he stayed in the new place, he'd sneaked into the bedroom at night to sleep between the couple a few times. After the second night, the woman no longer shooed Pippo away, had even made space for him to snuggle.

Pippo crunched a mouthful of the kibble, swallowed, and washed it down with several laps of water. The bowl would be here all day; he didn't have to empty it at one setting. Proper cats munched up to eight tiny meals a day. Not like Magic, who gulped everything in two or three mouthfuls to empty his bowl. And then tried to eat the cat food, too.

Licking his whiskers clean, Pippo began his ritual bath before hesitating when his eyes locked on Lia's satchel resting on one of the chairs. With a graceful leap, he reached the interesting object. Pippo reached out to paddle a bright metal tab, which swung back and forth in response.

A small opening right next to the metal tab grew a bit larger as he batted the zipper. Too tempting to ignore, he inserted a white paw into the hole. The opening spread wider, and soon Pippo could insert his entire white foreleg deep into the zipper pocket.

Pippo continued playing with the opening until it grew wide enough for him to stick his face inside and explore with delicate sniffs. He pulled back out, not liking the close feeling of the fabric pressing his face and delicate whiskers. But he couldn't resist further exploration.

Golden eyes wide, he pushed his head back through the opening, continued wriggling, and finally squirmed enough to pull both back legs into the pouched knapsack. His tail hung out of the opening, twitching with excitement. Pippo pulled his tail inside just as the suite's door swung open.

Lia dashed back into the room, Magic by her side. He whined and tried to grab her hand to slow her down. He knew something bad had happened.

"Can't believe it, not true, can't be right." She mumbled to herself, leaning back against the closed door, expecting pounding fists on the other side at any moment.

Class canceled. Did that mean it was Drummond dead in the garage? Only a matter of time before they came to question her. Heck, they didn't even need to speak to her, just access the security cameras to see who visited her last night.

They'd want to take Magic away…

Classmates could attest to the friction between her and Drummond. Oh God, this would derail her police career just like Drummond threatened. She despised the man for how he treated her. But she'd never consider murder!

How inconvenient.

She laughed bitterly at the thought, tried to stop, and the laughter morphed into gulping tears. Last night, September warned her the police wanted to question her. But that was about something in Heartland. That had nothing to do with her.

Why would someone frame her?

She didn't want to deal with the hotel's security chief. Jackson Glass scared her; she didn't trust him. She needed to think, get away somewhere without distractions, to puzzle out next steps.

Thank goodness she could collect her truck from September's private parking slot and avoid the police. For now.

She'd drive back to Heartland, get Doc Eugene to treat Magic—hide the dog, protect him. God, she couldn't have the authorities confiscate her dog! She'd have to find an explanation to convince Doc Eugene. Gunshots had to be reported, but she'd make him understand.

Then she'd hole up at Corazon Kennels. No way would she go back to Grandfather and Grammy's place. That'd be the first spot the police would look. She wanted to talk things out with September before going to the authorities. Of course, she'd talk to them. She had nothing to hide; she'd done nothing wrong.

And she might have been the last person to speak with Drummond. If it was Drummond. Maybe it was somebody else? *Breathe, Lia, get the facts before you imagine the worst.*

For now, she needed to get out before anyone thought to stop her. She grabbed the heavy knapsack sitting on the chair, noticed the open zipper and closed it before she shrugged the strap over one shoulder. Lia glanced around the room for Pippo. The cat had disappeared.

Damn! Once they saw the video of Drummond visiting her suite, the police would want to search the room. She couldn't take the time to corral Pippo but she didn't want the cat escaping into the hotel, either.

Lia called Magic with a silent hand signal and crossed to the door. Like every morning, she hung the sign on the external handle, cautioning hotel staff that her pet remained loose inside. She smiled. Nobody knew about Pippo. They'd assume Magic guarded the place, like always. Nobody would dare enter without her here.

Chapter Twenty-Two: SHELLY

A hot shower and change of clothes had done little to improve the way Shelly felt. After finishing with the call girl he'd returned to the motel to clean up and rest. None of the cold medicine seemed to relieve the congestion or the harsh cough that settled deep in his lungs.

No time to get sick.

He refused to let the stupid bug shove a stick in the spokes of his plans. He never got sick, prided himself on a wiry constitution that could get by with little sleep. Lots of cigarettes, and less food, but he still got jobs done. Shelly's skill at pulling the strings kept him well above the fray, a spider spinning webs while dancing along on the most fragile thread to escape. By now, Dallas PD had likely circled the wagons around Drummond's body. Shelly needed to control the narrative.

The Corazon bitch had tarnished his biggest win. That jeopardized Shelly's future. The people he answered to—who'd retreated into the darkest corners—still ran the show, and quickly grew impatient with loose ends. Lia had to pay. He couldn't let a woman best him. *Never happen.*

His motorcycle rolled into the *no parking zone* across the street from the Grand Chisholm and Shelly stuck his "officer on duty" sign on the bug screen. The police already had the hotel's garage ribboned off, but getting in didn't worry Shelly. He held up one hand to stop traffic as he jogged across the street. An officer stopped him at the entrance, but Shelly flashed his detective badge and the officer ducked his head and waved him inside.

He crossed to where crime techs collected evidence. They'd already moved Drummond's body to the ME's van parked just beyond the police tape. Shelly kept his expression stoic. There was plenty to document, but nothing would trace back to him.

Detective Greer looked up, and his eyes narrowed as he recognized Shelly. Still wearing gloves, Greer didn't offer a hand to shake. "What are you doing here?"

Shelly had taken personal leave time. As far as the department and his partner Greer knew, he'd been on his way to New York for a funeral and to resolve the estate of his elderly mother. His connections had multiple ways to make the fiction look real.

"Heard about this on my way to the airport. Figured I'd stop by to see if I could lend a hand. I postponed my trip. It's not like Mom will know I'm late." A cough tickled the back of his throat and Shelly covered his mouth, turning away until the fit passed. To soothe his throat, he shook out a cigarette. The *snick-shshsh* of his lighter echoed in the expanse.

"That's right, you partnered with Drummond back in the day, caught that big murder case right here. Sorry for your loss, man." Greer shook his buzz cut head. The case had been before his time. "Staged to look like a drowning, right? Brother, must be *déjà vu* for you." He tilted his head. "You look wrung out. Don't sound so good, neither." He frowned at the cigarette. "No smoking here. Evidence and all." As an afterthought he added, "Butts'll kill you, man."

"I'm full to the gills with NyQuil, DayQuil, whatever kind of Quill I could find. Nothing's touching this crud." Shelly hacked and spat, far enough away to keep from contaminating evidence, and ignored Greer's grimace of distaste. "So what happened?" To punctuate the words, and rub it in Greer's face, he took a deep draw on the cigarette.

Greer walked away from the technicians, stripping off his gloves, and mopped his brow with one sleeve. "Somebody must've had one hell of a grudge. They nearly decapitated the man."

Shelly had dropped that particular blade into the Trinity River, after using it on the woman last night. Sad to lose such a fine knife, but one made sacrifices from time to time. "You find the weapon? Any suspects? What about cameras?"

The other man shook his head. "The security guy, man named Jackson Glass, says he'll give us access to video. There are cameras all over the place, so gotta be something helpful. But he's dragging his feet." Greer rubbed his face and watched as the techies wound up their collection and prepared to leave. "Wong Enterprises owns this building.

You know the name. With all the sketchy biz they run, no wonder Glass slow rolls us. No transparency there." He didn't notice his unintended play on words. Greer had no imagination, no smarts. Not like Shelly.

"Anything else?" Greer hadn't mentioned the obvious clue Shelly had planted. His head increased its rhythmic throbbing. Greer had never been the sharpest pencil in the box.

"A couple of things, yeah. Drummond had a dog toy in his hand. Little red squeaker ball. Weird. And on top of that, one of his ankles got crunched by some major tooth action. The ME said it looked like a big dog, though—not one that would play with such a little toy."

Shelly fought the urge to roll his eyes. As scratchy as they felt, they might get stuck under his lids. "So who in the hotel has a dog?" Greer was so damn slow! Did he have to spell it out?

"We already got a list from the front desk. More mutts than you'd think for such a fancy place. Apparently new rules went into effect a couple months ago, including creating that dog relief station right outside." He jerked his head toward the area. "Before that, dogs weren't allowed—except service mutts, obviously. Something to do with Sorokin Glass, new head of the Wong organization having a service dog." He whistled with appreciation. "I've seen pictures. Sorokin's a knockout, and has a big black German Shepherd, just the sort to take a chunk out of Drummond, but staff say she's not here. A friend of hers is using the owner's suite." He pulled out his phone and thumbed through notes. "Apikalia Corazon, goes by Lia. And get this, she's got a big mutt, too. Drummond was her instructor over at the police training academy." He pocketed his phone. "They canceled classes, and she's already left."

"Sounds like we need a conversation with this Api-watsis Corazon." Finally! It'd taken Greer long enough to paint by dots. Or connect the numbers. Gaw, his head hurt, hard to think. Anyway, maybe Greer'd do his job now, take the Corazon bitch into custody, and free Shelly to finish cleaning up the other loose ends.

One of the technicians came back holding a cell phone in a plastic baggie. "Detective Greer, you should see this." The techie got Drummond's phone open by holding it to the victim's face. "Check the video on the text message it was on." She held it for him.

Shelly took a step closer to peer around the bigger man's shoulder. He recognized the video he'd sent to Drummond. The police had the tools, and sometimes the skill, to delve beneath even the masquerade shown in the video. It would take time, though, and give him more cover while they tried to figure out motives and identity.

"Son of a…" Greer didn't touch the phone.

Shelly whistled, feigning surprise. "That's Clarence Walford. We just caught that case what? Three days ago?"

"What the hell did Drummond have against them? What's with the costume? That's creepy as hell."

Shelly blinked. It took a moment for him to understand. "You think Drummond dressed up like a clown to take out Walford?"

"Crazy, right? Gotta figure out how this fits together." Greer nodded at the technician. "Get me copies of everything in his recent texts. And let's see who else he's been calling. I want a report ASAP; I've got the captain breathing down my neck already for Walford."

"Who do you think targeted Drummond? Someone who knew about the Walford attack?" Shelly kept pace with Greer as he strode toward the lobby entrance.

Greer paused at the door. "I'm gonna meet with this Glass fella, get a look at his videos."

"What about the Corazon girl, and her dog?"

Greer blew out a breath. "I'll talk to her eventually. We know where to find her. For now, this takes priority."

He knew where she went? For the briefest moment, Shelly felt the pounding of his head subside, and clarity descend. "I could take that off your plate, get some preliminary questions answered by the Corazon girl." He did his best to make it sound unimportant. "Or maybe you prefer taking your time and catching up with her later. That is, if she doesn't decide to rabbit."

Greer pulled open the door, speaking over one shoulder. "Sure, just send me your report before you leave to take care of family stuff. Oh, and sorry for your loss."

"You said you know where to find her?"

"Heartland, north of here. Runs a dog boarding kennel up there, or so I've been told. I'll let the PD there know to expect you."

Chapter Twenty-Three: SHADOW

Shadow burst through the back kitchen door as it swung wide. Ever since the early morning messages and later call with Jack Glass, September's nerves had thrummed with agitation. Shadow's sharp ears didn't understand the words but recognized the man's voice.

They'd left Combs in the shower and the kids fixing themselves breakfast. Still licking his lips from his own breakfast, Shadow zoomed to the ornate metal gate leading into the rose garden. He paw-danced before it, impatient for September to open the entry. She carried her bo staff with her. That meant lots of time alone while she practiced zipping it through the air.

He loved their morning routine, alone time together without kids, Combs, or Macy. Briefly, he wondered when Macy would return from Doc Eugene's. He'd missed teasing the big cat, and nose poking him in all the good-smelling places after the cat's morning litter box visit.

Macy stayed behind when they visited the clinic. Shadow liked the people there but not needle pokes. He put up with them, because September said he should. September was always right.

Well, almost always.

She drew abreast of him, dropping one hand to stroke his brow and he leaned into her touch. September unlatched the gate, so it swung wide for a good dog to pass through.

"Shadow, *check it out.*"

He launched himself, enjoying the stretch and pull of muscles beneath his fur. Shadow followed the grassy pathway surrounding the perimeter of the garden expanse. His nose and ears took in every detail. He detected only the usual evidence of bunnies, birds, a burrowing armadillo, and several squirrels rustling in the overhead branches of the red oak. Shadow expanded his search to cover each bisecting path that crisscrossed the center of the garden like spokes on September's car wheels. After clearing the area, Shadow raced back and sat directly in front of her, tail sweeping the brick pathway, to announce *all clear.*

"Good dog, Shadow. *Chill,* baby dog." He sprang to his feet on the release word, pacing by her side as she entered the garden. "Go *take a break.*"

Shadow raced to his favorite place and took care of business. Later, Willie would clean up after Kinsler made his own presence known in the same place.

He gathered his haunches and zoomed. Around and around the garden he ran, kicking up sod with each sharp turn, just for pure joy of the wind in his face. Here and there he stopped to lift his leg to scent mark. In one place, he nosed beneath a prickly rosebush, pressing forward despite the thorns to get a closer sniff of the rabbit that huddled, frozen in place, underneath. It quivered, thumped warnings with back feet, and finally exploded outward in a burst of bunny energy. With delight, Shadow barked as he chased after the zig-zagging critter.

As he passed September, she laughed. The sound made his tummy leap with a happy feeling.

At the distraction, the bunny easily ducked through the fence to escape. Shadow abandoned his bunny chase and instead swerved and skidded to a stop before September. He waited until she finished whipping the long stick through the air, knowing the damage the heavy staff could do. She stopped for a moment and dropped the staff; Shadow rolled onto his back to beg for a tummy rub.

She instead patted her chest with both hands. Eagerly, Shadow rolled to his feet and placed his paws on her shoulders. He basked in the warmth of her arms wrapped around his body. He sighed, resting his chin on her shoulder as she stroked his head and neck.

September already smelled less upset, calmer. Shadow liked to think he had something to do with that. She certainly made him feel safe.

He followed her to the nearby water outlet where a long hose looped around a wheel. She twisted the knob that stuck out of the brick wall, and Shadow tipped his head, watching with interest as the hose made funny noises and expanded.

"We need to water the new roses. Then we'll play some *hose tag*, okay?"

With a play bow, butt high and paws dancing in the dirt, he shouted his joy. He loved chasing water from the hose!

She smiled, and pursed her lips, and Shadow came to attention. He waited, tail flagged and eager for whatever game she proposed.

"Shadow, where's *hose*?" She waited, grinning.

This new game offered a combination of fun challenges. It was different from the *show-me* game, where September held a different item in each hand, like *book* or *pencil*, for him to identify. Similar to the *seek* game where he got to track and find missing people or pets, this game asked him to point out named items he'd learned. And sometimes, to *fetch* that item.

Like Frisbee fetch. He'd quickly learned the game only continued if he would *fetch* the item back to September to throw once more.

"Where's *hose*?" She waited patiently.

He knew this. That, right there, was *hose*. He nose-poked the coil.

Click! She made the tongue-click noise that confirmed he'd done something right. "Good dog, Shadow, you're so smart!" She waited a beat, then added, "Shadow, *tug hose*."

He knew and loved games of *tug*. And he understood *hose*. She wanted him to play *tug* with *hose?* Shadow found the snake-end of the hose and gingerly picked it up. He stood uncertainly for a moment, holding it in his jaws. Water dripped from the nozzle.

Click! "Good boy. *Tug*."

He walked forward while holding the hose, but the weight stopped him, and he dropped it. Shadow retrieved the end again, this time backing away as he pulled harder on the hose.

To his delight, the coil unrolled from the wheel. He wagged harder, tugging and growling with excitement.

Click! "Yes! What a smart dog, Shadow! Before long, you'll water the flowers all by yourself." She laughed, gave him the hand signal to *drop it*, and retrieved the end of the hose. "Let's play *hose tag*, good boy." She grinned and laughed, and that made him feel so good he didn't want her to stop.

For the next little while, September sprayed water into the ground beside the roses. Shadow watched avidly for the times she turned the hose his way, spraying a stream high into the air. He sprang after the elusive stream, his jaws snapping hard to catch the glittery shower. Before long, his head and neck dripped, and he panted happily in the morning breeze.

She shut off the water and rolled the long hose back to its home on the big wheel. Shadow shook himself hard, and September squealed in the spray. "Let me finish up here. Willie will be out any minute with Kinsler, so enjoy the solo time you have left." She retrieved the bo staff, and within minutes it again made a whistling sound as it whickered through the air.

 Shadow shook himself once more for good measure. Time to patrol his garden.

He sniffed the furrows the armadillo left behind as it sought bugs attracted to the water feeding each rose. The strange animal had routinely uprooted plants and sod during the night, making September mutter strange angry words as she replanted them each morning. She'd finally accommodated the armored invader by heavily watering one corner of the garden without roses, creating a legal digging spot for the creature and keeping it away from her roses.

She'd also added several shepherd hooks to the area, some had hanging glass cups of liquid for tiny, jeweled birds, others held containers with seeds for birds and squirrels. Shadow liked to hide behind a large shrub to ambush unwary thieving squirrels. He hadn't caught one—yet.

A different odor made him bristle. Fur stood off his hackles. His tail wagged high and furious, and he approached the bird feeders with a stiff legged gait. The armadillo had plowed a swath of the earth around the bird feeders, hiding and partially burying what lay in the dirt.

Shadow pawed the ground, uncovering a large bird's body. He sniffed it with interest and poked it first with his nose then a paw, hoping to make it move. But the creature, feathers clotted with damp earth, didn't move. Smelled sick. Dead.

He whined deep in his throat and looked up at the tallest tree where he'd seen similar birds perch. He had never got a chance to fully examine one of the feathery creatures. As soon as one detected a presence, it flew away, teasing Macy-cat and Kinsler with flapping feathery antics.

But this large creature preyed on the smaller birds. He'd never seen one on the ground. It hadn't been dead for very long.

Sometimes Macy caught small creatures and fetched them to September. She always praised the cat and accepted the gift. Macy never ate them, though, the way Kinsler did one time. Melinda had screamed for ten minutes. Shadow had wondered why.

Shadow knew what to do: he'd *fetch* his prize to September, like when they played Frisbee. Carefully Shadow picked up the red-tailed hawk in his mouth. He raised his head and trotted proudly to present the bird to September. She'd know what to do.

Chapter Twenty-Four: LIA

The drive north from Dallas to Heartland had moved in fits and starts thanks to road construction along the way. By the time Lia reached the vet clinic, Doc Eugene's back-to-back surgery schedule meant hours-long delay to see Magic and she had to leave him there.

Doc Eugene promised to get Magic's wounds cleaned up and have him ready to release late afternoon. She'd lied to him, felt terrible about it, but better that he thought her reckless with her own service weapon than have questions about someone shooting Magic.

She sat in her truck in the clinic parking lot, holding the

dog's harness with the attached K9 badge, feeling adrift without him—hung over, without the nebulous fun of alcohol or celebration. The horror of nearly losing Magic set in, leaving her hands shaking. On impulse, she removed his police badge and slipped it into one of her pockets. Somehow that made her feel closer to him.

Lia fished out her phone and called September. With every local news channel spilling the tea about Drummond's murder, she had no reason to hold back her version of what happened. Besides, she trusted September as an honest sounding board for the next steps. Her career, and possibly her freedom and life, were at risk. September had survived similar, more than once.

"Lia. Where are you? Jack called me. Are you all right?"

"In a word, no. I'm angry, I'm scared, confused. Somebody's targeting me, September, and I don't know why. I'm in Heartland, just heading to the kennels. I…" She swallowed hard. "I really need somebody to talk things out with, help me figure who's coming after me. And why."

A short, bitter laugh. "Well you've come to the person with lots of experience."

For as long as she'd known September, the woman had worn an invisible target on her back. Yet she managed not only to survive but to navigate the upheaval and come out whole on the other side. Well, mostly whole. September still struggled with her own demons, many known only to herself. Shadow helped her with that. Dogs always helped.

Lia took a big breath. "I don't know why Molingo mentioned me. But now that Drummond's dead they've got me connected to two murders."

"Combs knows of Drummond. Not particularly respected or well-liked, so there's that. Some folks questioned borderline stuff from earlier in his career, but nothing concrete ever got pinned down." It sounded like September took a swig of coffee. "So far, there doesn't seem to be any link between Molingo and Drummond except you." She paused, her voice full of concern. "Chatter says Drummond had a bite wound from a big dog. Everyone at the hotel knows about Magic."

Lia groaned. "I don't know why he rode my butt nonstop. I couldn't do anything right according to Drummond. But taking that sort of crap goes along with police work, it's part of the training. Even before the academy, I had my share of dealing with jerks."

Drummond seemed convinced the video incriminated her in some way. "He tried to show me a video on his phone..."

"Don't tell me any details, Lia. The police will ask, and I'll have to tell them." A low voice murmured in the background. "Combs says you should get an attorney."

Whoa. That put things in perspective. She didn't know any attorneys except Combs's aunt. "What about Ethel Combs? She works with y'all, right?"

September didn't hesitate. "Ethel does corporate work and only came out of retirement to help set up the Paladin Group. And Lia, we're not ready to take on any cases. You need somebody who specializes in criminal defense." She hesitated. "Your grandfather knows everyone in the county. And he has the funds to help."

Grandfather. That would mean dealing with Grammy, and a rehash of the birthday stuff. Now with class canceled, her dance card looked wide open. Yeah, right. She choked on a laugh, wondering if she'd celebrate this year behind bars.

"Where are you? Staying at the kennels?"

"Yeah. Just leaving Doc Eugene's. Had to drop Magic off

for a quick check up. I pick him up later this afternoon." No need to share more than that. "They canceled classes for the rest of the week, so I took off." She'd hunker down in the little island of safety and peace she'd created for herself. "But I'll need somebody to check on Pippo. When I left the hotel this morning, he'd hidden somewhere. He's got a clean litter box, and plenty of food for the next day or two. I warned housekeeping to stay out of the room."

"Won't keep the police out." September hesitated, then spoke softly, maybe so Combs wouldn't hear. "Jack said I may need to go down there to talk with the authorities. If so, I'll see about collecting Pippo for you." She laughed. "That cat sure keeps folks jumping."

Maybe things would settle, and she could go back to her normal life after the weekend. *Please God.* Lia wasn't religious, but figured prayers couldn't hurt. Hopefully God wouldn't hold it against her for reaching out unexpectedly like this.

"Detective Brummitt, the local PD, will want to talk to you, too. Make sure you find representation before that. I don't know what's going on, either, but stuff like this spirals out of control awfully quick. Just hang out at your kennels, decompress. I'm already at the lake house with Combs and Teddy, but tomorrow I'm meeting with Doc Eugene about Macy. How about I swing by after that? You can always call if you need to talk."

Lia felt her hunched shoulders start to loosen. "Okay." Having someone in her corner to talk to helped. She disconnected.

She shoved the truck into gear and pulled out of the lot. Along the way, she stopped for extra-crispy KFC with her favorite sides. No French fries this time, so she'd have to wait to snack once she got to the kennel.

She spent the twenty minute drive second-guessing her past decisions to pursue law enforcement. If she had never joined the academy, Drummond wouldn't have targeted her. And whoever targeted Drummond wouldn't be trying to blame it on her.

The knapsack on the passenger seat slid off into the foot well with a soft bump as the truck turned into the dirt road. The cat inside struggled a bit but managed to poke his head out of the top opening. Pippo strained to pull himself out of the constricting container. He eeled out of the bag, and crouched silently, motionless, in the footwell.

When the truck came to a stop the overhead light came on when the driver-side door swung wide. Lia grabbed up the bag and food, then turned away from the truck.

Before she could close the truck door, Pippo hopped out, unnoticed by Lia. Fearing the girl would snatch her up, and cut short the adventure Pippo craved, he dashed under the car. He watched as Lia headed toward the low building.

Home! Pippo recognized this beloved place. He knew every nook and cranny of the kennels, the front office, and the apartment up at the top of the rickety stairs. Mice and squirrels played hide and seek in the fields, sometimes sneaking indoors to tease cats and dogs alike.

Pippo peered out from under the car. He tucked paws beneath his white chest, wrapped his long tail about his gray body, and purred with satisfaction, watching and guarding his domain.

Chapter Twenty-Five: KAI

Kai panted softly and leaned forward to peer from the brushy overgrowth. She'd trekked many paw-steps to reach this faintly familiar area. It smelled of Lia and her big Magical-Dawg, but they weren't fresh scents, so Lia wasn't here.

She'd watched the woman with the big cat find and retrieve her friend Pippo. How strange. Kai would have come out to make friends, except the woman had her own big black dog. Then lots of cars arrived with flashing lights, and Kai decided to stay hidden.

But after hiding for a long time, and shivering as the sky

had turned from sunny to night, and back again, she worried nobody would come back for her. The sammich she'd stolen from the man had become a distant memory. Kai's tummy rumbled with pain until she found several dead birds and ate them. They smelled better than they tasted, though.

When the sky turned dark and then sunny once more, and several more strangers invaded the pumpkin patch, she decided to look for Lia. It hadn't taken long once she set her paws and nose to work. But when Kai arrived at the kennel, nobody greeted her. She couldn't find any sammiches. Or birds.

So when at last a big vehicle appeared, Kai watched with a hopeful wag. The car stopped, Lia stepped out, and Kai leaped to her feet, tail beating hard. But she hesitated, expecting Magic to hop out and chase her away.

Lia belonged to Magic, and he rightly protected her from interlopers. Kai stayed here when very young, before going to live in the big house with the fenced backyard. She whined softly under her breath. Kai didn't remember how she first came to live here, only that one day, Lia took her to the big house.

The people there treated Kai okay at first. But after lots of harsh words, she was relegated to the yard. Lia used to spend time with her, but not so much lately.

No big black dog appeared. But a much smaller creature—Pippo?—slipped out and dived under the vehicle. Lia didn't notice. Sometimes people missed the obvious. Lia closed the door and started toward the building.

With joy, Kai burst out of hiding and raced to meet Lia at the door. She danced her delight and play-bowed before the girl, enjoying Lia's gasp of surprise and laughter.

"What the heck…? Guess they still haven't found your

escape tunnel?"

Kai nudged Lia's palm, wanting her touch. She wriggled when the girl smoothed her pointed dark ears. Lia met her eyes, and Kai's heart swelled. Kai waited for Lia to open the front door and step inside. Her tummy growled. She licked her lips, eager for laps of water from a bowl instead of puddles.

The rustle of many critters scurried away, vanishing into the undergrowth. But Kai heard something outside, something that didn't belong.

"Well, come on inside. Last thing I want right now is an argument with Grammy about you. We'll hang out here tonight."

But Kai hesitated. She lifted her head, nose tasting the breeze, scanning the immediate vicinity. Squirrel scent made her whiskers twitch, and tummy rumble even louder. Across the fence she detected deer droppings. She'd eaten some last night but they weren't as good as dead birds. Neither spelled danger.

Magic wasn't here to protect his girl, to sniff out danger and threat. The fur rose on her hackles. Kai felt compelled to keep Lia safe. She'd run around the property, give it a quick sniff, *then* join Lia inside.

"Silly dog. I'll leave the door ajar for when you're ready for treats. I got sammiches."

At the word, Kai nearly changed her mind. But sometimes a dog had more important business. Like making Lia proud. Her ears flicked but she didn't slow her pace. Loping along the fence line, Kai circled the building. On her second circuit, she stopped to sniff the outside area of each of the dozen kennel runs. Though empty, they still held the stale aroma of their most recent occupants. She began a third round of the property and paused in several places to squat, pee, and declare her presence to any who might challenge.

This time, tires crunching on the gravel drive caught her attention. So soft, she knew Lia would never detect them, but clear as a flock of grackles to her keen ears.

A low growl bubbled deep in Kai's chest. This vehicle had two wheels instead of four. The suspicious movement made the fur bristled along a good dog's shoulders.

Kai whirled to face the threat. She stood her ground, voicing warning barks at the interloper.

"What is it? Coyote maybe?" Lia stepped out of the doorway, her silhouette stark.

The rough growl of a motorcycle split the air.

Kai roared and launched herself at the threat. The sound hurt her ears, and the smell burned her nose. Both shouted *danger!*

Another grumble-growl sound, but nothing slowed Kai's pounding gait. Before she got within tooth range, the intruder spun gravel and sped away.

"Kai! *Come-a-pup*, good dog."

She felt proud. She'd chased away the intruder. Her heart pounded, and breath raced but at least the boredom also ran away with the threat. And now she'd get sammiches and belly rubs. Oh joy!

Shelly departed, satisfied by the reconnoiter. He recognized the girl's truck and confirmed empty kennels with only one dog present. He grinned. Complacency did that to a person.

Alone, she'd never hear him coming. He'd wait until nightfall. And take his time.

Chapter Twenty-Six: LIA

K ai, *come-a-pup!*" Lia smiled when she heard Kai's thumping paws returning swiftly at the summons. "What a good girl, you chased off that dangerous motorcycle gang." More than likely, somebody got turned around on these old unmarked gravel roads. She felt bad because Kai spent most of her time locked in the backyard. Grandfather ensured she was fed but had no time for training. Grammy wasn't a fan of dogs, and surprised Lia when she offered to adopt the abandoned pup. And Lia's classes got in the way of helping out.

She'd chosen the Hawaiian name Kai as a

promise and a hope for the little dog. The literal meaning referred to the sea, but the little dog's soul spoke of so much more. The name *Kai* resonated with the vastness and mystery of the ocean, of tranquility, strength, and adaptability. For sure, the pup had to adapt to Grammy.

With the business on hiatus, the indoor/outdoor kennels attached to this main building contained only the ghosts of past barks and meows. Lia spent several minutes making sure the front door latched. She needed to rework the mechanism, a major reason she'd agreed to stay weekends at her grandparents' house. As a stopgap, she'd installed a deadbolt but that only worked from the inside.

She set down her backpack and takeout bag on the bench that lined two thirds of the main room and crossed to the small refrigerator, grabbed a bottle of water, and poured half in the bowl on the floor for Kai. "It's not sammiches but it'll have to do." She shared the chicken—no bones or fried skin—with Kai, prompting endless wags. The little dog also got to lick out the remainder of the mashed potatoes and gravy while Lia cleaned out the mac and cheese. She dug her phone and truck keys out of pockets, set both on the counter, then plugged in her phone.

Lia wanted nothing more than to head upstairs to the tiny apartment, climb into bed, and pull the covers over her head until September showed up tomorrow. She kept waiting for the crunch of tires on gravel. At any minute she expected former police colleagues to arrive and escort her away. At least Magic had a safe haven at the vet clinic. She might leave him there for the time being. Better than having animal control confiscate her boy.

And no, she didn't want to call Grandfather to help. That'd just reaffirm her as their perennial disappointment.

Grandfather and Grammy couldn't help their feelings toward Apikalia—Hawaiian for my father's delight—an unwanted baby with a criminal father. She fingered the name bracelet she always wore. They'd never wanted her, denied her heritage, lied to her over and over, until she learned the truth a year ago and met her half-sister. Living on her own gave her some respite. Then inexplicably, Grammy kept trying to make up for her horrible actions.

Her lack of sleep made it hard to concentrate. Maybe after a nap, she'd be able to think more clearly. Lia trudged upstairs and Kai scrambled to follow; together they sank into the small bed. Within minutes, she was asleep.

Lia woke with a start, and an idea. She scrambled downstairs and approached the small desktop computer. She hadn't spoken to her half-sister, Tee Teves, in many months. The last time, Tee mentioned the Innocence Project had taken up their father's case.

She waited impatiently for the computer to boot up. She'd saved information about Wyatt in a desktop file but with iffy internet out here, she might need her phone's hot spot to get online for contact information.

Would she really make a cold call to Wyatt's criminal attorney? What an intro. "Way to keep it in the family, Lia," she whispered. At least, she wouldn't have to go to Grandfather

Lia had never met her father in person, only via online Zoom. She had always ached to know more about her history as her 16-year-old mother had died giving birth. Now she knew her parents had met on the Islands and married secretly, but Dub and Cornelia Corazon got the marriage annulled and Wyatt arrested for statutory rape. As Lia grew up, they'd refused to share any information about him. She still hadn't forgiven Grammy for her part in her mother's death. Not even Grandfather had known about that.

As soon as the computer screen cleared, Lia found the file in question. It'd taken some convincing for her cop sister to want anything to do with Wyatt, who swore he'd been framed. That thought gave her shivers, since now someone appeared to be orchestrating something similar against Lia. Because he was her father, despite all evidence to the contrary, she wanted to believe him.

She located the name of the attorney: Brianna Lockhart, in Lubbock, Texas, worked with the Innocence Project. Lia wondered how often the attorney visited him. Maybe their interactions remained virtual, like hers.

Wyatt was serving time in Beaumont, close to 600 miles away from Lubbock, and 350 miles from Dallas. The Innocence Project focused on those they believed had been wrongly convicted, so Lockhart probably couldn't represent Lia, but maybe the woman could recommend a defense attorney in the DFW region. "Worth a shot." Gritting her teeth, Lia dialed.

"Lockhart."

"Yes, uhm, Ms. Lockhart? My name is Lia Corazon. I understand you're representing my father, Wyatt Teves through the Innocence Project?"

"Oh yes, Ms. Corazon. I've been meaning to reach out. Some interesting movement on your father's case, and I've been in communication with —"

Lia interrupted her. "I appreciate everything you're doing for Wyatt. But this is another matter. Could you recommend a defense attorney? I… Seems that I've run into a problem, and I need legal advice." She took a breath, hands playing with the mouse pad. She forced herself to be still, but not before the truck's key fob took a dive off the counter.

No answer from Lockhart.

Kai discovered the waste basket and grabbed the KFC bag full of chicken bones.

Lia spun to stop her. "No, pup. Drop it." Lia confiscated the trash and set it on top of the computer monitor. She bent to retrieve the keys but the fob rested halfway under the counter; she'd have to get down on all fours to reach. She took the other woman's silence as an invitation to go on. "The police say my name's connected to a local murder investigation. But I didn't do anything wrong!" *Didn't everyone say that?*

"Yes, I know about Clarence Walford in Dallas. Detectives Greer and Savatch lead that investigation—"

Her brow wrinkled. She hadn't heard anything about the Walford murder. "No, somebody killed an investigative reporter named Ricky Molingo on Friday in Heartland—about sixty miles north of Dallas. Now, my instructor—that is, my Academy Instructor, Detective Kincaid Drummond—somebody killed him last night, right after he forced his way into my hotel room talking crazy…"

"Kinkaid Drummond's dead?" Lockhart didn't hide her shock.

She knew his name?

"Where are you? No, don't tell me that. Are you in a safe place?" Lockhart covered the phone for a moment, speaking to somebody else in the room before coming back on the line. "That's three dead. Don't talk to anyone. Don't say *anything* to *anyone*, until I get there. Ms. Corazon, you're in grave danger. If you're somewhere people know to find you, get out. Get rid of your cell phone. Get a burner that can't be traced if you must, but for God's sake, Ms. Corazon… Lia… Get out now, before the killer finds you, too."

Chapter Twenty-Seven: MAGIC

Magic's head lifted. His tulip ears pointed forward, tail stiffened. He sniffed but detected only antiseptics and other fearful animals. He whined, a gargling sound deep in his throat.

Lia needed him.

He knew. Even though she left him to have his hurts tended. He knew something now made her heart race and breath quicken. He must find her, protect her. Lia meant everything.

Although he liked the kind man with the white coat, and the girls who helped him, they weren't Lia. They patted his head and called him handsome. And they'd fixed the hurty-sore that ran across his neck and down one shoulder, tsk-tsking how brave he acted.

Magic's job was to act brave, especially when Lia asked. He hadn't minded wearing the muzzle, either. Lia taught him to wear one, turning it into a trick for treat game with a yummy inside. The man with the white coat smeared peanut butter in the basket so Magic pushed inside to lick it up. He couldn't bite while wearing it but he knew these people meant no harm.

He'd do anything for Lia. Playing wonderful fun games like finding nasty-smelling boom-flash objects or biting games in case people threatened Lia. Magic loved their exciting games. Even more, he loved to sleep snuggled tight against Lia's side. He'd missed their bedtime cuddles last night.

She'd left him here, where he couldn't see or smell her. She'd taken away his harness that held her scent. Yet Magic still felt the connection. He felt her sudden throat-clenching fear. The emotional connection told him everything: she'd fled their home-place. Without him.

The thought grew the grumble-whine in his throat into such big feelings they spilled out in barks of concern. He placed a forepaw against the bright metal bars of the kennel, paw-thumping it over and over until it rattled and chimed, echoing in the small space.

He must reach Lia. Protect her. Guard Lia. Escape this place, get out, out, OUT!

Other dogs in similar cages around the room joined in the barkfest. One howled, and Magic tipped his own muzzle to the ceiling and sang a counterpoint.

The attendant hurried into the kennel area and switched on the lights. "Settle down, big guy, sheesh. So impatient.

You got everyone riled up, Magic, you silly troublemaker, happy with yourself? You need a potty break?"

Magic banged the cage door again. People took forever to understand what he wanted. What he needed. "Stop it. You'll tear your stitches. You're gonna unravel Doc Eugene's good work."

Lia always knew immediately. Well, sometimes Lia delayed or said "huh-uh" to his requests, but she always understood. This lady, though nice, reminded him of squirrels chasing pigeons, without a single brain between them.

He needed out-out-OUT!

"Hang on, let me get you hooked up." She took her time.

She approached with the lead, and he yelped happily, and jittered with anticipation. She unlatched the door. The loop slipped around his bare neck, high up behind his ears to avoid his healing hurts. "You'll get your collar back after the wound heals, Magic. They tell me you're a super smart trained police dog, so I'm expecting perfect manners." She laughed. "All that barking, throwing a fit? I guess your training wore off with the sedative, eh?"

Usually, he'd do as Lia taught him. Magic needed no leash to stay at heel with Lia. But this wasn't Lia, and he had to get back to her. He knew the way to their home at the kennels. So Magic towed the girl behind him as he headed to the back exit doggy relief station.

She pulled the handle, the heavy door swung open, and Magic yanked hard against the tether. It snaked out of her hand.

"Wait! Hey Magic, stop. I mean, *stay*! Magic, *stay*!" She ran after him, tripping as she grabbed for the end of the leash snaking in the grass.

The familiar command and his training paused Magic's

paws for only a brief moment. She had no claim on his loyalty, even if she knew the right words. She didn't matter. The nice man in the white coat didn't matter, either.

Lia mattered.

Magic put down his head and ran into the night. Three leaps traversed the tiny square of sod that smelled of dog pee, sickness, and fear. He bounded across the sun-warmed pavement, dodged cars with screaming swerving tires. He dragged the leash that had slipped down, and caught on brambles here and there until now it bit into his neck hurts.

But hurts didn't matter. Not when Lia needed him.

THURSDAY,

October 31

Chapter Twenty-Eight: SEPTEMBER

September and Combs had argued all the way to the lake house. She wanted to support a friend, he didn't want to get involved. She waited while Combs levered himself out of the passenger side, lips tight, clearly frustrated.

Paladin Group had limited ability to help Lia, or anyone else, and certainly weren't in a position to represent her as legal counsel. But Lia was chosen family, as much as Teddy, Aunt Ethel, or Doc Eugene. All had helped September, no questions asked, when she needed it most. No way would she turn her back on the young woman.

She rolled down her window. "See what Teddy can come

up with." The morning breeze blew chilly air across the lake fanning dark hair away from her cheeks. The fickle weather varied from year to year, sometimes heating up to the high eighties. Cooler this year, though, with forecasts predicting maybe mid-fifties for Halloween. Behind her, Shadow shoved forward to stick his nose out the window.

"Brummitt will stonewall us. And rightly so." Combs limped around the car to her open window. "Just because I retired from the force doesn't mean we can go renegade." He leaned down to brush her lips then started to turn away.

She reached out the window, catching his hand to stop him. "I've no intention of going vigilante. We follow the rules and let law enforcement do their job. But Lia deserves our support. Something's off. I know it." She squeezed his hand, then let go. "You know it, too."

He half smiled and gave a quick head nod of assent. "I've got your promise you'll head back here after checking in with her? You're not going off on your own, right?" He smoothed the white streak accenting her chestnut hair.

She blinked. She deserved that. Had gone solo on more than one occasion, but those days were over. Creating the Paladin Group meant reliable backup, no lone rangers. The question revealed more about Combs's feelings than her own.

"I promise. I'm going to talk with Doc Eugene about Macy. I promised to meet up with Lia today, but it'll have to be later this afternoon." She'd need to get Macy settled back home, then grocery shopping, not to mention dealing with Kinsler time. "Hopefully, Lia has legal counsel by now, and some sort of plan."

"We can't protect her without risking the kids. She needs to talk to the police, with counsel by her side. Clear the deck from the beginning. She just digs a deeper hole of suspicion by postponing the inevitable." He stepped back and patted the hood of the car like soothing a dog.

He'd ordered the specialized vehicle, complete with bulletproof glass and an engine able to outrun anything, to keep her safe. That's all he'd ever wanted. Sometimes his need to protect felt suffocating. With his bum leg he now had little choice but to let her run around on her own. Self-defense training had her better prepared than any time in the past. And of course, she had Shadow.

Shadow pulled in his nose as she closed the window. He woofed under his breath, easily reading her emotional state.

September backed out of the drive. "Yes, baby dog, I'm worried. About all the things. And about Macy."

The veterinary cardiologist provided Macy with the best care possible, but his exposure to the dead birds heightened her anxiety. It harkened back to the devastating "mad cow" wildlife scare over a year ago. She didn't think it affected birds. But between the waterfowl, and Shadow fetching the dead hawk yesterday, September didn't know what to think.

She reminded herself to talk about the bird issue with Doc Eugene. And she'd mentioned nothing of the birds to Combs. That would give him one more reason to cocoon her. Since his own injury, he'd become hyper-sensitive to protecting her from potential injuries or illness.

The dead hawk rested in a plastic bag in the rear of the car. If something endemic already affected their area, veterinarians already knew about it.

She pulled into the clinic parking lot, early for her appointment. The place already bustled with activity, clients dropping off pets on their way to work.

She took a moment to center herself, waiting while an older woman carrying a toy poodle in her arms, with an overweight Labrador on a leash by her side, crossed to her car and loaded up. She grabbed up a leash before releasing Shadow from the backseat and deftly hooked it to his harness.

She peered through the clinic door's window to check who waited in the area. For the moment, nobody waited. She swung open the squeaky door and allowed Shadow to enter first. He quickly scanned the room for potential danger, a reflex second nature to them both. September took a seat in the far corner and Shadow sat at her feet, leaning his shoulder hard against her knee.

An older woman behind the front desk looked up and smiled in recognition.

"I know I'm early. No rush," September said.

Before the woman could respond, another client exited from the hallway, dabbing her eyes with a tissue. Silently she took care of the bill.

"September, go on down to exam room one. He'll be right with you."

September nodded at the receptionist as she walked by.

Doc Eugene followed her into the exam room. He carried a chart with him.

"Yes, and how are you Mr. Shadow?" He bent halfway to meet the dog at his own level. "No needle sticks for you today, my boy. Today's all about the cat."

September leaned her elbows on the stainless-steel table as the vet opened the chart to discuss his findings. "Macy has done extraordinarily well on the previous medication. We've slowed the progression of his HCM more than I expected."

"So do we adjust his meds?"

Doc Eugene straightened and pulled a new page from the folder. He smiled. "We try something new. And I mean brand-new. I mentioned this when you dropped him off." He tapped the page. "A new drug. Used as an immunosuppressant in human organ transplant patients, Sirolimus delayed-release tablets just received conditional approval to treat subclinical HCM in cats." He cocked his head, probably noting her eyes swam with ready tears. "An animal drug gets conditional approval if it addresses a serious or life-threatening disease or addresses an unmet health need where testing poses complications."

"It's experimental?"

"Yes. The brand name is Felycin-CA1 and it's the first drug approved for use in cats with ventricular hypertrophy due to subclinical HCM." He'd highlighted the important parts on the sheet with a yellow marker. "The dose is 0.3 mg/kg orally once weekly. They did a vaccine response study that showed it shouldn't impact a cat's ability to mount an immune response. I've already screened Macy for liver disease. He doesn't have diabetes mellitus, either, so Macy's an excellent candidate."

She scanned the paper he'd handed to her. "It interferes with the cell growth that makes the heart muscle thicken?"

He nodded. "That helps slow down or even reverse the progression of HCM in cats…"

"…preventing fainting spells or other symptoms." She finished the sentence with a smile. "Oh my gosh, that sounds amazing. A chance for him to maintain his health."

"…Or possibly improve, yes."

"Let's do it." She swiped at her eyes, the tears now a happy, hopeful expression. "And I thought Macy caught something from all those dead birds."

Doc Eugene's eyebrows raised. "Dead birds?"

Quickly, September explained what she'd seen at the

pumpkin patch. "Shadow found a dead hawk in our rose garden, too. Maybe not related, but you know me, worrying about my animals." She grinned, but the smile faltered when he didn't smile back. "I have the hawk bagged in the back of my car. If you want to examine it?"

He nodded tersely. "We'll need to send it off. But it sounds like avian flu."

Her eyes widened. "Shadow had the hawk in his mouth."

He shrugged. "Not a lot to do about that now. Dogs appear a bit more resistant. But cats…" His tone turned grim. "Cats are highly susceptible to avian flu. Few survive infection."

She felt the words like a punch in the gut.

Chapter Twenty-Nine: SHADOW

Shadow eagerly rose to his feet in the backseat, tail thumping the upholstery in a ragged syncopated rhythm as they turned down the road to Lia's kennels. They'd lived here with the younger girl many months ago. He'd liked that and got to play with Magic and lots of other visiting animals.

They'd left Macy at home. He'd smelled funny after picking him up from the vet clinic—strangers' hands and clinic smells—but the cat would soon remove those tainted aromas by thoroughly washing himself whisker to tail.

September pulled to a stop next to Lia's truck, and sat for

a moment without moving, face in her hands. She did that sometimes and talked to herself to plan what to do. Not like dogs.

When Shadow needed to figure something out, he tipped his head from side to side to catch every sound and sniffed deeply of everything riding the breeze. People didn't hear as good as dogs, and they barely smelled anything at all. Sometimes Shadow felt sorry for September missing out on all the robust banquet of sniffy delights.

He whined and pushed his muzzle between the seats to cold nose her bare arm. She startled, like she had gone far away in her mind. Sometimes when she did that, September got lost down a deep dark place Shadow couldn't follow. He whined again. Shadow needed to be close to her to keep September connected to the here-and-now.

"I'm okay, baby dog. Just worried about you, and the dead birds. I should warn Lia, too. Pippo had even more exposure than you or Macy."

She cranked open the car door, stepping out and stretching to take the kinks out of her shoulders. Shadow waited impatiently for her to open his door, then leaped out, whining eagerly under his breath. He raised his head to the afternoon breeze, puffing his cheeks as he sifted through odors of a myriad of creatures.

Pairs of squirrels played tag through the trees. They flushed bright cardinals from the branches, a half-dozen adults with dull-feathered younger birds. The long grass hid multiple treats for birds and dogs alike, hosting hideaways for bunnies, pathways followed by deer, bobcats, and the occasional danger dogs September called coyotes that screamed fierce carols to the sky.

Shadow pawed September's leg. Her hand dropped to his

brow, gently smoothing one ear and caressing his cheek.

"Okay, Shadow." She grinned, looking around the large property. "*Check it out.*" She made a sweeping gesture with her arm, even though he knew the words and didn't need the signal.

Without hesitation, Shadow leaped away. He loped in a wide circle around the buildings, stopping to more thoroughly investigate a strange dog's urine marks. Nose alternating between ground and wind-carried scent, he continued and stopped at the far corner of the property, where Lia had joined the strange dog. He followed the trail for several paw steps, confirming the pair traveled directly away from the kennel.

Shadow puzzled over the absence of Magic's scent. His head tipped to one side considering what that might mean. They'd hurried away, too, not in a leisurely sniff-ari stroll to enjoy wildlife. He didn't find any indication Lia turned back to the building. Shadow whined beneath his breath and glanced back over one shoulder to where September waited for his *all-clear* signal.

He put his head back to the ground, inhaling deeply and debated whether to follow Lia farther. She smelled scared. He decided to follow a bit longer, just to be sure they didn't loop around to sneak into the back of the building.

Back when he was much younger, September taught Shadow the *seek* game. He'd learned that sometimes people did sneaky tricks to try to fool a good dog. But he was too smart to be fooled. Shadow loped ahead, swiftly weaving between thickets of rough grass and prickly cedars that grew in scattered islands across the landscape.

A strange scent stopped Shadow in his tracks. Fur bristled across his shoulders, and he carefully investigated the odor while ears swiveled independently in case the intruder gave themself away. The oily pungent exhaust meant a vehicle. Not a car. He turned away from Lia's scent trail to follow tire tracks pressing down the thick Bermuda grass.

He remembered a girl who rode an odd two-wheeled noisy machine. Had she returned? That made him uneasy, even though she'd acted as a friend the last time they met. Shadow learned the hard way that not all humans showed their true faces, or intentions. He was smart that way.

Loping along the motorcycle tracks, he could tell the trail didn't chase after Lia. Instead, the trail led Shadow around the backside of the property to where the long line of empty kennels sat. They looked wrong, empty and sad without furry inmates offering welcoming wags and yodeling yells. The kennel on the far end sheltered the stinky motorcycle, parked inside with gate still ajar.

Shadow could more clearly smell the stranger who rode the bike, the man's odor so pungent it cut past the burned rubber and oil stink. But he heard no footsteps, no whispered words, and detected no motion betraying the man's presence.

Cautiously, Shadow nosed open the wire kennel door to slip inside for a closer sniff. His lip curled as he examined the bike seat to memorize the stranger's signature aroma. Still fresh. Where had he gone?

The dog-size opening into the building proper allowed boarders to come and go from the indoor-outdoor runs. Sometimes, the little doors got locked to keep a good dog in one part of the kennel. Maybe the stranger sneaked inside; Shadow needed to *check it out* and warn September.

Now this was an adventure! So much more fun than staying at home and running around the boring fenced garden.

Shadow moved past the motorcycle and pushed his head and shoulders through the pet door. He squinted to see the dark interior hallway. He sniffed deeply, but the interloper hadn't come this way. And he could detect no hidden threat inside.

Snick-shshsh. Then the smell of fire, something burning.

Behind him, the gate to the outside kennel clanged shut, trapping Shadow.

Pippo crouched beneath Lia's truck. He'd enjoyed all the outside time, without any pesky human cutting short his explorations. He'd stalked a squirrel, hunted a mouse family with no success, and come across several dead birds that tempted him. But they smelled funny, so he left them alone. He'd caught several crickets—they weren't bad once you pulled the legs off—but Pippo missed his canned food.

He'd watched Lia and Kai leave the place earlier, in such a rush they ignored his belated meows. Lia even left the front door ajar. He'd already snuck into the building once and cleaned up the few kibbles Kai left in the bowl on the floor.

Maybe this person would fill his bowl. Smells of the strange dog kept him hidden until he recognized Shadow. But the dog hadn't intruded or stuck his nose to try and flush Pippo out. So once he loped away, Pippo crept forward to get a better look at the woman standing between the vehicle and the door into the building.

He wanted to go inside again, now that a human arrived who could fill up his bowl with yummies. Mice and chipmunks made a nice snack now and then, too. But they hadn't cooperated, and remained out of paw reach. His long fur kept Pippo warm in the cooling temperatures, but he'd prefer a nap on Lia's soft bed inside the building.

The woman walked slowly between the two vehicles. She watched for something, rocking back and forth impatiently from foot to foot, maybe waiting for Shadow to return.

Pippo decided to wait for the pair inside. Sometimes people didn't understand unless cats made their needs very clear, by meowing loudly next to empty bowls. Pippo pounced forward, racing toward the front door of the building. He leaped high and paws caught the handle, waiting for the anticipated result. Already unlatched from his previous inside visit, his weight pulled down the lever enough to swing the barrier open, just enough.

Pippo dropped to the ground and shoulder-bumped the ajar door. He eeled his way inside, stalked around the perimeter of the small room. In the corner, he scrambled beneath the cave-like knee hole under the counter and hunkered down to watch. A tiny rattling movement caught his attention when his fluffy tail brushed by. A solid paw-thwack sent the key fob spinning across the floor.

A flurry of barks paused the game. Pippo scrambled away, dashing through the kennel door to find a better hiding place. To wait. And to watch.

Chapter Thirty: SEPTEMBER

September waited for Shadow to reappear. She'd dropped Macy off at home, heartened that the new treatment could give him extra years. At the thought, one hand went to her pocket and played with the car keys and laser pointer Macy loved.

In most cases, Shadow completed his *check it out* quickly. She'd seen him complete the first circuit, nose barely skimming the ground and tail flagged high with interest. He began the second round and should have returned by now had there been nothing of interest. In his younger days, Shadow might get distracted by a bunny, but now September trusted him implicitly. He always completed his job before asking permission for extracurricular fun.

Her hand tightened on the haft of the bo staff and she pressed her inner arm against the gun secreted beneath her shirt. She still preferred the less lethal but effective staff so her ankle knife remained in her go bag. Besides, Lia and her protection dog were both trained for lethal force. *Lia should have heard their arrival...* September took three long strides to reach the rear of her vehicle.

An explosion of barks—five in a machine gun rhythm—broke the silence, followed by a pause, then three more in the staccato burst. All from inside the building. Shadow! September ran to the front door, which stood ajar.

Since the staff wouldn't work well in close quarters, she dropped it on the threshold and pulled out her gun, then kicked the door wide. September spun into the room, crouched nearly double, and hugging the wall as she scanned the small space. The waiting area looked empty, but someone could still be hiding or on the floor behind the computer counter.

"Lia? You here, you okay?" She kept her voice low, not wanting to betray her presence to whoever had Shadow upset in the kennel area. His alarm barks continued, a general BEWARE rather than pointed directly at an individual, and he wouldn't bark at Magic. She increased her volume. "Lia? Hey, Magical-Dawg, you here big guy?"

She scurried to the counter, peered behind it to confirm no one there. The whole building had a feeling of desertion. September straightened, inadvertently bumping the antique lariat hung in a place of honor above the computer. It unspooled onto the counter, jarred the keyboard, and brought the monitor to life.

A file on Wyatt Teves appeared. The name Brianna Lockhart, an attorney, was highlighted. *Guess she took my advice.* September blinked when she recognized the dog-themed cell phone resting next to the mouse pad. Lia never left her phone. With her truck still here, maybe she'd got hurt back in the kennel area where Shadow yelled.

"I'm here, Shadow. Wait, good boy."

His exclamations wound down, but he added an impatient yelp for punctuation.

September straightened, still gripping the gun in readiness, and continued her search. The narrow stairway led to the upstairs apartment, a place to check for Lia, but Shadow hadn't made his way to the front office. Maybe trapped by his harness catching on something? She strode to the kennel entry, pausing in the doorway to take in the long dimly lit hallway.

Corazon Kennels, although recently updated, remained old-school. No remote TV viewing, or swimming pool privileges, with the only bedding provided by the dog owners themselves. On each side of the wide corridor sat mirrored cement floor runs enclosed by chain link with a door-size gate for each entry. After one of her boarders managed to climb up and out of the kennel—September smiled, knowing Shadow could manage that trick—Lia had extended the chain link almost to the ceiling on each side, with the top of the fencing angled inward.

Lia had installed a washer and dryer in a closet area just past the doorway. As she walked by, September heard water running in the sink. She nudged the door open with one foot while pointing her gun with both hands.

"Oh for the love of all things furry!" She barked a laugh. "I thought Lia left you at the hotel." September holstered her gun and turned off the faucet. Pippo was curled up inside the sink. Playing with water faucets and door handles seemed irresistible to the cat.

September figured Shadow followed Pippo, maybe from an open outdoor kennel, and managed to trap himself inside. Lia and Magic clearly weren't here. They must've gone off on foot after speaking with the lawyer—running scared, if Lia abandoned her phone to prevent tracking.

"Oh Lia, you got yourself in bad trouble." She'd get Shadow out, then check upstairs to see if Lia left any clues. Maybe a call to the Lockhart woman would clear things up. To protect her friend, she needed more information.

September reached the last kennel and put hands on hips, staring at Shadow inside. "Got yourself in a pickle, too." She grinned.

On the other side of the kennel door, Shadow sat with his ears pasted against his head, doggy grin wide, and tail sweeping the cool concrete. Others might think him embarrassed or apologizing for his predicament. She knew better. Dogs quickly learned that appeasement gestures made angry voices and expressions go away. September reached to pull up the latch.

Shadow showed his teeth in a silent snarl, staring past her. She froze.

A loop of thick braided leather dropped around her neck, snaking to cut off her air.

Shadow erupted. He launched himself, banging against the metal door. The chain link jangled in a counterpoint rhythm with his angry frantic barks.

The hidden attacker cranked on the noose. Her hands clawed at the constriction.

A sibilant voice whispered in her ear, warm breath and

spittle making her cringe. "You're the Corazon bitch that caused all my headaches." His breath smelled rank. His respirations rattled with phlegmy congestion.

Shadow snarled. He bit the chain link and shook the door.

September forced her hands away from her neck. With her back pressed to his chest, she couldn't see him but reached behind to claw at his eyes. She tried to flip around to face him and relieve the constriction. She had only a short window before blacking out.

At least Lia got away.

Gun. Her gun, still in the holster. Within reach…

Shadow body slammed the gate again and again. Snarling curses became howls with each impact. The barrier rattled and jarred, a runaway percussion section following a crazy conductor's frenetic baton.

Abandoning the attempt to gouge his eyes or orchestrate a reversal, September fumbled for her gun, silently cursing the overshirt impeding her progress. She pulled it free.

He saw. Momentarily relaxed his grip on the noose to swat the gun away.

She gasped, gulped in three quick breaths before the pressure returned.

Shadow continued battering the gate. His voice faded as he channeled all energy into escape.

September stared into Shadow's gorgeous brown eyes, as dark sparkles filled her own vision. Her knees hit the floor, the bruising contact a dim echo of the pain in her throat. Tears streamed from her eyes, eyes she feared might pop out from unbearable pressure. After the many times she'd escaped death, how ironic she'd die being mistaken for Lia.

Her hands reached weakly to her throat, fluttered as effectively as moth wings at his grip. All energy drained, her spasming fingers dropped to her waist.

She felt a bulge, and in a last desperate burst of energy, snagged the jingling car keys, interlaced between her knuckles. September aimed the jagged bundle upward at the attacker's face.

The laser pointer on the key ring ignited, shooting brilliant streams against the ceiling, bouncing off walls, splitting into prisms of rainbow light as it hit chain link.

Shadow never enjoyed chasing laser pointers. Not like Karma. Cats liked chasing them…she couldn't remember, brain didn't work right. Cats and lasers…

September couldn't hear Shadow's barks anymore. Either he'd fallen silent, or she'd become deaf as her body shut down.

She gave up fighting. Her vision faded. Still, she angled the laser pointer unsteadily to focus on the kennel's door latch. It jittered there, like a bug that begged catching.

Pippo watched from above. He'd followed September from the laundry. Pippo liked to climb the chain link at the front of the kennel and tight-rope-walk the length of the hall out of nose-reach of pesky dogs. Lia always made him get down.

But Lia wasn't here. And September didn't know to look up. Or glance behind, when the foul-smelling man looped something about her neck.

Pippo didn't like the way Shadow barked and battered himself against the barrier. A cat could climb up and squeeze through the narrow gap at the ceiling. But big dogs must stay grounded.

When Shadow's noise faded to whines and whimpers, Pippo noticed the zooming streaks of light darting about. The elusive firefly he'd tried more than once to capture stutter-danced on the gate latch in front of the dog's nose.

Shadow looked up. Brown eyes met golden. Without blinking, Shadow backed slowly away from the front of the kennel. He whimpered, voice anguished. Pleading.

September slumped in front of the man, a man muttering to himself with words Pippo couldn't understand.

Tail twitching, Pippo danced forward, a furry ballerina on-point traversing the high wire. He scrambled down, behind the stinky man. He leaped high to capture-bite-devour-pummel the light-prey. His paws clutched the haft of the latch, jarring it up and out of its locked position—

Shadow's full weight slammed against the unlatched door. It burst open, slapped the attacker's butt, startling him so much he dropped the noose, and yelled.

Pippo's answering screech echoed as he dashed away, retracing steps to the lobby then scrambling up the stairs to hide in the bed.

Home. And safety. The bed that smelled like Lia. Like love.

Chapter Thirty-One: LIA

Lia had waited until dark to vacate the kennel, just in case someone was watching—maybe that lost motorcyclist?—then camped out in the scruffy hills, too tired to go far in the dark though she knew the area well. Once daylight bloomed, she'd tried to figure out next steps. Going back to the beginning seemed the best option.

As she walked, she thought of all the times she'd made the pilgrimage from her grandparents' homestead to the kennel property. There, she basked under the tutelage of Abe Pesquiera, and found her calling. The easy-going Hawaiian encouraged her to embrace her heritage despite her grandparents forbidding it. And taught her everything he could about training dogs.

In those days, Abe owned and ran the boarding kennel. Grandfather expected Lia to continue his passion of raising and training the finely bred horses for Corazon Stables. She adored the elegant creatures; according to her grandfather, had *the touch* with them just as her mother had.

But for Lia, her soul soared in a partnership with the dogs.

That's what attracted her to working as a police K-9 handler. Jobs that allowed you to partner in this way weren't common. Lia wanted to do more than offer training classes, basic obedience, and boarding services at the kennel she'd bought from Abe.

Now, she fled both dreams, her first love of training dogs, and newfound goal of graduating from the police training academy. The unnamed threat had become more real with the urgency in Lockhart's voice. Clearly, the attorney knew more than she shared. That urgency sped Lia's feet.

She jogged through the field, Kai ranging ahead and pretending to scope out danger. Lia missed Magic, but Kai gave her a much-needed smile amid all the angst. The pasture was bordered by ancient bois d'arc fenceposts strung with rusty barbed wire, and stretched as far as she could see. Generations of longhorn cattle had worn a path deep into the sod—and before them, deer—long before Corazon horses had taken their place. These days, Grandfather pastured the mares closer to the stables. Personal mounts and the working cutting horses were also stabled close to the house.

Prairie beardgrass, a variety of native grass that swayed and danced in the breeze, scratched exposed skin. She ducked through mounds of dried switchgrass and bunchgrass, and recognized the luscious turkeyfoot that cattle craved like kids jonesing for ice cream.

She rested for a moment beneath the blue-green foliage of a massive cedar tree. Cedars spread like a rumor and often took over entire pastures. Along the fence, yaupon holly trees bobbed and weaved in a line dance, the fall berries adding fruity bling to each graceful movement.

She crossed another pasture before the Corazon's massive home came into view, perched atop one of the highest hills on the rolling prairie. She shed the backpack and rummaged inside to find a small pair of high-powered field glasses. She spied only normal movements around the house—well, normal for a big event day—with nothing that raised suspicion.

Good. She'd steer clear until all this mess blew over. Whoever hunted her knew about the kennels. When they didn't find her there, they might target her grandparents' house.

She reshouldered her pack and set off toward the pumpkin patch. From studies at the academy, she'd learned most bad guys made stupid mistakes. They thought too highly of themselves and their skills. Lia understood her own limitations and she knew these pastures as well as Magic's tummy freckles.

At the thought, she glanced around for Kai. She'd fallen behind again, letting Lia take point while Kai protected and guarded the rear. Or so Lia imagined. She reminded herself not to ascribe too much to the pooch, certainly not the level of connection or understanding Magic owned. Kai had received little training.

But as if Lia had shouted, Kai lifted her head from the grassy hummock she'd just baptized and met Lia's eyes. Kai's tail wagged a happy message. Lia raised one hand, waving, and blew Kai an air-kiss, then grinned with surprise when Kai leaped high in the air as if to catch it. One of the many silly games she played with Magic. Kai must have seen and copied it. The girl was a natural. Imagine what Kai could do with dedicated training.

But no time for silliness, not with someone stalking her, and leaving bodies in their wake. Sweat trickled down her back under the weight of her pack. She had camping necessities, including extra clothes and ammunition. She wore her gun holstered for easy access.

Lia gasped as a feeling of imminent danger erupted like fireworks in her head. She winced, intuition or something like it sounding the alarm. She instinctively dropped to one knee behind a flimsy fence post while drawing her weapon.

A split second later, the dog's deep barks confirmed her instinct. Kai raced past Lia, fur bristled, and tail held high. She dived between rusty wire strands, leaping through the high grass then simply head-down bulldozing until only the vegetation's movement revealed her progress.

If she closed her eyes, Lia could imagine what the dog experienced, she knew them so well. Brittle grass switching against canine muzzle, dust motes stirred beneath broad thumping paws, and a musky-earthy sweat-sweet odor that brought Lia's childhood rushing back…

Kai's alarm barks shut off. Lia rose from her defensive crouch, shading her eyes, not needing binoculars to see the old friend being led proudly by Kai.

A red pony with dark mane and tail: Sebastian, her childhood companion.

Chapter Thirty-Two: SHADOW

Shadow erupted from the kennel focusing all energy on attack. He leaped high, jaws wide, making contact and crunching vise-like jaws on the man's nearest forearm. The attacker screamed.

A rush of salty wet filled Shadow's mouth. Ears slicked tight against his head, Shadow hung from the man's arm, his rear paws barely touching the cement floor.

The man dropped September. As she collapsed to the ground, the man flailed at Shadow's muzzle with his free hand.

Shadow clung to the meat of the man's arm for another

ten—endless—seconds, increasing the pressure to emphasize his power. Then he opened his jaws wide and dropped to the floor. He scrambled to straddle September's shuddering form, guarding her with teeth and snarls, threatening to escalate the attack.

"Good dog, Shadow." September's voice, though hoarse, increased Shadow's confidence. His ears twitched in acknowledgment, but his eyes never wavered from the bad man.

With a snarl of his own, the man backed away. "I'll kill you, kill you both, you'll spoil everything. Your own damn fault, you did this to yourself." His eyes darted around, alighting on September's gun. He lurched for the weapon.

"Shadow, *guard gun*." Her voice sounded broken, but Shadow understood.

He raced the man, beating him to the deadly object and standing over the gun. Shadow bared his teeth again; he didn't want to bite. He still had the man's nasty taste on his tongue.

September grappled the chain link kennel to slowly lever herself upright. One hand loosened the lariat around her throat and massaged the tender area.

"You're the Corazon bitch that hired that reporter."

She shook her head. "Lia's not here. She didn't hire him."

He startled, staring at her with bloodshot eyes, nose dripping and face flushed. Then he nodded, sneering. "You know everything? You're dead, too." He pulled a knife, but before he could use it, a coughing fit stole his breath. He staggered, nearly bent double.

"Black dog, white streaked hair—you're the Magpie. Sorokin Glass." He panted, brandished the knife, then glanced at Shadow's snarling face and reconsidered. He whirled and raced away, Shadow nipping at his heels, literally.

"Shadow! *Chill.*"

He skidded to a halt, whining under his breath. The bad man raced through the front office and banged out the front door. Footsteps pounded away.

Shadow yawned loudly, and shook himself hard, releasing some of the tension that still bristled his fur. He sniffed the leather cord the bad man used against September. He picked it up with a growl and shook it hard. Shadow fetched it to September.

She paused to gather up the rope—but she didn't bite and shake it, just lifted her lips as she coiled it and slung it over her shoulder. He stood close beside her as she collected her gun. Together they made their way back to the main office.

When the motorcycle roared to life, Shadow kept his attention glued to September. She shuddered and propped herself against the wall. He worried she might suffer terrible lasting hurts. He'd survived terrible hurts—like when the gun reached out and bit a good dog's ear. Or fire seared his paws. The pain eventually left but the scary feeling stayed forever.

September had more than enough scary feelings piled up in her life. It was a good dog's job to chase more scares away.

Chapter Thirty-Three: SHELLY

Shelly left the wire kennel door open as he raced away. Damn this bug! He should have easily finished Sorokin, dog or no dog. He'd meant to come back last night after casing the place, but the damn cold meds did a number on him. His eyes watered profusely, and the dog's bite left him throbbing in pain.

Just like a woman. Sneaky. Devious. Conniving, the two of them, with their rabid attack dogs. The Magpie probably put Lia…

Wait. She said the Corazon girl didn't hire Molingo, but he clearly spoke that name. Shelly hadn't made a mistake. With his dying breath, trying to delay his end, the reporter pointed a finger at someone "hiring" him to snoop into history better left buried.

Molingo and Drummond and Walford all brought this on themselves. Shelly had done his job before. He resented the forced do-over that opened him up to further scrutiny. Yes, all their own fault. The Corazon girl and Sorokin Glass sticking noses where they had no business. If they'd only shut up, and do as they were told…

But no, instead they second guessed their betters. They deserved what they had coming. And if not Lia Corazon, then another with the unusual name.

He swiped at his nose with the back of a hand. All those years ago, the elegant plan he'd conceived had worked brilliantly. Sorokin Glass dared dethrone his mentor, and now, with her Corazon disciples, planned to unravel his life's work.

He'd underestimated the situation. The blond girl hadn't the brains or experience to set this up. Now he knew the Magpie pulled her strings, a few minor adjustments would still accomplish his goal.

The clown regalia no longer mattered. He'd implicated the girl with the deaths of Walford and Drummond. That sparked another brilliant idea. He bared his teeth at the genius of the thought.

He'd add Sorokin to the Corazon girl's hit list. Based on the evidence he'd planted, she'd already wasted Drummond and the Walford snitch. Made sense she would turn on an old friend who trumpeted her allegiance to truth, the law, and righteousness. Ha! Once he orchestrated that little scenario, nobody would believe a wild story Molingo had uncovered.

He laughed out loud but stopped when it turned into a

hacking cough that nearly spilled him off the cycle. Shelly pulled off to the side of the road, clutching the handlebars as his midsection clenched again and again and he spewed onto the roadway. Once it passed, he spat, wiped his uninjured forearm across his mouth, and pulled back onto the narrow country road.

He needed to take Lia out before Detective Greer showed up at the kennel to debrief her.

She'd take refuge with her grandparents. It paid to know a person's weaknesses. Family took care of family, at least the good ones did. Not that he'd know about that.

Shelly gunned the cycle back onto the asphalt. He always looked for those connections so he already knew Dub and Cornelia Corazon owned a sprawling ranch only a few miles away. He smiled. He didn't care which one hired the reporter. Easy enough to take all out and silence any questions.

He'd take a short cut through the corn maze, a preposterous acres-large Texas-shaped monstrosity. He'd looked that up, too, and his cycle could easily navigate the acreage of the dried vegetation while staying under the radar. He could stake out the homestead, plan his attack. Then, when the time was right, he'd pay grandma and grandpa a visit.

Chapter Thirty-Four: SEPTEMBER

September used one hand on the chain link to help her balance as she navigated back to the office. She fought the urge to cough, fearing it would further damage her throttled throat. Shadow's hackles remained bristled, and he pressed hard against the side of her leg, whining under his breath.

In the office, she pulled a bottle of water from the small refrigerator and pressed the cold plastic against her neck, closing her eyes at the soothing sensation. She saw a dog bowl on the floor, so opened the water and poured out half for Shadow. She pointed, not wanting to speak, fearing if she started coughing and wheezing, she wouldn't be able to stop. Shadow obediently dipped his head to the bowl and took three or four laps before returning his worried gaze to her face.

She knelt on the floor and opened her arms. Shadow needed no further encouragement to press eagerly into her embrace, his back end two-stepping an emotional doggy dance of relief. They didn't need words. He'd saved her life. Again.

So had the cat. She made a mental note to find and check on Pippo before they headed out. They must leave, and soon. Her attacker could circle back to take a long-distance shot. She had learned to believe threats, both overt and unvoiced.

After an all too brief cuddle session, September levered herself upright. She drank the other half of the water, wincing with each swallow. It burned only part way down, but after the third gulp she gained some relief.

Medical attention must wait. It'd only delay what she needed to do: go after Lia, warn her. Then activate the full resources of Paladin Group. She'd been wrong to leave it to the police—strict adherence to the rules mattered, but sometimes you must bend or risk breaking yourself, or others.

September hadn't seen her attacker's face but would never forget his voice. He wanted Lia dead. So Lia had run, abandoned her truck and escaped cross-country with Magic. Lockhart must've warned her. She'd share the attorney's name with Teddy, and he'd unlock the details.

She retrieved a second bottle of water and drank half, still wincing at the rawness in her throat. She tested her voice. "It'll have to do." Sounded rocky, but texting fell short for this update.

>when R U home?

From Melinda. September groaned. Combs had agreed to compromise on the hayride. But September couldn't leave now.

<At Lia's kennels. Ask Dad

That answer would have to do. She called Combs to update him.

He answered on the first ring. "September?"

"I'm fine. But we've got a situation." *I sound like Jack.* She recapped everything, underplaying how close she'd come to checking out. "He's after Lia, don't know why. Thinks we work together." She massaged her throat. "Lia talked to an attorney named Lockhart, then took off on foot without her phone." She rattled off the attorney's number. "See if you or Teddy can find out more."

"Lia doesn't want to be tracked." Combs didn't sound happy, but at least he didn't insist on her coming in. "How'd she know Lockhart?"

"It's on her computer in a file about Wyatt Teves. Lockhart's with Innocence Project, must be working on his appeal." September knew very little except that he'd been convicted of killing her birth father, Henry Wong. God forgive her, but she figured Teves deserved a medal for that.

Combs set the phone on speaker so Teddy could talk. "What's wrong with your voice? You sound like me." The older man's tone always reminded September of swallowed glass. And at the moment, her throat felt like it, too.

She brushed the comment aside. "I'm going after Lia. Shadow can track Magic."

"Don't do that." Combs clearly hated the idea. "Wait till Teddy's wizardry gets us some answers. We need to know how to protect her. *And* protect you."

Combs made sense, but September couldn't leave Lia on her own. "We'll be safer together. He already got a taste of Shadow's teeth and won't risk getting that close again." *He wouldn't need to...*

At his name, Shadow's tail thumped a happy tattoo. September stroked his brow, comforted he'd stand by her no matter what.

Combs cut through her bull. "Doesn't need close proximity to shoot you, September. Wait for backup." Combs couldn't hide his frustration. "Lia's likely headed for her grandparents' place. We should warn them."

She shook her head, even though he couldn't see the gesture. "Cornelia's throwing her big Halloween bash tonight. It's Lia's birthday party, but she didn't plan to go. She'll steer clear, won't want to lead the killer there." Before she forgot, she added, "Melinda texted, don't know why; told her to contact you."

Before Combs could reply, Teddy weighed in. "It makes sense Lia dials up the only criminal attorney she knows. But something more made her run, when she'd clearly planned to hole up at the kennels. Just found one nugget, and betcha we'll find more pearls as we string 'em together."

"A nugget? C'mon, Teddy. I need to hit the trail to catch up with Lia..."

He chuckled. "May not mean a whole lot. But it turns out Drummond and his partner ran Wyatt Teves's criminal investigation. It made Drummond's career, back in the day."

Chapter Thirty-Five: LIA

Lia needed no saddle, and Sebastian needed no reins. Kai trotted ahead, leading the way, as if she knew just where they'd go. Back to the pumpkin patch, where it all started. Where September found Molingo. Where he'd met someone vital for his investigation. Where his interview turned deadly. And where the reporter had preserved his notes, according to Peter.

When all else fails, go back to the beginning. She knew her colleagues had scoured the area, looking for the evidence Peter swore he'd hidden. But Lia was convinced she could find what remained hidden from the others. Kai wasn't a trained tracking dog, but she'd already surprised Lia with her innate abilities. It wasn't in Lia's nature to run scared, and she hated that the attorney's words had spooked her, but she preferred to channel that energy into solving the current mystery.

She tongue-clicked at Sebastian and he picked up his pace. The comforting thump-thu-thump of hooves on the baked Texas sod matched the rhythm of her heart. Lia felt her shoulders drop, and breathing calm, as she swayed gently with the animal's motion. She let her mind free-associate, trying to decipher the puzzle.

Molingo's investigation got him killed. Wyatt's attorney mentioned three deaths: Molingo, Drummond, and someone named Walford. What did they have in common, other than herself? Why would Lockhart know, unless they all had something to do with her father's appeal? Also, if Lockhart's intel proved so dangerous, why hadn't she warned Lia, or contacted the police?

Or had the attorney conferred with Drummond? Was that why he'd accused her of doing something illegal? Unless Drummond himself had something to hide.

"Stop it!" She whispered the words, making Sebastian's ears twitch at the hissing sound. Just because she disliked Drummond didn't mean he was dirty.

And… dirty how?

Lockhart first mentioned Walford and that Detectives Greer and Savatch investigated the murder. Did Walford's murder happen before or after Molingo? Certainly Molingo's investigation poked a hornet's nest, leading to his own death, and that of Drummond and the mysterious Walford. But it still didn't answer why anyone would target her, other than being the estranged daughter of a convicted felon. As a police cadet, she had no juice to do anything, let alone funds to hire anyone.

They had to connect to Wyatt, or Lockhart wouldn't have told Lia to run.

Wyatt maintained his innocence, just like most convicted felons. Tee didn't believe him—had other issues with his behavior toward her mother and herself she refused to share—but Lia wanted to trust Wyatt's word.

So far, none of his appeals worked. But maybe the tide had turned. Once she found the missing evidence at the pumpkin patch, she'd happily turn it over to Detective Savatch.

Chapter Thirty-Six: SHADOW

Shadow's ears came forward to better understand September's words. He knew she spoke to Combs and Teddy through her phone. People did amazing things, like talking to each other even when they weren't here. He whined low in his throat when she mentioned his name. After the excitement of chasing the bad man away, Shadow wanted—no, he needed to do *something* to reset his emotions.

Like play Frisbee *fetch*. Or eat bacon.

September pocketed her phone and turned away from the computer. In four long strides, she reached the doorway to the stairs leading to the apartment overhead.

"Shadow, *check it out.*"

He didn't wait for her hand signal. Shadow sprang forward, leaping up the stairs two and three at a time, his sensitive nose revealing secrets even before he cleared the landing.

The open floor space had changed since the time he and September shared the area with Lia. The two twin beds, one on each side of the room, reminded him of late-night snuggles and the smells and sounds of critters in the old walls. One of the beds now served as a sofa with a multitude of pillows jumbled across the surface.

Pippo had burrowed a nest in the other bed, the one that smelled the most like Lia.

Shadow didn't bother investigating the cat. He could tell nothing lurked beneath either bed. He pawed a quick circuit of the small space, following the freshest scent left behind. Dresser drawer, closet with door still agape, and the window where she'd stood for long moments, perhaps keeping watch. The strange dog's scent mirrored Lia's path, speaking clearly of concern and excitement.

Shadow's claws clicked on the wooden floor as he returned to the top of the stairs and sat with great deliberation. He barked once. His tail swept the landing as September quickly climbed to meet him.

"Good boy, Shadow. Let's see what Lia packed. It'll tell us how long she plans to go silent."

She quickly retraced many of Shadow's own steps, learning important things without benefit of sniffs. People were funny that way.

September paused near the bed. "Appreciate your help, Pippo." She turned sideways and extended one finger for the cat to sniff.

After a perfunctory nose-touch, Pippo pushed against the finger to stroke his cheeks against September's extended hand. "Such an escape artist. I need to do something to keep you safe until Lia can take over." She laughed, massaging her throat. "Can't complain, you saved my life. But the front door won't securely latch, and we can't take you along to seek Magic."

Shadow whined. He loved playing the *seek* game. It wasn't as good as bacon, though.

September gently gathered the cat into her arms, nodded at Shadow, and led the way down the stairs. She tested the front door twice, but it still refused to latch from the outside, needing the inside deadbolt for security.

Shadow followed her out the door. She grabbed up the fallen bo staff, and he danced impatiently as she crossed the parking lot and unlocked their car. September opened the rear door, and dropped Pippo on the backseat before quickly closing him in. September climbed into the front seat, inserted the keys, and did something that made all of the windows roll down just wide enough for a good dog to stick his nose.

He whined, and did a paws-up against the glass, stretching his neck to sniff. She mentioned *seek*, and that meant tracking. Would they go in the car instead?

When she climbed back out, September hurried to open the rear hatch. He paw-danced when she collected the tracking gear. "This time of year, the temperature's not a risk. Pippo should be fine for a few hours." She glanced around, squinting to ensure the area remained safe for them. At the thought, he raised his muzzle to test the slight breeze, detecting no threat.

She attached the long lead to Shadow's harness.

September shrugged the strap of her go bag over her shoulder and adjusted the lariat on her other shoulder. She shut the rear car door and pushed the button on her keys to make the cricket sound.

He waited for the command. He knew what to do.

"Shadow, want to play *seek*? You know Magic and Lia. *Seek Magic*. Shadow *seek*."

His nose dropped to the ground. Tail beating the air, he cast back and forth. As before, though, he found no trace of Magic scent. Only Lia, and the strange dog.

But Shadow knew what to do. He was smart that way.

Chapter Thirty-Seven: MELINDA

Melinda sneezed, and her face flushed. *Please don't let my nose run.* How embarrassing.

The bales of straw they sat on itched the backs of her legs through the material. She tugged to adjust her jeans where the artful holes and tatters allowed straw to prickle exposed skin. Dust tickled her nose. A tank top with a hoody over top, and cute sandals completed the outfit but now she wished for better shoes. It had turned cold, not to mention spooky. Halloween night, with a crescent moon, and a cute boy by her side. She wondered if he'd want to hold hands? Melinda hoped so.

She glanced sideways at Delaney sitting next to her. She'd been surprised when he called but eagerly accepted the invitation to get together for the hayride. Dad had approved the hayride with her friends. He didn't know Delaney would be there.

Delaney said he had to get away. She knew what that was like. Even though Dad had retired from the force, he still had eyes on her at all times. She knew how suffocating it must feel to have police swarming Delaney's little brother, Peter.

"You snuck out? Do they know where you are?" She whispered, liking the idea of the clandestine meeting.

He shrugged and rocked into her shoulder when the horse drawn wagon lurched down and back up a trough in the land. She grabbed his muscled arm to keep her balance but immediately let go. Her face heated even more and she turned away.

Melinda enjoyed the delicious flutter in her stomach. This felt dangerous, not because of Delaney, but because of everything else going on. Well, maybe a little because of Delaney.

"Is Peter okay?" He wasn't much older than Willie. She blinked at the thought, the butterflies morphed into snakes roiling her gut. If anything ever happened to Willie…

"He's surrounded by cops." Delaney glanced sideways at her. "Police, I mean. A nice lady policewoman stays with us in this old apartment across town. Told her I needed my space, and she locked me in the bedroom. So I shimmied out the window. Not the first time, either. Uncle Ricky never found out when I did it at our house." He grinned, but the expression didn't reach his eyes. "Now he never will." His jaw squared. "If they wanted me to stay, they should've confiscated my keys. It was only a couple miles to collect my car. We run more than that in cheer practice."

She smiled back. Delaney was seventeen, a few years older than she was. She liked older men, especially the ones with rizz. She might even let him kiss her. He needed comforting, after all. She glanced around the wagon. But not while these kids were around.

Two other teenage couples plus many younger kids perched around the artfully arranged bales of hay. One couple had already got hot and heavy while younger kids snickered and pointed, whispering behind their hands. Some people had no class.

"Peter's stronger than he thinks. He got scared but he's holding the line. And we got a plan, too, to nail that SOB who killed Uncle Ricky." He glanced around at the other kids then leaned close to whisper in her ear. "Uncle Ricky gave Peter his notes on his phone. Peter hid it good, too. I just need to collect it. But I need your help."

The butterflies returned, and Melinda crossed her arms hard across her stomach to contain them. Delaney needed her help. "You can turn over the evidence to my dad. They started the Paladin Group, and it's dialed in. Gonna be kick ass awesome for getting justice."

He shook his head. "Not that kind of help. Uncle Ricky had an agreement. We'll get paid if we give the information to the Corazon lady. But I need your help to get it out of the hiding spot."

Melinda looked around, then leaned in to continue the fiercely whispered conversation. "What are you talking about? Why would Lia hire your uncle? He was an investigative reporter, not a PI, wasn't he?"

"Don't know. Don't care. Uncle Ricky said this could be a big payday for him, and Peter says Uncle Ricky told him everything's documented on the phone. Just before he died, he shoved it into Peter's hands. Made him swear to hide it in a secure spot." Delaney fisted tears from his eyes, voice rough with emotion.

"The police closed the pumpkin patch—Willie got all twisted over that—and searched it." Melinda wrinkled her nose, fending off another sneeze. The hayride route would loop past the pumpkin patch, then across one field and skirt the corn maze before returning to the stables. "Did Peter tell you where to look?"

Delaney nodded. "He's scared to tell the police. Says Uncle Ricky said some crazy stuff about cops being involved. Neither of us can make sense of it, but we can't take chances. If the killer finds that phone, then Uncle Ricky died for nothing." He took a big breath. "That's why Peter told the cops he hid the evidence at the pumpkin patch." He grinned. "He didn't lie."

"You're not making sense. Stop talking in circles." She raised her voice, and one of the couples eyeballed her for a moment before resuming their face-sucking gymnastics.

"He hid the phone in a car, shoved it through the back window. Said a big black dog inside barked at him—figured nobody would risk looking there." He cocked his head to one side, eyes narrowing as he stared at Melinda. "As far as I know, only one car was there that had a dog inside."

She blinked. "September's car? That's why you invited me?" She couldn't hide the hurt disappointment.

He nodded and grabbed her hand. It wasn't the romantic gesture she'd hoped for. "I need your help, Lindy. I gotta look in her car and find Uncle Ricky's phone. Please?" He squeezed her hand. "Peter says the killer promised to come after him. I got to stop him. I need your help, to save my brother's life. And nail that killer."

Chapter Thirty-Eight: SEPTEMBER

Good dog, Shadow." September's gloved hands clutched the end of the long tracking line, allowing him to tug her cross-country through the scrubby pastures. He picked up Magic's trail quickly, probably because he'd already found the trace when checking out the property upon arrival.

Combs should have already notified the police. They knew her attacker traveled on a motorcycle. If they didn't flush the killer quickly, an all-points would at least slow him down. Thank goodness Peter and his brother had police protection.

Lia was her priority. Never mind that events of the past

couple of years revealed they weren't blood family. Her mother Rose—adopted mother, she now knew—had been estranged from her sister Cornelia. That made September and Lia cousins, at least of the heart. Some things were more important than blood.

Shadow loved tracking lost pets, plus he adored Magic, and had even helped raise the young Rottweiler mix. With the two dogs partnering them, she and Lia stood the best chance of staying safe from the killer.

September had turned off her phone as a precaution but kept it with her. Once she found Lia, they'd brainstorm to identify their attacker and try to figure out why they'd been targeted.

Shadow paced quickly with his head held high. Every once in a while, he swerved off the direct route, mirroring the paw-steps the other dog had taken.

Like September and Shadow, Lia and Magic had an uncanny bond above and beyond that of many pet lovers. Lia needed no words to communicate with Magic.

Where Magic's energy exploded with bright teeth and deep throated threats, Shadow's strength arose from deep and selfless love that filled her empty places. He always knew when September needed grounding. Without training, he learned to alert her to an impending meltdown. Her connection to Shadow didn't work in the other direction, at least not as overtly as between Magic and Lia. She brushed off a fleeting jealousy. She wouldn't trade her relationship with Shadow for any alternative.

Shadow paused at the summit of a gentle incline, nose again dropping to the ground and tail beating the air. Clearly something of interest happened here.

September saw the Corazon's house in the distance. Cars

pulled up the long drive, parking in a nearby field for the big Halloween gathering. She wondered again why Lia's grandmother had been so adamant the girl attend.

"Shadow, *seek. Seek Magic.*" He'd stopped, taking more time than usual to explore the area. His ears slicked back with her encouraging words to carry on.

Maybe they'd crossed the fence line? She noted a bit of golden hair snagged in one of the old rusty fence wires and smiled. Shadow confirmed her guess, tugging her forward so he could wriggle through too.

He waited impatiently for her to carefully stoop and crawl between the rusty barbed wire strung between fence posts. Grass chewed down to bare earth along the fence revealed fresh hoof prints. That explained his interest, if a horse joined the pair. "Good dog, Shadow. *Seek.*"

If Lia traveled on horseback she'd move faster. September urged Shadow on, stretching her legs into a mile-eating trot. A motorcycle could easily travel cross-country even more quickly than a horse.

On foot, Lia could stay nearly invisible, especially once the sun went down. Even the modest moon glow would paint a target on her back with her riding high above the brushy field. What was she thinking? They needed to find Lia as quickly as possible.

September had a good idea where Lia headed, but wasn't sure why she'd visit the pumpkin patch. Maybe the girl had insight into finding answers hidden amid the spooky decor.

Shadow led September to the back end of the corn maze, where they fought through several rows of dried field corn, leaving September's bare arms itchy. They broke into the clearing, and she could smell the decaying bodies of the birds. She saw a single car in the parking lot. Had the motorcycle guy used a car this time?

"Shadow, *wait*." He whined but planted his tail, impatient for her next request. She squinted around the area, alert to any motion. She didn't want to yell and risk having the motorcycle killer alerted, in case he beat Lia here.

Moving quietly, September unhooked the long tracking line from Shadow's harness, rolled it up and stuffed it inside her go bag, so he could find them more quickly and efficiently, and with the least noise. She'd just hang back and watch. She gave the hand signal, silently telling Shadow to *seek*.

He launched himself, making a beeline for the overturned wagon midway down the field. As she watched his progress, September caught slight motion just behind the decorative wagon—the silhouette of a horse's head. She smiled and stepped forward.

The sound of the gunshot stopped her cold. September dropped to the ground and froze.

Chapter Thirty-Nine: SHADOW

At the sound of the gunshot, Shadow skidded to a stop and froze. His notched ear flicked, remembering. He lifted his head, nose seeking. He confirmed Lia and the big creature September called a horse waited by the overturned wagon. The strange dog's scent, not as potent, meant the other dog waited downwind, out of easy detection.

Why would Lia shoot at September? He could easily travel the rest of the distance between them. That way he could *show-me-gun* and knock it away so it couldn't hurt September.

But would that prompt the strange dog to attack? Magic

would defend Lia with his life, but Shadow didn't know anything about her new dog friend. He understood the imperative. He'd also protect September with his life. That's what good dogs did for their people.

Lia and September knew each other and had always acted friendly. So Shadow didn't understand what changed. He whined deep in his throat and slicked back his ears. People confused him sometimes. They said one thing and did the opposite. They didn't always clearly telegraph their intentions the way dogs did with the quirk of an ear, tail elevation, or scent.

Cautiously, Shadow took three slow paw-steps forward, ears pricked for any answering sound. He glanced over one shoulder toward where September now lay hidden. She didn't move, but her breath remained steady, and he knew she waited patiently. It was up to him to *check it out*, and clear threats, even if they came from a friend.

Lia peered over the edge of the wagon, bracing her service weapon against the wooden rim. Something moved out there, something that made the hair stand up on the back of her neck. She learned long ago to listen to intuition, not ignore it.

Kai had disappeared. She desperately missed Magic. He'd come running if she but called—silently or otherwise. Kai was an unknown and might pose a threat with her unpredictable behavior. If Lia could neutralize the attacker, she might get some answers, a good night's work.

She fired the first shot as a warning. Lockhart's warning had come to fruition, but Lia couldn't bring herself to simply shoot another human without specific cause. A stalker followed her out here on Halloween night. Not ghosts or goblins, but a very human ne'er-do-well.

A bit of motion caught her eye, and Lia squinted into the brush. She shifted behind the wooden barrier, keeping the gun aimed at where she'd last seen the threat. More than one? Her jaw tightened, and she had to consciously relax her shoulders.

"Don't move! I'll shoot, and this time won't miss." Lia steadied the gun, squared her shoulders, and prepared to shoot.

A familiar voice called, "*Show-me gun!*"

The big black dog leaped high, nose punching her hand. The weapon spun away. His chest collided with her shoulder, tumbling them both to the ground.

Shadow stood over the prone woman, tail waving with excitement, and pinning her to the dirt as he washed her face thoroughly.

September holstered her weapon, grinning ruefully. She and Lia had nearly taken each other out. *Should've identified myself to begin with.* Thank goodness Shadow never failed to have her back.

Before she could say another word, though, a dog bolted into her, knocking her sideways onto her back. The dog straddled her prone figure, back end wagging furiously. But her hackles remained erect.

She didn't dare move. She knew the training Lia gave and didn't want to risk the teeth of this strange dog.

"Lia, it's September. Call off your dog, will you?"

Lia barked a sharp laugh in response. "You call off Shadow first."

Chapter Forty: CORNELIA

Cornelia Corazon checked her makeup one last time. She turned away from the mirror, craning her neck to see the back of her costume, and nodded with approval. Dressed like a Spanish queen, the sky-blue outfit matched her eyes and made the perfect statement, with a nod to her heritage and position in the community: satin, brocade, lace, pearls, and a matching tiara. The massive skirt and tiny waist, a bodice that bared her still-elegant shoulders, made her feel as regal as she looked.

"Dub, hurry up. We must greet our guests." She had photographers waiting at the bottom of the staircase to catch them in their splendor as they made their appearance. She smiled. This year she'd outdone herself. And it'd all be worthwhile when Lia arrived.

She hadn't heard from the girl, but raised her right, and had no doubt she'd show up. Apikalia Corazon knew her duty. Sure, when Pippo disappeared, Lia became upset. Rightly so. But if the stupid dog hadn't panicked and run inside and made a mess, Pippo would never have escaped.

Cornelia refused to admit it to anyone, but she missed Pippo. With Lia gone weekdays, and Dub working long hours, she actually enjoyed the company. Sometimes Pippo sneaked into their bedroom at night, and Cornelia awoke to a purring presence sharing her pillow.

But never mind all that. However much Lia protested, she wouldn't disappoint her Grammy and Grandfather. Lia had a position as a Corazon, and Cornelia planned to honor her granddaughter in a public way, erase any perceived taint, to make up for… well, for a lot. She'd planned the evening down to the minute and refused to consider anything would fly in the face of what she wanted.

"I can't get the buttons fastened." Dub entered the suite from the large bathroom, jaw tight with aggravation. "What's wrong with my regular duds? Nobody believes me as a Conquistador."

"Don't wiggle, let me fix that." She deftly finished the problematic buttons on the blue and white striped shirt's accordion collar and stood back to see. He'd refused to wear tights, but compromised on the less stylish baggy pantaloons and boots. The faux armor dressed up the costume, along with the very real sword in the scabbard on Dub's belt.

He clutched the silver plastic helmet that matched the armor, a single blue plume that matched her dress drooping from the brim.

"Couldn't we just once dress as ourselves?" He took her place in front of the floor-length mirror. "Feel like a damn prize pony shined up for auction."

"It's for a good cause, Dub, you know that. We have a certain position in the community. Certain expectations." She'd hosted the Halloween party annually since Lia's high school years, back when the girl enjoyed the event. The fundraiser supported a different nonprofit each year, and she wanted Lia here when she announced this year's recipient.

Dub patted her hand when she took his arm. "I'm proud of you, Cornelia. We've both learned a lot over the past year. Never thought you'd make such an effort to make amends."

She sniffed. "Well, I hope Lia appreciates it. I still think that man's a liar and a criminal, even if maybe—*maybe*, I say— he got railroaded in some situations. The evidence should settle things for better or worse." Her lips tightened. "But jailbirds say anything to point blame elsewhere."

A couple of months back, Robin Gillette had rampaged through the Celtic Festival. Now she wanted to reduce her sentence any way possible. You couldn't trust such people to tell the truth.

Gillette's arrest filled the local news, better than a soap opera, with the woman spouting outlandish claims. Usually Cornelia paid such things no attention. She had no patience for outrageous behavior, but Gillette dropped a familiar name, one Cornelia had tried to forget, the man she'd never wanted Lia to know.

That's why Cornelia had contacted the investigative reporter with a juicy news tip—and the promise of a financial tip if she saw the story before he published it. Molingo should have delivered his report by now. Instead, he'd ghosted her, as the kids these days called it.

"Very open minded to look at the possibilities." Dub patted her hand again, and together they walked out of the suite.

Dub had encouraged her to reconcile with Lia. Their only granddaughter would inherit Corazon Stables and carry on the family name. Cornelia couldn't let the terrible words said continue festering. And if she could remove the horrible stain hovering over the girl's heritage, she owed it to Lia.

Over the months, Lia grudgingly met her partway. First, she'd agreed to adopt the stupid pup someone abandoned at Lia's kennel. At least she'd got rid of that menace, always running away so Lia would easily believe that. Then, she agreed to keep the cat while Lia attended class in Dallas. Cornelia prayed Lia would get thoughts of the academy out of her system soon. She needed to settle down to the real work of running the ranch, to meet someone steady, make an appropriate match. Dub agreed, even if not as vocal as she.

Cornelia didn't expect or want exoneration of Wyatt Teves. But going through the motions served two purposes, both far more valuable. Offering help aided her reconciliation with Lia, and learning the reality behind Wyatt Teves's conviction would crush any future hope the girl had for a relationship with that murderer.

She and Dub reached the top of the stairs. A gathering of guests, most in full Halloween regalia, stood and clapped with appreciation at the bottom. Cameras flashed as, beaming with benevolence, Dub and Cornelia Corazon descended the curved staircase to meet their guests.

At the midway point, they paused for Cornelia to address

the crowd. "Thank you for coming, everyone. My, the costume competition looks hotly contested tonight." She smiled, looking over the crowd. Nowhere did she see Lia. She sighed, it would still work even if the ungrateful child came late, or not at all.

She pasted the smile back in place. "As you know, each year we choose a wonderful charity to benefit from the ticket sales to our party. I'm delighted to share that, this year, all funds from the Halloween festivities will benefit the Innocence Project."

Chapter Forty-One: **MELINDA**

Melinda elbowed Delaney. "Look! September's still here." She whispered, not wanting the other couples to hear. That is, if they ever came up for air. Ew!

The hay wagon rumbled across the gravel, passing by the Corazon Kennels sign. "We'll have to kick it to get away without the driver catching us. We got lucky September's still visiting Lia but let me do the talking. Otherwise, it's sus."

"Yeah, we can collect Uncle Ricky's phone, turn it over to Lia and get paid. One stop shopping, I love it." His lips twitched at the labored joke. The humor fell flat. "That phone evidence buys Peter and me our future. No cap, she owes us, cuz it's her fault for getting him murdered."

Melinda's mouth opened then closed. She knew for a fact Lia had no money, that's why September let Lia stay at the Grand Chisholm. Better he hear it from Lia, though. She was dialed in with the police. No way she had any part in murder. Police were the good guys.

Dad would have a cow if he knew Delaney came on the hayride with her, but September might overlook the omission if they came bearing gifts of evidence. "They're not expecting us. Sometimes she's a PITA but at least you can trust September to do the right thing."

He nodded. "I read about September Day in the news. She's dope."

Melinda glanced at the wagon driver, making sure his attention stayed glued to the horse and road ahead. She scooted to the back edge of the wagon, ready to drop off. They'd need to duck and hide quickly, or else he could stop and make a fuss and spoil everything. They didn't need drama alerting September before they even made their pitch.

Delaney hopped off first, reading her mind and scurrying into the ditch. He steadied her when her sandals slipped as she followed. His hand on her bare arm made her pulse quicken. *Stop it, he doesn't like you that way.* But maybe if she helped him out, he'd want to hang out again. More than that, though, helping him and his little brother felt like the right thing to do. Like what the Paladin Group did for people. She was part of that. Well, almost part of it.

They crouched together, waiting for the hay wagon to trundle out of sight. The horse nickered, and looked back over one shoulder. Melinda held her breath the driver wouldn't pick up on the gesture. They'd catch a ride home with September, after their discussion. Nerves made her stomach roil, no longer the pleasant butterfly tickle. She liked the nervous kick during cheer squad practice. But this felt way different.

"Come on." Delaney stood and grabbed Melinda's hand to pull her up. Her stomach repeated the Herkie. She trotted beside him, pointing ahead to the rustic building. No lights inside, either downstairs or overhead apartment lights, but outside security lights spilled out into the night.

They walked past the parked cars in the drive. She recognized September's tank of a vehicle. The older truck with the kennel logo belonged to Lia. Delaney waited as she knocked on the door. The latch gave way, swinging open on squeaky hinges. Melinda took a half-step over the threshold. "Hey! Lia? September? Surprise…" Her fake cheerful tone wavered.

The room felt empty, and sort of creepy. And dark. She switched on the lights, illuminating the waiting area. The doorway to the stairs in the far wall betrayed no lights, either. She'd never been here when the place didn't echo with barking boarders, and Lia's cheerful banter. "Anybody here?" She hurried to the stairs, switched on the light, and called louder in case Lia slept upstairs. "Hey, it's Melinda. I got news you want to hear."

Nothing.

"Nobody?" Delaney walked into the room, hands clenched at his sides. "Where'd they go?" His jaw trembled. His shoe kicked something across the room.

Melinda grabbed one of his fists in both of her hands, pressing gently until he relaxed his grip. "They're gone. Don't know where. I told you, September's hard to predict." She couldn't text her now, and spill the tea about Delaney and what he needed. "Lia's got no money. Makes no sense she'd promise a big payday to your uncle when she's got next to nothing and has to borrow stuff to make ends meet."

"Uncle Ricky said the Corazon lady hired him. Who else could it be? And Peter put the phone in a car with a dog in it." He noticed the key fob he'd kicked. "Hey, maybe we got lucky after all. Is one of the cars September's?" Delaney collected the object and hurried back out the door. He thumbed the button.

"That black one, the SUV. That's September's." The older truck blinked lights. The black SUV stayed silent.

With frustration, he dropped the keys and sprinted to September's vehicle to try the doors.

"Dad got her car special made for security." Melinda scooped up Lia's keys and ran after him. "You can't get in without a key. Bullet proof glass and everything," she added as he hammered on the windshield with one fist.

"But all the windows are partway down. Look."

How odd. "She never does that." Her brow furrowed, and she cupped hands to peer through the dark glass into the car.

"I got an idea. I need a stick." He held his hands apart. "About yay-long, sturdy." His voice transformed from angry dejection to hopeful excitement.

She shrugged and gestured toward the field across the gravel road. Melinda watched as he dashed into the darkness and shuffled beneath a cedar elm. In less than a minute, Delaney returned carrying several stick candidates. She watched, curious. "Lia's grandparents live in that big mansion with all the horses."

Delaney stripped twigs and leaves off the first branch and approached the driver's door. While grasping the end of the stick, he pushed his arm through the window opening. "Yeah, so?"

"Lia's got no money, but they're rich." The richest people she knew, anyway, except for September. But September didn't act rich, not like Mrs. Corazon. "And they all have the same last name. So…" Seemed clear enough to her. "They're the ones hosting the Halloween party tonight. And the hayride. And…"

Almost immediately, he lost his grip on the stick. It fell onto the driver's seat. "Dang! My arm won't fit." He turned to look at her. "It's not Lia Corazon. Her grandmother?"

"Bet!" She grinned.

The window was barely opened three inches. She saw what he intended, but his forearm, let alone the bicep, couldn't pass through nor reach far enough. "Let me try." Her much slenderer arm could reach through the narrow gap and use the stick to press on the auto-lock to open the doors.

Melinda stood on tiptoe but still could barely reach the high-set window. Without warning, Delaney reached one arm around her waist. She squeaked then consciously calmed her voice. "Boost me up a little more." With his help, her arm easily slipped through the narrow opening. She tried to ignore the scary-awesome feeling of his hard arm around her waist as she fished with the blunt end of the stick. It took lip-biting concentration, and forty-five seconds of manipulation that felt like years (*Delaney's holding me up, oh my gosh!*). Finally, the *whisk-click* sound announced success.

"Yes!" He waited for her to safely withdraw her arm before gently setting Melinda down.

Impulsively, she threw arms around him in a brief hug before dropping the stick. "Now what?"

"We search the car." He tossed his long hair out of his gorgeous eyes, a smile finally reaching them. Delaney gestured at the back door. "It's not my car, so maybe better if you do the honors. You know, open it up. 'Kay?"

She nodded. "Peter said he dropped it through which window?"

"One of the back ones. He said the dog sat on the back seat with windows cracked open sorta like this. Hey…you don't think that's why September left 'em down like that?"

Melinda shook her head. "Shadow never leaves her side. If she's not here, they're together." She reached for the rear door. "She would've seen the phone on the seat, unless it slipped down the back upholstery. Or maybe fell on the floor and scooted underneath somehow." She pulled the door wide open. "Go 'round to the other side to look."

It made her nervous to search September's car. The sooner they got done, the better. She switched on her phone's flashlight function to illuminate the interior.

Yellow eyes glowed from back seat. Melinda squealed and dropped her phone.

Chapter Forty-Two: SEPTEMBER

Thought you wanted to meet up, but you'd already bailed by the time I got to the kennels. Why'd you bolt?" September asked as she joined Lia beside the overturned wagon. September massaged her throat, the ache had settled into a muted pulse, increasing when she spoke.

She shucked the go bag off her shoulder, and leaned the bo staff against the wheel. What in daylight looked decorative and fun, at night took on macabre shapes with the jack-o'-lanterns' empty eyes and gaping fanged mouths. She hadn't noticed the solar-operated lanterns lining the whole area before, but now they offered a spooky glow to the whole area. Hairs rose on the back of September's neck, and she felt for the gun beneath her loose shirt to reassure herself.

"Wish I knew." Lia pushed hair out of her eyes. She took off the white cadet cap, rebound her braided hair with an orange hair tie, and situated the hat. Her grim expression gave little away. "I reached out to Wyatt's attorney. Only criminal law person I know. Like you said, I needed some advice."

"Lockhart, right? Saw that on your computer before we left." Shadow nudged her hand, understanding she included him in the comment. "I asked Shadow to track Magic, but I guess he focused on you instead. And this one." She scratched Kai's white chest when she flipped onto her back. "Where's Magic?" September smiled, always intrigued and impressed by how much Shadow figured out on his own. "And holy cats, you collected a horse along the way?"

"My pony from days long ago. Sebastian's notorious for getting through fences, and betcha Grandfather has some of the guys out looking for him come morning. Kai alerted me to him." She grinned. "We used to ride every day when I still lived at home, and he knew me right away."

September respected horses, admired them, but knew next to nothing about them. Lia had grown up riding. September knew folks developed just as strong bonds and connections with equine companions as canine or feline.

"Kai just showed up. She's Grammy's dog but likes to dig out of the back yard. She'd lick you to death, has no special training." She shrugged. "Had to leave Magic at the vet to clean out a bullet wound."

September gasped. "Who shot him?" She touched Lia's arm, commiserating. "Doc Eugene will take good care of him." She grimaced and again touched her throat. "We had a run-in with your stalker back at your place."

"Crap! Are you okay?" Lia's eyes widened. "Couldn't be the same person as shot Magic, because Drummond's dead." She added drily, "I assume you know, since they found him in your hotel."

"Wait… Kinkaid Drummond shot your dog?"

"Yep. My academy instructor from class."

September found an oversize pumpkin, not yet carved, and took a seat. "Jack called from the hotel." She still had trouble saying Uncle Jack. "He texted at dark-thirty in the morning. Said a Detective Greer will investigate Drummond's murder. They think Magic bit him. He wants to talk to you, Lia."

Lia groaned and hunched her shoulders. "I know, but not my dog's fault. Drummond shoved his way into my hotel room, drunk as a hero, accusing me of I-haven't-a-clue-what. Magic took issue, bit him, and the gun went off." She rubbed her face. "At least Magic's okay. Bullet grazed his neck and shoulder, carved out a long divot of skin. I didn't notice right away, with that long fur on his neck." She impatiently dashed away tears. "Drummond wasn't a good guy. He wanted me gone, tried to make me quit the academy. That's all I've ever wanted!" She took a seat on the edge of the wagon, and took off her hat to fan herself. Kai hopped up beside her, and laid her head in Lia's lap.

"Wish I had answers." September felt helpless. According to Jack, the police had more than enough evidence to hold the young woman for questioning. "We've got to trust the process, Lia, and let the detectives do their work. Come into the police station, talk to the local detective; Paige Brummitt already knows you. You don't want folks thinking you're running."

"Drummond'll get what he wanted." She sounded bitter.

"This could wreck my career before it even starts." She sighed, stroking Kai, who wriggled and gargled with joy. "How did everything go sideways so fast?"

September knew the feeling. She felt responsible anytime someone got hurt. "Combs will have alerted Brummitt about the attack at the kennels, so the Heartland PD knows a killer's after you." Whatever his reasons, she didn't think he'd stop.

Lia's concern stayed focused on her dog. "Doc Eugene had to sedate Magic to clean everything out, so I had to leave him. Drummond threatened to send animal control, so at least Doc Eugene will protect Magic." She shuddered. "I feel naked without him. Know what I mean?"

"Absolutely." September paused, gathering thoughts. "Like I said, the attacker thought I was you. He thinks Molingo gave you something and he wants it. Nearly choked me with your old lariat." She gestured to the loop of rope she'd shrugged over one shoulder just in case. You never knew when a rope came in handy.

Lia held out her hand for the braided leather and handled it with reverence. "This belonged to Wyatt back in the day." She shrugged the lariat over her own shoulder. "Lockhart warned me to run. She had new information in Wyatt's case but had no time to share." She looked at September and wrinkled her nose. "Sorry, I know the subject's sensitive."

September laughed, gallows humor. "Your dad killed my dad… maybe. Neither of us knew our fathers, and I suspect Wyatt did the world a favor if he's guilty."

"He didn't kill Henry Wong. He got framed."

"Whatever you say." This wasn't the time for discussion. "You think Lockhart's new information has something to do with Drummond's murder?"

"I don't know!" Lia stood and Kai rolled to her feet,

watching and hoping for more attention. "I've never been stalked. I'm just one of dozens who signed up for the police training academy. Why'd Drummond pick on me?" She sniffed. "Everyone in class knew he had it in for me." She paused to scratch Kai behind the ears. "If Magic was here, we could search the place more thoroughly. I gave the place a good looking over before the sun went down. But the police already combed through everything. Peter said his uncle gave him a phone to hide. Somebody showed up earlier, and left that car." She nodded at the distant parking lot. "I hid, wanted to see what they'd do. But they didn't stick around. Besides, lots of places to hide something that small."

September nodded. "It'd be like hunting for a needle in a—"

"Pumpkin patch." They finished the phrase together and smiled.

Sebastian nickered and walked closer to the pair. The big creature reached out to nuzzle Lia's shoulder, and the young woman stroked the pony's neck. Lia grinned, then wilted again. "He was a reporter, right? Hell, if I knew anything about the three deaths, I'd share it with the authorities."

September wrinkled her nose. "Three? Who's the third?" She pointed over one shoulder, "Found Molingo over there by the pond. Number two is your academy instructor, Drummond."

"Lockhart mentioned a Clarence Walford. First I've heard about him, but if she knows him, he's connected to Wyatt's case. She said Dallas PD has a Detective Savatch investigating both of those deaths. With three, chances are they'll loop in the FBI, if they suspect a serial. We need to find the link and get answers."

September debated switching her phone back on. Combs

and Teddy would want the Walford name to cross reference. "If you didn't contact Molingo, do you think Tee might've…"

Lia pulled loose the bright orange hair tie and shook loose her mane. The light of the crescent moon transformed the blond hair into a halo and her pale face into an otherworldly glow. "Tee isn't easy to mistake for me." Tee had distinctive Hawaiian features, complexion, and accent. "She'd've told me. Besides, she's not exactly on board the Wyatt-is-innocent train." She quickly smoothed her hair and re-tied the ponytail. "The guy who attacked you thought it was me?"

"The name of your business sort of shines a spotlight on the name, so yep, he expected to find you there. He kept saying stuff about going after *the Corazon woman*. I tried to convince him you had nothing to do—" Her eyes widened. "Oh my God, Lia, you don't suppose?"

Her already pale face drained of remaining color. "Grammy's been on my case for a month about a special birthday surprise. A big-whammy announcement at the Halloween party." Lia stopped, both hands going to the top of her cap, as if to keep her head from exploding.

Kai hopped off the wagon and jumped up at Lia, mouthing her clothes, trying to get Lia to play.

"I wouldn't listen. I have no patience for Grammy's secrets. She makes a production out of everything." She pulled her hands away from the leaping dog, spinning to stare into September's eyes. "There's only one other Corazon woman. He's going after Grammy."

She vaulted onto Sebastian's back, and took off at a canter, disappearing into the corn maze.

Chapter Forty-Three: MELINDA

Melinda cradled the cat in her arms and backed away from the open car door. "The cat explains why September left the windows down." The animal shoved its face hard against Melinda's lips, leaving fur stuck to her lip gloss. "You'll have a pink forehead." She smiled, though. She'd always preferred cats to dogs and got a kick out of Macy's tricks besting the dogs at their house. The metal name tag suspended from the collar said PIPPO.

Delaney searched the back seat and floor. "Found it!" he crowed, brandishing Uncle Ricky's phone. "It's locked, but I recognize the case. And that Corazon lady better pay up for it. Trick-or-treat, baby!" His eyes glimmered.

Melinda nodded. The man paid with his life. "We should take it to the police, and they can get her to pay." You didn't mess around with evidence. Dad taught her that.

He glared. "You're not gonna wimp out on me, are you? They won't do any—"

"They'd use it to catch whoever killed your uncle. Don't you want that?"

"Sure. But why not both? Uncle Ricky said this would set us up good. He isn't… I mean, he wasn't rich. And remember, he said cops were in on stuff. What if they just want to bury his notes? I gotta think about taking care of Peter. Otherwise, I got to quit school, get a job."

Her heart lurched.

"But if Mrs. Corazon pays like she promised then we got a buffer. Can't you see?" He held the phone in both hands, knuckles white. "Just want what he deserved, what she promised. She owes us, it's only right. After Mrs. Corazon pays me, *she* can give it to the cops and be the hero. That'd be better anyway. Don't need 'em to know about this." His eyes narrowed. "You got to swear you won't tell your dad. Or other cops."

Melinda's lips tightened. "I can't lie to my dad." Not like that, anyway. Okay, sometimes by omission, but never anything big. She sighed. "But I won't bring it up, Delaney."

He shrugged. "If that's the best you can do." He stared at the cat in her arms. "Should we leave it in the car? We could try to lock the doors again." He looked around. "We've got to walk back to the pumpkin patch where we left my car."

Melinda nuzzled the cat with her chin, hiding her grin as she clicked the key fob. Delaney startled when the truck flashed its lights. "Why not drive?"

He smiled and took the offered keys. "Brilliant. If she and September are on foot, we can beat 'em to the Halloween party to have a private talk with Mrs. Corazon." He pulled open the driver's door and climbed in. "This truck is so lit! Old school manual transmission. Love it."

Melinda hurried to join him on the passenger side, settling Pippo on her lap. A ride over to the house beat hoofing it. And winner-winner-chicken-dinner, she'd go to the Halloween bash with Delaney after all. Melinda's heart fluttered with anticipation. Anything could happen!

Chapter Forty-Four: MAGIC

Magic panted as he loped along the shoulder of the road. He and Lia rarely ran long distances together, but his training prepared him for sprints when needed. The distance from the clinic back home to the kennel meant traveling at a slow steady pace that ate up miles. He'd traveled for hours, rested during the coldest hours last night, determined to rejoin Lia.

And Magic knew—he didn't know how—that Lia's emotional distress had calmed. He still padded on, but the siren alarm jangling his brain subsided, allowing him to think and plan.

Return home. Find Lia. Together, he felt powerful and fierce. Alone—not so much.

He whined deep in his throat, speeding up a bit as the goal drew nearer. Magic ran along the side of the roadway. Even after dark, the smooth car path held an uncomfortable level of heat for paws. Soon he'd reach home, and Lia.

His paws raced faster, ignoring the hurty stones under his galloping stride. There! The lights from windows spilled into bright islands on the front lawn. No tiny pee-and-fear-soaked potty area here, but grassy fields farther than good dogs could see. And two vehicles, the truck oh-so-familiar.

The roar of the engine turning over played a familiar song to Magic's ears. Lia's truck rolled backward from its sleep-spot, to slide and skid on the gravel parking lot. Lia was leaving in the truck. Without him!

Magic always rode in the seat beside Lia, propping his broad muzzle on the half-open window. As a team, they could do anything together. Nothing stopped him with Lia by his side.

But she'd left Magic behind at the medicine-smelly place. And now she'd drive away. He'd be alone all over again. Dog paws couldn't keep up with her truck.

Magic barked. He barked again, paws churning to catch the departing truck. Saliva splattered as his cries increased, yelling and begging for Lia to stop-stop-STOP and wait for him.

The truck turned around, gravel spitting from the rear tires as it sped out of the driveway. He dodged to one side as it approached him. The truck's eye-lights switched on, blinding Magic in the beams. One skewed to the side, the other nailed him in place, and he skidded to a stop, waiting frozen, gulping gasps, chest heaving—

"Stop! Stop the truck!" A girl's voice. Not Lia, though Where was Lia?

"A dog, just a stray dog." The engine rumbled. The truck swung wide, as Magic stood frozen in place for a dozen heartbeats.

Lia's truck pulled away, speeding faster as it traveled down the gravel road. Magic knew cars raced much faster than he could run.

"He's running after us." The girl's voice again.

His panting jaws snapped closed. He gathered his haunches, muscles bunched. Magic sped after the departing truck, using all his energy and determination and heart to outrace the vehicle.

"On this gravel, I can't go faster than twenty miles an hour, but he won't catch us."

Magic didn't know or care what the strange voices said. That truck belonged to Lia. She must be inside, too. Nobody drove the truck but Lia.

With an extra burst of desperation, he drew close enough. When it slowed briefly at the turn-off onto the highway, Magic leaped high, reaching with his paws.

He landed—ker-THUMP!—in the bed of the truck, just as it accelerated away.

Chapter Forty-Five: SHELLY

Shelly parked his motorcycle at the edge of the massive fifteen-acre cornfield maze directly overlooking the house proper. The Corazon homestead featured a long, twisting drive currently packed with cars making slow progress into adjacent parking areas on each side of the drive. He silently congratulated himself on holding back, rather than rushing into the place. Easy to get blocked in, although his bike surely would prove more nimble than the majority of the high-dollar vehicles vying for access. Some kind of swanky event, he remembered, with people dressed up in the most outrageous costumes. A Halloween party. That's right, tonight ghosties and ghoulies and all things devilish roamed.

Too bad he had to use his clown get up to point the finger elsewhere. Oh well. He could always go as the plague. He laughed at the thought, and a cough doubled him over for a full minute. Finally he straightened to wipe snot onto his sleeve. Soon enough, he'd check himself into an urgent care. But he'd toughed out worse situations.

Tonight would tie a tidy bow on his legacy and his future, nailed in place with bullets if need be. He'd wait until the traffic thinned before infiltrating. He'd flash his badge for a private one-on-one with the hostess.

"Gotta see the hostess… with the mostest," he muttered. His head felt swimmy. Was that a word? Shelly blinked, his eyes strained to focus through a fog of mucus. Shelly coughed again and spat. He tasted blood. His head throbbed, and his throat felt like raw meat.

Didn't matter. Focus, focus.

Once inside the place, mixing with flamboyantly dressed revelers, his presence wouldn't raise an eyebrow. Hell, he could play the part of ax murderer and be welcomed.

Shelly settled back to watch. He had time, and needed to wait to clear out the late-comers. He reviewed other entry options. It looked like the back of the house hosted guests on an expansive grassy lawn. A smaller area, segregated by a fence, looked interesting. He could clear that fence in ten seconds, mix with the party-hearty crew, and make his way into the house proper.

Nobody had located Molingo's notes yet. May be gone for good; he was due some luck, but he couldn't leave his fate to luck. Slitting the Corazon bitch's throat would eliminate that loose end. The Molingo kid hid in police protection, but he had ways to get past that, too. Nobody believed kids anyway.

If the boy got too loud, he'd finish him after he shook this stupid cold. Then he'd pull the trigger on that sweet retirement beach property and take his time to relax and heal. He coughed and honked again, sticking a hand out to catch his balance against the bike.

All around him, the wind shivered dry corn stalks. They rattled like a snake's tail. His arms itched. Did corn act like poison ivy? Shelly scratched, now imagining spiders tickling the back of his neck. Maybe crawling in his scalp.

He raked fingers through his hair, untying the blond ponytail to shake out his long locks. Same color as Lia's, go figure…made the clown costume that much more convincing. Once satisfied no buggy intruders lurked, he smoothed and gathered the hair to reestablish the bad boy trademark look. But his fingers fumbled the hair tie, and it disappeared into the corn stalks.

Never mind. More important issues mattered like…like something about a woman. Yes, a sneaky snitch of a creature sniffing into his business. Corazon, that's right, that's right, the name itched his brain worse than imaginary spiders. He fingered the hair over the top of each ear, smoothing it down into some semblance of tidiness. Gonna crash the Corazon's costume party. He'd go as a plague detective and infect everybody. He snickered.

A thumping rhythmic sound grew louder as it drew near. What was that? A horse.

"Cowboys, yee-haw…" He giggled. God, he felt boiling hot one minute, then freezing the next. *Thumpity-thumpity-thumpity…* like a herd of buffalo.

The Corazons kept cattle and horses, but would they stampede at this time of night? "Move 'em out, rawhide… where's my whip?" Now he wished he'd kept that lariat he found, would've been a great souvenir. Even if he hadn't managed to lights-out that Magpie creature.

The hoofbeat drumming grew loud. Any minute now—

Shelly took cover behind his motorcycle, drew his gun, and watched. He blinked, clearing his watery eyes, and relying on muscle memory for an easy shot.

The horse and rider burst from the corn. Stalks split before the beast with the sound of breaking bones. The horse shied sideways and rose on his haunches at the sight of him and the bike.

He ducked, dodging flailing hooves. His shot went wide. How'd he miss such a huge target? Shelly aimed again, but his arm shook. Damn fever.

"Whoa… steady, steady!" The rider—a girl?—clung tight to the creature's back, arms flung about its neck. A dog danced beside the pair, barking loudly, the alarm a danger to Shelly's stealthy play. He couldn't have anyone alerted to his unexpected presence. And besides, he felt so awful somebody else should pay for this feeling.

He stood from behind the cycle, blinking hard to clear his vision. At this range, the kill shot couldn't miss.

Her eyes met his. He recognized the Corazon woman, the young one, the girl from the hospital. "Lucky me," he muttered, and fired.

She fell from her mount with a small cry, body swallowed up with a rustle and crunch of crushed stalks. With a shrill neigh the horse loped away.

Magic howled! A sudden fire-hot pain seared his thigh. He whipped around, nearly losing his balance in the back of Lia's truck. He checked, sniffing and licking the spot to soothe the hurt.

There should be blood, but he tasted, smelled nothing. The pain pulsed, a deep throbbing ghost-ache that made him whimper. And worry…

Worse than the ghost-pain, Lia's sudden fear flooded his whole being. The emotion stabbed bloody daggers into his heart. Lia hurt. Lia in trouble.

Lia needed Magic!

Shelly grinned. "Make sure, make sure." He holstered his gun, and found the knife, stroked the blade with reverence. Cleaner, more elegant, knives had personality and finesse, not the blunt mayhem of bullets. Shelly waded into the sea of corn, pushing stalks aside to find his fallen victim.

The dog continued haranguing him, and he slashed out, catching an ear as it raced by. With a yelp, the pooch fell back, whimpering and crying. "Give you something to cry about." A bullet. After taking care of the woman.

She lay on her back, rocking back and forth, both hands clenching tight to her thigh. The wound spilled black wet, staining her light colored pants. Her attention flicked sideways.

Shelly looked, and smiled at the sight of her service revolver, fallen well out of reach. Newbie mistake. Gotta secure your weapon, cadet.

"Why?" She stared at him from beneath the white cap, chin raised in defiance, refusing to flinch.

He stepped closer, bent to finish the job. Her pale neck, so pretty and delicate… too bad he couldn't take more time—

A pounding gallop announced the horse's surprise return, the animal blowing and squealing with anger. It looked like a blood-red phantom born of the waxing moon as Shelly whirled to face the creature.

The horse reared, front hooves churning the air, aiming to clobber him.

The dog joined the defensive dance, dashing in to nip at his heels and his arms, leaping to target his knife hand. The horse wheeled, inadvertently knocking the dog off her feet.

Backing away, and breathing heavily, Shelly stared at the odd trio, girl on the ground with the horse standing above and dog guarding her flank.

He sheathed the knife, debating for several heartbeats. He could shoot all three. But the devil horse could still cause damage unless the bullet hit just right. And more gunshots drew additional attention he couldn't afford. Better to move on.

"You'll bleed out soon enough." He crossed to collect her gun and then mounted his two-wheeled steed and kicked the motorcycle to life. "I got a date with your grandmother, sweet cheeks."

The damn Corazon woman started this whole mess. He'd make sure she paid dearly. Shelly rode down the hill toward the party-hearty house. "Trick-or-treat."

Chapter Forty-Six: MAGIC

Magic balanced himself in the back of Lia's truck. His leg still throbbed, and his heart raced from feeling Lia's hurts and fears.

He growled, confused and frustrated. Lia should drive her truck, but a stranger sat behind the wheel. But Magic recognized the girl in the passenger seat. She turned around to stare through the back window at him, eyes wide and showing the whites, like a dog fearful of attack. He lifted his lips in response, showing teeth so she'd know he meant business.

The truck bumped up onto the smooth pavement. It

hurried faster, wind lifting his floppy ears until Magic slicked them back to avoid the sensation. He lifted his muzzle to the air current, inhaling and seeking a beloved familiar scent.

Now he'd gained a ride, Magic didn't know what to do next. Finding Lia meant everything.

Magic felt her pull like a beacon shining through the darkness. He debated leaping off the truck and striking out across the field, but four fast paws couldn't beat the truck's speed. And so far, the vehicle moved him closer and closer to Lia.

His fur bristled with excitement, and he yearned to push his face into his girl's arms, feel her hands smooth his brow and reassure him, call him "good-boy-Magic" and "honey-boy" so he knew he pleased her.

He lived to please Lia. To keep her safe. Make her smile and laugh when he won the sniffy-games or bite challenges. Right now, Magic wanted to bite something or someone, bite hard, and shake. If he couldn't find Lia soon, he'd explode!

The girl in the truck stopped looking at him, turning back to talk to the boy who drove the truck. Magic heard the murmur of words but ignored them until he heard Lia's name. He whined and pushed closer to the glass barrier.

Yes! Speaking her name meant they would take him to her. He paw-thumped the glass, wanting the truck to go faster and faster.

"What's he doing back there? Why'd he scream?" Delaney's knuckles whitened on the steering wheel. "Never heard a dog sound like that. Don't want him falling out the truck. Sheesh!"

Melinda shivered. She'd never heard that sound either, not from Kinsler or Shadow. The wind through the half-open window blew hair into her eyes and mouth. She wished she'd tied it back but considered her hair her best feature and had wanted to impress Delaney. Stoopid… like that even mattered anymore. All the hair product in the world wouldn't survive the windy blast.

Magic belonged to Lia. She had no idea why the woman left without her truck or her dog. Or Pippo. Dad said sometimes people just wanted to disappear, but Melinda couldn't imagine Lia abandoning her animals.

The feline snuggled in her lap, purring. Stroking the fur made Melinda feel better. A long feather tied to an elastic band fluttered from the mirror, and the cat stared at it, enthralled. Impulsively, Melinda grabbed it, and offered it like a toy, and Pippo grabbed it with greedy paws. September said just sitting in the same room with a dog or cat reduced stress. Unless the dog was bratty Kinsler.

The truck slowed and turned off the highway. Melinda swiveled in her seat, looking around, red hair flying. "Delaney, this isn't Corazon's place. The police still have the pumpkin patch closed."

He grinned. "The parking lot's still open. That's where I parked, then hiked over to catch the hayride. Didn't want to get trapped with all the mom-mobiles in case we needed wheels." Truck tires spun in the gravel, bumping her up and down. He winced. "I don't want to mess up Lia's truck. We'll swap rides and take my car to the Corazons."

"What do we do with Magic? He won't fit in your little car." She looked over her shoulder at the Rottweiler. "I don't think he'll want to do what we say, either."

Delaney parked beside his car. "He hitched a ride here. He can do whatever he wants."

As if the dog understood their words, Magic vaulted out of the pickup. Without looking back, he galloped off, disappearing into the pumpkin patch after dodging the police barriers.

The big dog accelerated across the field and vanished into the corn maze. He acted like he heard someone calling him. *What in the world…* She tightened her hold on the cat, fearful Pippo would struggle out of her arms and get lost in the field. Again.

As Delaney climbed out, Melinda saw movement in a different spot near the middle of the pumpkin field. A silhouette of the big dog stood ghostly sentinel.

Sudden nerves sped her movement. He trained as an attack dog, after all. Such big white teeth… She didn't want to be on the ground with Magic, without Lia to keep him under control.

Quickly, she climbed down from the truck, letting Delaney shut the door as she hurried to the smaller car, fingers wound in the cat's harness. She'd breathe again once the car door slammed shut, with her and the cat safely inside.

Melinda waited impatiently for Delaney to join her. Now that they had his uncle's phone, and a plan, Melinda wanted it done. She wrestled the feather hair toy from the cat's paws and used it to gather up her hair. "Hurry up."

But he paused. "Somebody's over there. Coming this way." He stood beside the car, squinting into the darkness at the movement in the patch.

"Let's go already. It's giving Casper vibes." Uncle Ricky probably haunted the place. Starlight turned the bois d'arc tree into witchy talons clawing the sky. "Come on! It might be the killer who hurt your uncle, let's go!"

The shadowy figure waved arms, and loped across the field, clearly intent on stopping them. Melinda's breath quickened.

"Spooky, no cap!" He got into his car. "Tell Lia we only borrowed her truck. I left the keys in the ignition." He started his car and peeled out of the parking lot.

"You left the keys? Are you mental?" She turned in her seat. The spooky figure couldn't catch them on foot—but could easily run them down in Lia's truck.

Delaney's car slipped and slid as he accelerated down the narrow drive, and back onto the country road. Melinda twisted in her seat, staring out the back, watching, watching for twin beams set slightly crooked to follow in their wake.

Chapter Forty-Seven: LIA

Good girl, Kai. Whoa, Sebastian." Pain colored her world, and Lia struggled to make sense of the last few minutes. If not for her four-legged defenders, she'd be dead.

Will be dead soon enough. The bullet missed the bone and passed through the outer fleshy portion of Lia's upper thigh. The initial pain had transformed into a radiating constant burn. Her leg felt leaden, weighing at least twelve tons. The exit wound beneath her soaked the hard-pack ground.

Gotta stop the bleeding. Before I pass out.

"Kai, move pup. Good dog." She pushed her gently aside

when she wanted to shove into her lap. Without a phone she'd dug her own grave.

Stop the bleeding. Get help. Warn Grammy.

Her grandparents wouldn't have a fire-breathing horse or snarling hero dog to keep the killer at bay. Heck, with his wild hair and scarlet eyes he'd fit in with the party guests made up like zombies. "And stab Grammy in the back."

Kai barked at her words, dancing in again to land a slurp across her face. "Enough." The pain, dear God, the pain… she wanted to dissolve into a sobbing mess. Her leg felt cold. She'd shed the duty belt, or it would have served as a dandy tourniquet. The holster strap wasn't long enough. What else?

Her father's lariat slipped from her shoulder. She stared at it, blinking, wondering how… then remembered September fetched it along.

Lia fingered the old, braided leather. She shook out the coils, hefting it awkwardly from her semi-reclining position. Debating, Lia eyed Sebastian. With a properly tossed rope around his neck, he could tow her out of the maze and closer to the house, where folks might see her. Maybe he could pull her far enough, she could yell for help and be heard.

She stared at her bloody thigh. The lariat would make an even better tourniquet to stop the bleeding. But she'd have to sit here for who-knows-how-long. That gambled someone found her before the inevitable happened.

Tourniquet and wait, or have Sebastian tow her out? She had no way to cut the lariat to serve double duty.

Lia's hat had slipped off. She skinned off the hair tie thinking the orange elastic might offer enough pressure to slow the bleeding. But the fabric wouldn't stretch far enough. "Dammit!" She dropped the tie and replaced both hands around her thigh over the bullet hole, hissing with the pain.

Kai barked and pranced away, clearly still overwrought by the whole experience. She ducked down, grabbed up the hair tie, and bounced away, shaking it like a toy.

Lia's eyes widened. Kai could take a message to the house for help. Kai always returned after her walk-abouts. She'd use the lariat to stop the bleeding.

She dug in her pockets, finding what she needed. "Here, girl. Good Kai, c'mere honey-girl." Shoulda spent more time on her training. "We get through this, and I promise you'll get the attention you deserve. Here, Kai."

Kai play-bowed, forepaws dancing in the dirt with butt and tail high, hair tie clutched in her teeth. Kai shook it with a ferocious snarl, danced forward and dropped it in her lap, then waited for Lia to toss it in a game of fetch.

"Such a good dog." She picked it up, dabbed it in the blood welling from her wound, then beckoned the dog closer. "Hold still, pup."

Kai's cut ear bled freely, but nothing Lia could do about that now. Ears always bled a lot but weren't particularly dangerous. Deftly Lia unbuckled Kai's collar. She threaded the blood-soaked hair tie, along with Magic's K9 police badge, onto the strap before re-fastening the collar. Grandfather would understand.

Now, to get the dog to carry her message home. "Kai, such a good girl. Go home, pup. You saved me once, now save me again. Go home. *Timmie's down the well. Go!*"

Kai danced away, and back again, once more play-bowing in the universal invitation to fun. Her ear stung, and she shook her head, spraying wet against the girl's face.

The smell of blood excited her, the shouting and gunshots, Sebastian's bruising hooves. Most of all, she loved spending time with Lia. The girl talked to Kai, patted her, let her lick her face. Finally, a human with kind words and praise. It made her tail move so fast, she nearly lost her balance.

She heard the words, "go home" and had a vague understanding. But Kai didn't want to leave Lia. Not when "go home" meant a fenced yard and loneliness. Yes, she wanted to please Lia. But this feeling of belonging meant more. She couldn't bring herself to obey. Instead, she snuggled close to her, and rolled onto her back when Lia's hand stroked her chest.

"Magic! Oh thank God, you're here!" Surprise, relief, joy, and love filled Lia's voice. But not for Kai.

Kai bounded to her paws, backing away when the other dog lifted his lips in warning. She didn't wait for Magic to attack. She knew better.

Without a backward look, Kai tucked her tail, yipping a high-pitched lament. She'd "go home" after all. She understood Magic's gruff warning clearly.

Lia belonged to Magic. Kai wasn't welcome.

Kai belonged to no one. She was nobody's dog.

Lia didn't question how Magic appeared in the middle of the cornfield. It didn't matter. If she got out of this—no, *when* she saved herself—she'd figure out the mysteries. "Good boy, oh Magical-Dog, I'm so glad to see you."

He tried to climb on her lap, and she shrieked in pain.

Magic recoiled, and threw himself on the ground, echoing her own whimpering.

Sebastian nickered. Magic rolled back to his feet. Something trailed from his neck.

"Come-a-pup, here big boy. Let me see."

Magic pressed close, licking her tear-smeared face. He wriggled from one end to the other as she smoothed his face and head. Stitches bristled along the line of his own wound, and her fingers came away wet. He'd torn one or more of the stitches trying to reach her.

Lia lifted the slip leash over his broad head and couldn't help grinning. "Ran out on Doc Eugene, did you? Bet they're going crazy looking for you."

She ran the long strap through her fingers and threaded one end beneath her injured leg, wrapping the leash around her thigh just above the injury. Lia struggled and finally released the loop carrier on her trouser waistband for the police baton.

Lia tied the end of the leash around the baton, then stifled her cry as she twisted it to tighten the strap around her thigh. The constriction stemmed the blood flow but increased the throbbing pain. She tied it in place and breathed heavily for several moments to plan next moves.

Chapter Forty-Eight: MELINDA

We gotta park and walk in." Melinda craned her neck around, taking in the sea of mostly high-end vehicles. Delaney's old car stuck out. For that matter, so did the two of them, him in scruffy jeans and hoodie, and her in distressed jeans and cheer team sweatshirt. She pulled the hood down, and pulled straw off the fabric.

She watched a costumed couple, glittering with sequins and bright masks, exit a golf cart at the front entrance. A man wearing a suit along with a SECURITY badge on a lanyard stopped the couple. They produced a ticket. Melinda twirled her hair, and the cat batted at the feather tie holding her ponytail. "We don't have tickets."

The golf cart bumped away from the house to meet them. Probably another security guy.

"We'll get in. We don't need tickets; we're not here for the party. We got to talk to Mrs. Corazon." Delaney parked next to a Mercedes convertible and climbed out.

"Wait. I'm coming." She juggled Pippo as she opened the door. It wouldn't do to lose Lia's cat now.

He turned around. "Leave the dang cat in the car. Let's go."

She shook her head. "Pippo is our ticket into the house. Mrs. Corazon had September searching for Pippo recently. Returning an AWOL feline will get us through the door."

She hooked two fingers through Pippo's harness and snugged him tight. As the security person in the golf cart approached, she whispered, "Let me do the talking. I got this."

He raised his eyebrows but nodded once. She could read his mind. He'd give her the first shot and if she failed, he'd try to bulldoze his way inside. Melinda knew from hearing about the Corazons that wouldn't get him far.

The man blocked them. "This is a private party, kids." He looked them up and down, disapproval clear.

Delaney bristled. She put a hand on his arm before speaking.

"Sir? Sir, hello. Uhm, I have Mrs. Corazon's cat. He ran away again. Returning Pippo, see?" She gestured with her cradling arms and Pippo meowed on cue.

He frowned. "I don't know anything about it running off again. Who are you?"

Delaney started to speak but she cut him off. "Melinda Combs. Maybe you know my dad, Detective Jeff Combs?

Retired now." She smiled, dimpling.

The security guy scowled and spoke into his com-unit. "I got two kids here. Say they're returning the family cat. Yes, again."

"We just want to do the right thing." Delaney stuck his hands in his pockets, slouching and trying to look innocent. "Hey, if you want, you take the cat to the house for us. I got things to do." He nudged Melinda with his elbow when her mouth dropped open.

"Oh…uh right, Delaney. Good idea." She took a step closer. "Just hook fingers through the harness, or he'll climb up to your shoulder and maybe launch another escape. Pippo likes to perch."

The guard flinched and shook his head. "Hey at the house, repeating, I've got Detective Combs's daughter and her friend returning the cat. Let the boss know." He stared hard at Melinda. "I'm gonna trust you to do just what you propose. Walk on up to the house, and another guy will take you inside. Don't try nothing funny. Your dad won't like me reporting his daughter tried to sneak into the party." He smiled for the first time. "Although I gotta admit, that's a great trick if it works. Now, go on." He waved them by and eyeballed another guest arriving behind them. "I got to check this guest in, so I can't take you up, unless you want to wait."

"That's okay, we'll walk. Thanks!" Melinda tightened her grip on Pippo's harness. She and Delaney hurried down the driveway, increasing their speed to a jog until they reached the front door. Behind them, the throb of a motorcycle echoed as it found a parking spot and shut down.

As promised, a carbon copy of the security guy met the pair at the front door. "Mr. Corazon agreed to let you return the cat, says his wife is quite fond of the critter. Follow me."

He closed the door behind them and led Melinda and Delaney past the fancy entryway toward the rear of the house. They could hear loud music, lots of laughter, and saw fabulous costumes from shabby to chic with couples dancing and snagging yummy-looking treats and cocktails from circulating waiters.

Someday I'll attend, too, dressed up in the most spectacular gown…

"Well now, I'm simply astounded. Pippo escaped again? And you're the pair who found him?" Mrs. Corazon swept into the room wearing an outfit Melinda would simply die to try on. She looked like a queen in gorgeous blue satin and lace. With a bejeweled crown! She had the haughty attitude nailed, looked down her nose at them, even though both Delaney and Melinda stood taller. Mrs. Corazon held out her arms. "I'll take him upstairs and close him in the bedroom. He won't want to be out with all these strangers in the house."

Delaney stepped in front of Melinda, blocking Mrs. Corazon. "We need to talk first. Privately. And then you'll get your cat back."

When she started to protest, his voice turned hard. "You can call the security guy if you want, but I think you'd prefer this conversation to stay private."

Shelly climbed off his motorcycle. He saw the last couple jog toward the house. He waited until a security man escorted them inside and out of sight. One outside, one at the door, probably more inside. He nodded. Good to know.

The fellow on the golf cart pulled up next to him. "Got your ticket? Party's already in full swing. Most everyone's already checked in." The man got off the cart and thumbed his phone probably to find the guest check-in list. "Man, I've seen all kinds of costumes tonight. Even those two kids had a great story. But you're the winner."

"Kids?" Shelly squinted, vision still bleary from inflamed eyes. Was one of 'em that boy who got away? "Yeah, need to talk to them." He flashed his badge.

"Great costume, man. You look like death warmed over." He grinned and held out his hand for the expected ticket.

"Thanks. Here's my ticket." Shelly pulled out his gun and fired.

Sebastian moved closer. The big pony would have crawled into Lia's lap alongside Magic if he could. He lowered his head, snuffling and pushing his red velvet nose into Lia's neck. She reached high to encircle his head in a gentle hug. "Wanna help? I know you do."

She shook out the lariat and quickly dropped it over his head. He startled a bit, raising up so the loop of the rope fell around the base of his neck over his dark mane. "Whoa, big fella. I don't know if I can stand up on my own. You're gonna help, okay?"

Lia doubted she could climb back onto Sebastian's back with only one good leg, though she'd sure give it a try if she could find a step. But with his support, she could at least get herself out of this cornfield one limping step at a time, and make it easier for searchers to find her.

If they were looking. *Please let them be looking…*

She pulled herself up to a sitting position. Less than an hour ago, she'd vaulted astride without a thought and rode bareback without a care. With her injury, pain, and growing dizziness she'd need help just to keep her balance standing, never mind climbing aboard.

Within minutes she cobbled together something similar to a dog harness, snugging the rope around Sebastian's red neck and chest, making sure his chocolate mane wasn't caught. "Good boy, such a great fella, thanks for your patience." She murmured a soft litany, praising his steadiness and gentle nature. *This might actually work.*

Magic sat close by, cocking his massive head from side to side. It made her smile, despite the pain. Such a good dog, he'd known she needed help, escaped the vet clinic despite his own wounds, traveled miles to find her… *Focus, Lia, focus!*

Something steady and immobile to brace against would help as she levered herself up. Without a word spoken, Magic rose and came to her side. He planted his paws and waited for her.

"Love you, too, honey-boy." She rested her left forearm on his broad back, while grasping the trailing lariat with her other hand. Lia grunted and couldn't help letting loose a scream as she pushed and pulled herself up onto the knee of her good leg then hopped upright. She leaned against Sebastian, panting and trying to blink away the dark sparkles filling her vision.

"You got this, Lia. You got this." Not only to save herself, but to warn Grammy and her guests, Lia had no choice but to push through the pain. Police work protected and served the public. Tonight it turned personal with her family targeted.

Chapter Forty-Nine: KAI

As the house came into view, Kai slowed her pace. Many cars, trucks and motorcycles—her hackles raised at their presence—clogged the long drive. Noisy voices of laughter, conversation, the occasional shout, spilled out of the building, too, with loud music mixed into the cacophony.

The blood smell on her fur made Kai growl and want to snap, bite hard at anyone too close, especially the scary-funny people wearing odd clothing. Some covered their faces with masks or wore hats that turned them into threats.

Her tail tucked tight, and ears pressed flat to her head. She wanted to act brave but felt unsettled and out of her depth. Best to find her tunnel and hide.

Hide from Magic. She didn't blame the other dog. Lia and Magic belonged to each other. If she belonged to Lia, Kai wouldn't want another dog to try and steal her affection, either.

Lia's hurts made her worry. The girl sent Kai away like she'd done something bad. Did she cause Lia's hurts? Kai scared the motorcycle man away once before. But this time, she failed.

If Magic had been there, Lia wouldn't have got hurt. Magic knew how to protect his person.

Not like Kai. Maybe that's why Lia sent her away. And why the man who fed her, and the lady who yelled at her, made Kai stay all alone in the fenced yard. All alone, so she couldn't hurt anybody else. She didn't want to hurt anyone…

Bad dog! She whimpered. She'd never dig out of the backyard again. At least locked away from people she couldn't cause them hurts.

At the thought, Kai padded in a wide circle, staying beyond the spill of light from the many bright windows. She avoided the costumed people. Most congregated in the vast back yard some distance from the small, fenced portion she called home.

When she reached the hidden tunnel, Kai sniffed thoroughly. She listened for several heartbeats, making sure the hidden enclosure remained vacant. Kai wanted—no, she needed—alone time, to find one of the battered chew toys and bite it, bite it hard and shake it. Maybe that would help. Later, the man would come fill her food bowl. Not sammiches, but okay to fill the empty ache in her middle.

Kai entered the tunnel, diving headfirst, and shoving hard

with pistoning rear feet to squirm shoulders through the tight space. Her head poked out beneath the greenery.

Before she could climb the rest of the way out, floodlights bathed the space in brightness. She blinked, holding still. She watched and listened, sniffing carefully, as the woman who lived here appeared in odd clothing, flanked by two young humans Kai didn't know.

She sniffed again. One of the kids carried her cat friend, Pippo.

The trio moved slowly together, dog and pony matching pace with Lia's hobbling gait. At one point, they stopped while she vomited and then stood panting while the rank odor continued making her heave. Finally she conquered her stomach and pain and proceeded.

Time ran together. The sliver of moon climbed higher. She panted, staring at the distant glow she knew pinpointed her grandparents' home.

Astride Sebastian, she'd get there more quickly, if she could stand the speed. She had to try.

Lia looked around: mostly scrubby cedars, with rolling pastureland. Over there. A misshapen tree slumped close to the ground before turning and reaching for the stars. A natural step ladder.

Urging Sebastian to turn took a bit of persuading. He'd set his sights on the homestead, too, where better eats than dry grass awaited.

His herding heritage showing, Magic added his own suggestions, pushing into Sebastian's space to exert invisible pressure. Together the three meandered to the twisted tree.

Lia grabbed one of the branches, leaning against it while again catching her breath. Her leg, now a leaden weight, had no feeling. She should loosen the tourniquet or risk permanent damage. But she wouldn't have the energy to tighten it again and couldn't continue without the tourniquet.

Keep going.

This next maneuver meant life or death. If she fell trying to mount Sebastian, she wouldn't get a second chance.

Gritting her teeth, she clung to his makeshift harness, suspended against Sebastian's side. Her feet hung in the air, the injured limb as good as dead, while the other sought to find that elusive cedar step. Sebastian stood steadfast, rock solid, as if he understood what she needed.

Her good leg and foot found the needed support, and she stood on the swaying tree bough. Little by little, she inched her way higher, grasping overhead branches with one hand to keep her balance. Her other hand kept Sebastian steady, until finally, she'd climbed high enough to attempt the transfer.

Do it quick. Grab and hang on. She must vault astride the pony's back and pray Sebastian didn't shy away from the predictable rebound of the tree limb. "Steady, steady…"

She crouched on her good leg, and began to gently bounce, using the spring action of the tree to boost her. On the third bounce, she sprang onto Sebastian's back. Lia grappled the straps of the lariat and wrapped arms around his arching neck. She lay prone, flat on her stomach, her face pressed into his dark mane, with both legs hanging down both sides, afraid to try and sit up.

As she feared, Sebastian shied sideways away from the flexing tree. "Whoa, whoa, steady. Good boy." On the ground, Magic danced around, woofing with excitement.

The gentle rocking rhythm of the horse's gait matched the

throb of her leg. God, she wanted to sleep. Her hands and feet felt cold. Lia bit her lip, fearing the lethargy spoke more of blood loss and shock than anything else.

Her eyelids drooped. Sebastian headed down a slight slope and stumbled but immediately recovered. Lia's cold hands lost their grip. She clutched at his mane, instinctively tightening both thighs to maintain her seat, and screamed at the resulting flash of pain.

Lia slid off. She landed with a teeth-jarring jolt. Of its own volition, her body curled into a fetal position, shivering, shivering.

Sebastian stood motionless, head drooping to nudge her with his soft nose.

"Not your fault…" She'd tried. Done all she could.

Chapter Fifty: CORNELIA

Cornelia swept into the fenced backyard, holding up the skirts of her fabulous costume to avoid soiling the fabric. Every year, party crashers did their best to spoil things for everyone else. She couldn't see Dub—probably outside enjoying cigars with his buddies—and the security had better things to do. She could handle these rude delinquents and teach them a lesson in the process.

She whirled, standing with an imperious pose that suited both her position in the community and the costume. "You wanted a private word. Well? Get out here, and let's have it. I have guests who need my attention."

The girl looked familiar, with her riot of red curls spilling about her shoulders from a messy ponytail. "What are you doing with him? Did Lia send you?" Her granddaughter had taken Pippo back to Dallas. And apparently stayed there, simply to thwart Cornelia's birthday surprise.

"We're not here about Pippo." The girl's arms loosened, and Pippo leaped to the grass, sniffing delicately before padding over to Cornelia.

The cat stroked his body against the brocade of the costume, leaving fur behind. Surprising herself, Cornelia found she didn't care and scooped him up to cuddle. "I appreciate you returning him." Her words came stiff and proper, her throat suddenly tight. How long had Pippo been out on his own this time? "Come back inside. I'm happy to give you a reward for returning him."

The boy, a few years older by her estimation, shook his head, too-long hair hanging in his eyes. She'd never seen him before. "Like she says, we're not here about the cat. I have something else you want." He pulled a cell phone from a pocket.

She frowned, snuggling the cat closer. Both kids looked dingy and frazzled, straw stuck in the girl's hair suggested they'd come from the hayride. "I don't understand. Now, I've been patient. Your clothes tell me you can't afford the ticket price to this event, children. While I'm grateful for Pippo's return, I must ask you to leave. Now." She waited, and when they didn't move, added a sharper note. "I can get security to escort you off the property."

"Don't you dare! My dad—"

The boy's hand on her arm stopped the girl mid-sentence. He had quiet dignity about him, despite his youth. "You made a deal with my uncle. With Ricky Molingo. He did the work, and I'm here to collect payment due." He gestured with the phone again.

"The reporter? He's your uncle?" She sniffed and turned to go back into the house. "That's between me and Mr. Molingo. But he's been a disappointment, hasn't delivered as promised." Cornelia didn't want the cat to escape again. She'd had enough of Lia's scornful assessment of her care-taking responsibilities.

"He's dead because of you!" The boy's words ended in an anguished choked off sob.

She stopped, arms reflexively constricting. Pippo squealed, and wriggled away, dashing across the grassy yard. Cornelia took two quick steps after him, then returned her full attention to the children. "What are you talking about? I gave Mr. Molingo a lead and might have suggested an incentive to see his research. But he—what's the word you kids use?—ghosted me. Haven't heard a word from the man, after he promised results in time for my granddaughter's birthday. That's today, by the way." She shook her head. "People shouldn't make promises they can't keep. Sad."

"Listen to him, Delaney's telling the truth. Don't you watch the news?" The girl fairly shook with outrage. "Ricky Molingo got murdered in your pumpkin patch."

"Don't be ridiculous." She knew about the death, of course, but Dub handled that, said it was a homeless person. Her brow furrowed. Why hadn't he told her about this? Never mind she hadn't told him about the reporter.

"September found him while searching for your cat." The girl crossed her arms.

"Uncle Ricky did as you asked. And he got murdered because of it." Delaney waved the cell phone at her again. "My little brother nearly died, too. So if you want the research on his phone, you gotta pay for it, just like you promised."

Cornelia laughed. "Just as I thought. A pathetic shakedown. Get out. Now, before I call security." She turned back to the house, shaken, but wouldn't dare let them see. The bows sewn into the hem danced and fluttered in the evening breeze as she lifted her skirt.

Yes, she suggested Molingo investigate Wyatt Teves's murder conviction and report back. She'd also reached out to an attorney, but that didn't make her culpable if the man got himself killed.

"It's not a shake down. You hired him, he did the job. Don't you want his research? You owe it to Delaney and his brother." The girl caught Cornelia's arm. "You really are cold hearted. I can see why Lia hates you."

Cornelia gasped as if slapped. She pulled her arm away.

"Leave her be, Melinda. If she's not interested, the cops will love to hear about her part in all this." The boy's chin trembled with anger, frustration, or both. "Bet she woulda stiffed Uncle Ricky, too. C'mon." The pair pushed by Cornelia to reach the patio doors.

A disheveled man with bloodshot eyes appeared in the doorway. "You're right, kid. I'm Detective Sheldon Savatch with Dallas PD." He flashed a badge. "I'll take your evidence."

Chapter Fifty-One: SEPTEMBER

"Wait, wait, hold up." September's voice came out as a croak. She ran across the pumpkin patch, go bag slapping against her back, and bo staff clenched in her hand. She couldn't run full speed, to avoid twisting an ankle, and slowed to a walk when the car pulled out of the lot.

Shadow paced beside her, silent and stoic. Whoever just left the parking area saw her approach and clearly wanted nothing to do with her.

She stopped, breathing heavily, and spoke again to Combs. "I'm here. Somebody just took off in a car. There's a truck here, too but nobody else around."

"Sit tight. I've called the Heartland PD. Brummitt's sending a patrol car for you."

"What about the Corazons' party?" She'd already told him about Lia racing away on horseback. And hearing gunshots not long after. "Cornelia's the target, but I worry about collateral damage." The guest list numbered hundreds.

"Brummitt has it covered, September." His voice grew louder. "She's coordinating with Dallas PD. Must be a connection to Molingo's death, but Brummitt didn't share details."

"Yeah, Lia said Lockhart mentioned a Detective Savatch investigating the murders. But it'll take at least an hour for him to get here." September matched his frustration.

"C'mon, September. How far d'ya think Brummitt would get trying to cancel Cornelia's party plans? The shindig's in high gear already. It'll take more'n what-ifs and maybes to close it down. Lia has the best chance to petition the Corazons."

As she reached the parking lot, September stopped abruptly, recognizing Lia's truck. "Shadow, *check it out.*" If a bad guy hid inside his nose would know.

"Wait for the ride. An officer will bring you home." Combs paused to speak with someone.

September watched Shadow cautiously approach Lia's truck. He sniffed, circled the vehicle, did a paws-up on the passenger side with wide loose tail wags, and returned to sit before her with a soft woof. Based on his all clear, she walked closer.

"Willie's upset he didn't get to go on the hayride, too. He's making up for it eating too much candy. Melinda won't be home for a while, but with everything going on, I just want you home. Teddy's here, too."

Her jaw tightened. She'd agreed the authorities should handle everything. But where were the blaring sirens? The blazing light bars atop police cars? He wanted her to twiddle her thumbs and wait for a ride home while the killer stalked Lia, and threatened hundreds at the Corazons' home? Combs wouldn't sit on his hands. She'd trained for situations like this.

She took a breath before speaking. To be fair, she hadn't shared all the details. And if roles were reversed, she'd want him to wait for back up. "Has Teddy found anything helpful?"

Combs relayed her question, then put his phone on speaker.

"Clarence Walford worked for the Grand Chisholm Hotel in a number of capacities and ended up head of concierge services." Teddy ticked off the facts. "Walford retired early, supposedly after winning some sort of lottery prize. Bought a small house, refused interviews, and ever since, he and his wife lived quietly in a modest suburb of North Dallas." He hesitated. "Several people from the hotel retired about the same time, within weeks of Henry Wong's murder."

September shuddered. "Please tell me he didn't die in the presidential suite." Everything led back to Henry Wong.

And to her.

Teddy chuckled. "Don't want to sleep with Daddy's ghost roaming around? Sorry, it's Halloween, so I couldn't resist. But no. Walford discovered Wong's body floating in the pool."

And Wyatt Teves got convicted of the murder. "Did Kincaid Drummond work the case alone?"

Combs interjected. "We can talk about it later. Just come

home, September, wait for the ride." Frustration and not a little anger crept into his voice. He'd jump in the car to fetch her himself, if not for his bum leg. "No need for heroics. The police have it handled. It's not always about you, babe. Please."

Her phone pinged with a text. Melinda. A series of emoji's—Halloween pumpkins, devilish clown face, and a gun—preceded a capitalized three-letter universal emergency message:

>SOS!!!

A hard swallow. "Combs, I just got a message—" September felt a nearly audible click in her head as puzzle pieces fell into alignment.

"So did I! She's in trouble. D'ya know the hayride route?" His shouted demand betrayed a father's terror. "Teddy, we've got to—"

"She's not on the hayride. She's at the Halloween party." Without waiting for his response, September disconnected and pocketed her phone.

She couldn't wait for Brummitt's officer to appear. September had to get to the Corazons' ASAP, before something unspeakable happened to Melinda.

With desperation, she checked the doors of Lia's truck. Shadow danced beside her, barking with excitement. September grabbed open the driver's door, peered under the steering column. Could she hotwire the old truck? Her training included that skill although modern vehicles required equipment she didn't have. *Mental note, add to go bag…*

She saw keys in the ignition. No time to wonder why or how. "Thank God"

Chapter Fifty-Two: MELINDA

Melinda kept her phone out of sight so Detective Savatch didn't see. You were supposed to trust the police, but despite his badge, he scared her. Delaney wasn't having any of it, either.

"What evidence? I was just mouthing off, Detective." The boy swallowed hard, his Adam's apple bobbing. His knuckles whitened on the phone as he tried to slip it into a pocket.

"It's on the phone, kid." Savatch held out his hand. It trembled a bit, then steadied. "You want me to arrest you? Withholding evidence carries serious consequences, boy." He took a couple more steps toward them. "Hand it over."

"Now see here." Cornelia drew herself up to her full five-feet-two-inch height. "This isn't the time or place for such things. Take this business downtown to the police department."

Mrs. Corazon sure knew how to play the stuck-up queen.

So Melinda played along. "Great idea, Mrs. Corazon." She turned to the detective. "Go to the police station and we'll follow you there. I'll get my dad, Detective Combs, to meet us." She squeezed Delaney's arm hard when he would have protested and offered a tiny head shake. They wouldn't *really* follow him. She just wanted to delay until help arrived. And name-dropping couldn't hurt, either.

She shrank back when Savatch rounded on the older woman. "Mrs. *Corazon?* You're the bitch that started this whole mess." The night wind whisked his long hair around his pale face. He sure didn't look like the button-down detectives Melinda knew.

Savatch coughed, then spat something nasty onto the grass, before drawing his gun. "Give me the phone now, or I'll scatter what you call brains all over the grass." He pointed it first at Delaney and Melinda, then aimed it unsteadily at Mrs. Corazon.

She flinched, staggered backward, and tripped over the long skirt. Cornelia landed on her side in the grass, face pinched with pain and surprise. "I don't know what you're talking about." She held up one arm defensively. "I don't have anything to give you."

He leaned over her, pushing the gun into her face.

Melinda wanted to squeeze shut her eyes, not wanting to see. But they had to do something to stop him. She looked around the lighted yard for anything...

"Yes, all right it's true. I asked Molingo to look into that old murder." She spoke quickly, words running together. "Teves claims his innocence, you know. I never believed him, no, not at all. But wanted to be sure, so…"

At her admission and mention of his uncle's name, Melinda felt Delaney shiver.

The detective sputtered. "You had no business sticking your nose—"

"I have my reasons. Personal reasons. For my granddaughter, Lia."

Melinda shuddered as his gun moved closer to Mrs. Corazon. The barrel stroked her cheek. Her breast heaved, and the pulse in her thin throat thrummed a staccato rhythm.

What to do? Melinda looked around frantically for anything… and saw Pippo watching, in the classic feline stalking pose, butt high, tail twitching. Following the cat's gaze, Melinda saw the fluttering ribbons on Mrs. Corazon's skirt, beckoning like a feather cat toy.

Rear feet trod in the grass, revving up for the dashing pounce.

Delaney shuffled closer to the patio door, but Melinda was frozen in place. He mouthed silent words, urging her to make a break for it.

She mouthed, "No." Savatch would shoot them in the back before they reached help.

Mrs. Corazon blabbered on, words spilling one on top of the other. "Molingo never delivered anything. No evidence one way or the other." Her eyes narrowed, and she pointed. "But *he* says he has something, that boy there. *He* has Molingo's phone, wanted me to pay him for it. Threatened me, too." Her chin trembled. She wouldn't meet Melinda's eyes.

Savatch laughed. "Trying to save your precious Lia? Left

her in the corn field. She's dead."

The world stopped for three heartbeats. Party noises faded into static. Then Mrs. Corazon shrieked. She screeched, again and again and again. Melinda thought the whole county must hear.

Coyotes answered back.

Savatch aimed his gun at Delaney. "Gimme!"

The detective, if he actually was a cop, would kill everyone as soon as he got the phone. Melinda knew that. She saw the same understanding in Delaney's eyes.

Delaney tossed her the cell phone.

Savatch whirled, pointing the gun at her.

She lobbed the phone back to Delaney. As soon as the man's focus moved, Melinda skinned off her feather hair tie. In the same motion she sling-shot it between the boy and the man's gun. And yelled, "Delaney, run. Run now!"

Pippo streaked toward the flying feather, just as Savatch stepped after the pair. The cat changed course, grappled his leg, clawing and biting, scaling his torso like a live oak, with ears pinned back and murderous intent in his eyes.

Melinda gasped, she hadn't expected that. As Mrs. Corazon's shrieks dissolved into sobs, Melinda ran toward the door. She glanced quickly over one shoulder. He couldn't be a real police officer, not acting like that. Police were the good guys.

Savatch yelled and threw the cat off. The gun cracked. Mrs. Corazon crumpled. Pippo hissed, and jumped atop the woman's fancy bodice, puffing up to twice his size, ready to take on all comers.

Melinda prayed somebody heard the gun over the party music. Delaney grabbed Melinda's hand and tugged her toward the door. They nearly made it.

Kai scooted fully out of the tunnel, the heavy metal tag Lia attached to her collar shifted. She sat to scratch at it.

At first, the interplay between the woman and the two kids created tail-wagging entertainment. She especially liked the cat smells, even if it was long-distance. Sometimes Pippo sneaked into the yard, and they got to play together.

But when the sick-smelling man appeared, with his foul noisy gun, Kai's hackles rose. She remembered his smell, an indelible impression that made her want to squat and pee to proclaim *no threat no threat!* Her low swinging tail transformed to high-held wags of agitation. The bad man who hurt Lia followed Kai here. How had that happened? Had Lia come, too? And Magic?

She lifted her head, nose testing the wind, but she could only detect the blood-taint she still carried on her collar.

Bad dog! No wonder Lia and other people wanted nothing to do with Kai. She brought bad scary danger to them. She whimpered, a low growl mixing with the worry-whimper.

Then Pippo raced toward the bad man. And attacked him. Yes! Even though Pippo's tiny teeth and small form couldn't compare to a dog, the feline bravery mustered Kai's own courage. If Pippo attacked with no fear, Kai could make up for her mistake leading the dangerous man here.

The wild-eyed stinky man tackled the boy, both rolling to the ground.

Kai launched herself, a roar of defiance fueling her paws.

The bad man screamed. He pointed his gun at Kai.

With the loud awful POP! an invisible fist reached out to punch Kai in the neck. She yelped. The blow slammed against the borrowed metal tag on her collar.

It hurt. Ached worse than the fire of her knife-sliced ear. But Kai shook off the sting. That's what brave dogs do, to protect and defend. Defend her territory, and the people within. This fenced area belonged to Kai, and the people needed her help.

When he pointed the gun again, Kai danced away from the man's stumbling movements. She dashed in circles around the man, and bit him again and again, right where his tail should be.

Chapter Fifty-Three: SEPTEMBER

It took September what felt like forever to master Lia's cantankerous truck. She'd rarely driven a stick shift, and her hurry made things worse. She let out the clutch too fast. The herky-jerk motion threw Shadow forward, and he yelped when he nose-bumped the dash. "Sorry, baby dog." Her voice still sounded gravelly and her throat ached from the attack.

Her phone rang as she saw the turn-off for Corazon Ranch. Combs. She switched it to speaker and propped it on the dash.

"The officer called from the pumpkin patch. Where are

you?" She could imagine him pacing, limping up and down the dining room.

In the background, Teddy called loudly: "Put her on speaker. Tell her we're better off helping from here."

"Lia's truck and keys were in the parking lot. I'm on my way to get Melinda. Lia's probably already at the party. We'll coordinate once I arrive." She massaged her throat with one hand.

Combs cursed. "That damn party, I'm sick of hearing about it. And now—"

"She went with Delaney." Willie's young voice piped up.

He should be in bed by now. "What?" September put both hands on the steering wheel, fingers gripping so hard her hands ached. "Delaney and Peter are in police protective custody." Surely, even a hormonal teenager wouldn't risk his life over a date.

Well, yes, he probably would. Holy crappiocca, it got worse and worse.

"Go finish your homework, Willie. Now." Combs's exasperation told her this wasn't the first request. "A little late for tattling."

The expansive Corazon estate came into view. Shadow sat up in the passenger seat, front paws propped on the dash. His head swiveled with rapt attention at all the lights and activity. He whined under his breath, and his tail swept back and forth on the old truck's worn upholstery.

"I just got to the house, Combs. Dammit, still no police presence. You sure Brummitt's on top of this?" She weaved down the narrow drive, finally parking some distance away from the other cars. September didn't want to get trapped in, should she need the truck to head out quickly.

"Don't know why nobody's there yet. Look for security

on site. The Corazons used to contract with off-duty officers for their big events." Combs couldn't keep the worry from his voice. "Please watch yourself." He knew better than to ask her—again—to wait.

He wanted to be here, breaking down doors to find Melinda and whisk her home to safety. Combs couldn't fault her for doing the same. In the best of all worlds, she'd leave everything to the police. But not with Melinda at risk.

"I'll be careful. Update me with anything pertinent." September disconnected.

Melinda was the only daughter September would ever have. Despite head-butting, she loved the child with a fierceness that sometimes surprised her.

The truck door squealed as September climbed out of the vehicle. She grabbed her go bag and checked her holstered gun. She hesitated then grabbed the bo staff. Couldn't hurt. "Shadow, let's go." He still wore his tracking harness, but she didn't hook on the long lead. To do his best, Shadow needed full freedom of movement to track, to protect, or escape.

He hopped out, tail high and waving with happy excitement. Without prompting, Shadow's head swiveled to the house. He sniffed the quickening breeze. Wagging stopped abruptly. Hackles bristled. His whine of anticipation transformed to a low warning growl.

"I hear you, Shadow. Good dog. *Check it out.*" She waved a hand forward, indicating the pathway before them. Regimented lines of cars parked on each side of the narrow drive felt like an enemy army watching in silent disapproval.

Shadow galloped forward, head high and nose reading the air. After passing a dozen cars, he skidded to a stop and swerved between two cars. He barked once, sharp and high pitched.

September's grip tightened on the bo staff, and she unholstered her weapon, then trotted forward. Her own attention swiveled from side to side, acutely aware of the unprotected target she presented. Surprising that Corazons' security didn't have more of a presence, especially based on the high-dollar vehicles crowding the space. A golf cart, looking wildly out of place, sat nearby, probably used to ferry late-comers from parking to the house.

"Good dog, Shadow." She came abreast of the dog, looking around one last time for potential threats before turning her attention to what he'd found.

Someone had dragged a man into a hidden culvert between two parked cars. Blood soaked his shirt, so much blood… It stained the security badge he wore on a lanyard.

She knelt beside him, felt for a pulse. Her own heart trip hammered so loudly she couldn't tell what was his or hers.

He moaned. Still alive.

September dropped the staff and holstered the gun. Where the hell was Heartland PD? She pulled out her phone to text Combs.

>Security man down, north side driveway. Shot? Call 911.

Maybe calling the emergency number would light a fire under Brummitt's team.

The man moaned again. She bent to speak to him. "Help is on the way."

But he grabbed her arm, pulled her close. "Warn them. Those kids, he's after the kids." He licked his lips. "Bastard shot me. Hurts, oh God it hurts… Tell my wife, my kids I love 'em—"

"No, no, no, you'll tell them yourself. Hang on." She looked around frantically. They were alone, no help in sight. He moaned again. She couldn't see his injury. Maybe a doctor at the house could offer emergency care quicker? If she could get him onto the golf cart…

His hand gripped her wrist with bruising strength. She bent to hear final whispers from blood-flecked lips. He gasped. "He's got a badge."

"Got it. He's wearing a policeman's costume."

He coughed, spewing red. "No. Detective's shield. From Dallas." He took one last shuddering breath. His hand fell away.

Magic whined, and licked Lia's face, knocking off her police cadet cap. He lay down close to her, snuggling against her side, sharing his warmth.

"Sorry, good boy, we tried. God, I love you…"

Sebastian had a home with Grammy and Grandfather for life. But who would take care of Magical-Dog? A highly trained police dog needed a special human partner. *I don't want to leave you…*

Her eyelids fluttered. The black abyss beckoned.

Magic barked and barked again. She felt his cold nose goosing her neck. He didn't want her to go, either. His warm tongue washed her face. She blinked, opened her eyes one last time.

Magic stood above her, holding the white cap in his mouth, and pawing her arm again and again. Suddenly she knew what he wanted, what she must do. She took the cap, and, using one index finger dipped in scarlet from her wound, scrawled the four-letter message. She gave the cap back to the dog.

"Magic… bring help. *Timmy's down the well—*"

As he dashed away, cap firmly in his mouth, she smiled. *What a good boy…*

Chapter Fifty-Four: MELINDA

Melinda waited for Delaney to scramble upright. They had to get help. Mrs. Corazon's crumpled form remained motionless on the grass, Pippo spitting and hissing, ready to attack.

Kai continued dancing around the shooter, dodging in to land a well-placed nip time and again. Delaney stared at the man, chest heaving. "He killed Uncle Ricky." His face turned red as his fists clenched.

"Leave him alone. Let's go." She shook him. He'd kill them both if they didn't run. "You've got the evidence on the phone. You'll get him that way."

The killer kicked hard at Kai, and the dog dodged. But a second kick landed hard; the dog yelped and scooted out of range.

They'd hesitated for too long. The man whirled, gun still weaving in his hand, but quickly settling on Delaney. "Give me damn phone."

Instead, Delaney disappeared inside. Kai dashed after him.

Melinda sprinted in their wake. Her left sandal slipped, tripping her just as she reached the door. A clawing hand caught her hair, yanking her backward off her feet. She squealed, then shuddered on smelling the sickness of the man in his stale breath and fevered sweat.

Spittle wet her face when he yelled into her ear. "Got a knife at your pretty throat. Don't say a word, don't struggle, princess, or I'll slice you from one end to the other." He held her before him as a shield. "Do you hear me?" He shook her by the neck.

She spoke, barely a whisper. "Yes. Yes, I understand."

He pushed her ahead of him. "I can slit your throat quicker than you can cry out for help. These cretins will buy it as a Halloween stunt and watch you bleed out. Understand?"

Melinda swallowed hard as she stepped through the patio door.

"Better pray your boyfriend does nothing stupid. I want that phone. And if you wanna live to go your prom, he'll swap the phone for you. C'mon." He forced her across the threshold, one hand still knotted in her hair. He moved the knife down to her side, hiding it from view, but she could feel the sharp blade against her side.

Savatch hurt from head to butt, not to mention injuries inflicted during the battle with Sorokin and Lia's animals. His brain stuttered like a car stuck in low gear. One driving goal remained—recover Molingo's phone. Destroy it. Escape. Then time to recover.

His illness put everything into slow motion. He weaved through the costumed revelers, snarling when they bumped or impeded his progress. As expected, they startled first then grinned with delight at the spectacle. Who needed a costume? His badge prominently displayed on his belt, and the pale-faced beauty in custody played into the crowd's fantasy.

"Not a word, girl." He hissed into her ear.

She grabbed hold of a column, stopping their progress. "But how—"

He yanked her forward. "Shut the hell up. Let me think." Where was the boy with the phone? Savatch looked around, long hair flying, bleary vision searching for the kid who held his future. Over there—yes, hiding behind a big man wearing a ludicrous Conquistador costume. That stupid mutt pressed against the kid while the boy pointed at Savatch.

The big man took several steps toward them. "Hey, you… Detective? That's Melinda Combs, isn't it? We need to talk."

Savatch grinned, shook his head, and pushed the girl to a side door and out into the fall night air. He knew just where they'd go, so she'd get the full Halloween experience.

The boy would tell Don Quixote everything, and they'd figure out what he wanted. Demanded. Needed… if they wanted to save Detective Combs's daughter.

Cornelia slitted her eyes, peering into the bright floodlights illuminating the fenced yard. She fought to keep her body still.

Pippo crouched on her chest, snarls fading to a self-soothing purr, paws snagging the fancy fabric. *Cat didn't belong outside. Lia said coyotes could kill and eat Pippo… Lia wouldn't like that.*

That man, the detective, shot at her, wanted to kill her! So she'd played dead. She held her breath for ages, then breathed shallow and silent, praying it wouldn't betray her, betting on an academy award performance to rival her late-sister Rose. Cornelia waited endless seconds after everyone left. She finally levered herself onto her elbows, dislodging Pippo.

With a swift stroke, she silently thanked Pippo, before struggling to her feet. The massive amount of fabric, corset boning, and jeweled bodice must have put him off his aim. If the bullet passed through the costume, Cornelia didn't know where. She didn't question, simply embraced the lucky break to struggle to her feet.

Dub, she must find Dub. For a moment, anger bubbled at the security who let this man into the place. And he'd taken that girl, the policeman's daughter, with him, demanding ransom.

The fault came from that Molingo boy, clearly a common type. Just like his loser of an uncle. And what of Lia?

Tears flooded her eyes. Cornelia dashed them away. The nasty man boasted—BOASTED—he'd killed Lia, her only granddaughter. She'd done everything just to make things right with Lia, and now… now, she'd never see her again.

Pippo played with a bit of sequined fabric he'd found in the grass. Cornelia scooped the cat back into her arms, hugging him close.

Find Dub. But they must keep things quiet. Otherwise, it

could ruin the fundraiser, not only this year but taint future events. They'd muster the security people, send them out to find Lia, her dear sweet Lia. Clean up this mess.

And press charges, oh yes! He'd pay, that horrible man would pay for taking away her precious Lia.

Chapter Fifty-Five: SEPTEMBER

September messaged Combs to confirm she couldn't revive the fallen security man. Text so she didn't have to argue. She must focus on the living. On Melinda.

"Let's go, Shadow." September resettled her go bag, grasped the bo staff and hurried down the long drive to reach the house proper. So far, she detected no undue activity, just loud music from outdoor speakers and intermittent raucous laughter. After Melinda's SOS-text, she'd not heard another word.

By this time, Lia and Sebastian should have arrived. With the younger woman's police training, they stood a chance of apprehending the doer before he caused more damage.

Until she learned otherwise, September chose to believe Melinda safe. *For I wish it to be so.*

At the front of the house, a security person stood guarding the door. He smiled. "You're a little late, but still lots of party to go. The bonfire's on schedule for lighting up soon." He lifted an eyebrow at Shadow. "Got your tickets? You must be September Day; I recognize Shadow." He checked the screen on his tablet.

Everybody knew Shadow. At his name, he sat up and waved his paws, something usually guaranteed to prompt smiles all around.

"No ticket. But this is an emergency situation. I need to speak with the Corazons."

He scowled. "Again? First a couple of kids with a lost cat. Then a raggedy-looking detective." He glanced around. "Don't tell him I said that, though." He thumbed his comm device. "Mrs. Corazon demands tickets then lets 'em sail through without 'em." He spoke into the device and waited. Waited some more. He repeated his inquiry. "Come back? You want I should let her and the dog come in?" He waited, then gestured to her with the device and shrugged. "Sorry, they're tied up. You'll have to wait."

She stared at him, wanted to scream, but held her temper when Shadow pawed her leg. "So's ya know, your security partner back at the cars also met that *raggedy detective*. Now he's dead."

The man startled. "Detective Savatch's badge looked real."

"I can't speak to that." Savatch? Detective Greer's partner from Dallas. The man sent to question Lia… She tried to make sense of that. Maybe the killer got the jump on Savatch and stole the real detective's credentials. "Your partner managed to tell me Savatch wanted to speak to the kids you let in. They're in extreme danger, along with everyone else in the place."

His eyes widened. "I wondered why a detective snarled his way in to a friggin' costume party. Wish somebody'd clue me in." Her words finally landed correctly. "Wait. My buddy's dead?"

She nodded. "Already called 911. We don't want to cause a panic. But we need to get these people out of harm's way."

"Good thinking." He peered through the door into the nearly empty entryway. She could see a mass of costumed people through the archway to the grand ballroom. Party goers spilled out onto the lawn beyond. "Mrs. Corazon's gonna hate shutting this down."

"Oh for the love of—" September shoved past him into the marble-floored foyer and hurried into the crowded ballroom.

Shadow followed close, then stiffened when Kai skidded into the area, clearly upset. Shadow whined, arched his neck with a high-held tail wag.

The security guy ran after September. "Wait. Wait, you can't—" He stopped short seeing Kai. "Oh hell no, not another mutt."

The two dogs circled each other, vying for the best tail-sniff access. The side of Kai's face and neck shined red in the glare of the chandelier. *Her own, or someone else's blood?*

"Later, Shadow. Let's go." Thankfully, he immediately came to her side. Before September could make her way through the crowd, a tall boy in jeans and tee shirt under a hoody jogged into view. He stopped short, eyes wild, when he recognized her.

Behind him was an elaborately costumed older gentleman,

craggy face set in a perpetual scowl. *William "Dub" Corazon.* Dub waved them back into the entry foyer and took the time to close the ballroom's elaborate double doors, giving them a measure of privacy.

"Didja see them? They come out this way?" Delaney managed to look both stricken and hopeful, face wet with tears, elbows of the hoody colored with grass stains. "I never meant any of this to happen. She owed us the money, that's all. I never meant…" He dropped to his knees.

Kai pushed into the boy's arms, frantically licking away the tears.

"See who?" September held up her palm—*wait*—to stop Shadow in place.

"Boy says some yahoo in a police get up took off with his girl." He glared at her. "What're you doing here, September?"

Cold fingers scraped the length of her spine. "Delaney, he took Melinda?"

Delaney's shoulders shook. He hugged Kai. "And he shot Mrs. Corazon."

"Cornelia!" Dub spun on his boot heels, heading back to the double doors. "Shot her? Why didn't you say so? What the hell—"

September knelt beside the boy. "Focus, Delaney. Tell me, slowly. Is Melinda hurt? Where'd they go?" Her throat still ached, but now the burn of tears threatened to choke her.

"I don't know! He had a badge. I think he killed Uncle Ricky. For this." He held out a phone. "Uncle Ricky's phone, all the stuff he found out, it's on there. Peter hid it in your car. So I got Melinda to help me get it back." He sobbed. "I'm sorry!"

September took the phone from the boy. "Where'd he go?"

Dub returned, grabbed Delaney's shoulder and shook him. "Where's my wife, boy. You said she's shot?"

A small, bedecked figure appeared, swaying on clicking heels into the foyer. Cornelia clutched Pippo in her arms like a living muff. "Lia's in trouble, Dub." Her carefully coiffed hair fell in messy swirls past her shoulders.

"You got shot?" Dub caught her just before she would've slipped to the floor.

"Yes, but I'm fine. I played possum. But Lia… that terrible man said Lia's dead." She choked on sobs, hiccupping on her words.

Lia dead? Dear heaven… but Melinda wasn't, at least not yet.

"I only wanted to make her happy… oh God!" She looked frantically around and elbowed away from her husband's support. Cornelia stalked over to glare at September. "Your dog tracks people, right?" In her arms, Pippo bit and pawed a sparkly feather toy.

Shadow responded to the stare with a low growl, ears slicking back, until September put a hand on his side. She rose to her feet. "Where'd he take Melinda, Delaney?"

The boy shrugged. He fingered Kai's collar, and something attached to it.

September bent to look closer. Someone had threaded a bloody orange hair tie onto Kai's collar. Also a K9 badge. She fingered the dented shield. Something had nearly shattered the metal, but she could still read Magic's name. "Good dog, Kai, Lia gave you this, didn't she? A message?"

Kai wriggled and wagged at the attention. How September wished she could speak.

Cornelia moved closer to hiss into September's face. "Find my granddaughter! You and your dog, find her!"

September stood. "Why'd he take Melinda? Where'd they

go?" September stared back without flinching.

Dub grabbed his wife's arm. "If you know something—"

She shook him off, and Pippo sprang free, dropping the toy to race across the slick floor to the staircase, and disappear.

Cornelia stared at her empty arms, letting them drop to her sides in a helpless gesture. "He went out the back way. Toward the bonfire. Said he'd trade the girl for that." She pointed at the cell phone in September's hand. "Never mind them. You've got to find our Lia."

September stared at the cat toy, walked closer and scooped it up. Familiar red curly hair caught in the sequins on the elastic. Without another word, September whirled, giving a hand signal to Shadow. She shoved Ricky's phone in her pocket. Time to make a trade.

"Wait, no wait!" Cornelia ran after her, grabbing at September's arm. "That girl can wait. Lia's hurt, she's dying. You've got to find her." Her eyes glinted. She turned to Dub. "She can't die; she can't. I did all this for her."

September shook off her hand. Lia was her dearest friend. But Melinda was her daughter.

"Lia isn't dead." *For I wish it to be so.* She pointed to Kai's collar. "That's her signal, means she's alive. That K9 badge looks like Magic may have taken a bullet for her. Tell Detective Brummitt when she gets here." She rounded on Cornelia. "Which door did they go out, show me!"

Cornelia pointed, hand trembling. From fear? Anger at being thwarted? September didn't care.

Dub put an arm around his wife, supporting her figure. "Through the ballroom, door on the far left leads to the back lawn. Everyone will be heading that way soon. For the bonfire."

"Keep everyone away."

She ran with Shadow through the ballroom, blowing past clueless revelers to burst through the indicated doorway. Once outside she paused for only seconds, taking time to offer Shadow Melinda's sequined hair tie. The scent told the dog everything he needed to know.

Find Melinda. "Shadow. *Seek!*"

Chapter Fifty-Six: SHADOW

Shadow didn't hesitate. Usually, September fixed a long line to his harness when they played *seek*, but he didn't need it to know what to do. He put his head down, sifting the air currents and telltale clues left on the ground.

Many people passed over the area. Dozens of small groups in funny clothes were scattered across the wide grassy expanse. Odd-smelling flames on poles flanked a pathway leading down the hill, their dancing illumination failing to fully light the area. Not that a good dog needed light. Night birds called, and in the distance, coyotes added their praise to the night moon.

Shadow's nose saw clearly, and ears narrowed the focus. He could have closed his eyes and still easily followed the Melinda-bright scented pathway. There… and there again, she stumbled.

Fear.

He whined, paws hurrying as he unraveled the puzzle path to reach her. Deep in the thrill of the hunt, Shadow almost forgot to check in with September. He paused, glanced over his shoulder, and saw her far behind him, back up the hill, trotting in his wake.

"Shadow, *seek!*" She carried the long bo staff in one hand, and the gun in the other.

With her encouragement, he continued to track, an easy assignment compared to earlier. The lawn unrolled before him down a gentle slope, and he could guess the destination. On the summit of the next hill perched a bird's nest of logs and straw, with a weird figure stuck on the very top.

"Hey, look, a dog! Didn't know we could bring our dogs." People walking toward the hill noticed Shadow and tried to lure him away from his job.

Shadow ignored them. He'd wanted adventure and reveled in the excitement. Melinda's scent, her terror, screamed louder the closer he drew to her location. The pungent aroma of the bad man made his fur itch. His hackles rose of their own accord. His tail flagged high, churning the air.

Behind him, September called out to the people. "Clear the area. Go back to the house. Active shooter situation."

Gasps, then hurried feet sped away. But Shadow never wavered. He followed the spoor. He *must* find Melinda, and the bad man with her. *Seek* Melinda. *Guard* the girl. He must not fail. September asked and he'd do anything for her.

He slowed to a more cautious gait ascending the hill. To

one side of the pile of logs, a large barrel of water stood with the top open, and a hose trailing out.

Shadow scanned and pinpointed the bad man who scurried around, keeping the stack of wood between him and a good dog. The man couldn't hide, not from Shadow.

"Get away, get away. I'll burn her, burn you, burn everyone!" The man screeched, the very image of an evil clown with hair fanning about his shoulders. He climbed up the pile of lumber, dragging Melinda with him.

Guard Melinda! Protect her!

Shadow barked and barked again. He ran to the base of the pyramid, and sat, his signal of success. But he immediately stood again, whirling to race halfway down the incline to meet September, urging her to hurry, and then turned to run ahead of her, barking all the while. The wood pile smelled bad, too, a pungent odor that reminded Shadow of oily cars.

"Yes, good dog, Shadow, good find. Melinda, you okay?" September's voice remained steady, but her worry and fear-stink poured off her body in waves.

Melinda's voice cracked then steadied. "I'm okay. But he shot Mrs. Corazon!"

The clown-man pulled her hair and she shrieked. He pressed his face close to hers, saying something, then pulled away.

"He wants the phone. Ricky Molingo's notes." Melinda held her hands in an awkward pose against her stomach. Shadow saw something bound them together. "Delaney has the phone."

"He gave it to me." September drew closer to the pile of wood as Shadow continued to bark. "*Chill*, baby dog. Good boy."

He immediately fell mute but kept a watchful eye. Melinda

and the bad man perched like birds atop the spindly nest.

"I have what you want, Detective Savatch. Here's Molingo's phone with all his research notes, got it right here." She held the small object high so he could see.

Humans relied on sight. Even September. Shadow felt sad people missed out on so much.

September called again, her voice strained. "The phone? With all the notes. You can have it. Just let Melinda go."

"I know you, Sorokin Glass. I know what tricks your whole family plays. Liars, you're all liars!" He hauled Melinda even higher on the stack of logs. "I did my job. Now everything's unraveling, all your fault."

He smelled bad. Sick. Shadow watched his wobbling figure. Only his grip on Melinda kept him upright as he wove back and forth like a snake questing prey. Shadow placed paws up on the first tier of stacked wood, half expecting the man to topple all the way down.

"No trick. Just want Melinda, and us all to walk away tonight."

He stumbled, caught himself on one knee, but never loosened his grip on Melinda, keeping her between himself and September. "Throw away your gun, Magpie. Into the stack. Do it now, or I'll light her up."

Snick-shshsh. Shadow's ears twitched. He lifted his head, sniffed. Fire. He whined.

Shadow hopped up onto a big log at the base of the pile, and looked over his shoulder at September. Did she know about the fire in the man's hand? Fire could burn a good dog. He remembered… paws and other parts hurting so bad…

The man grappled his pocket and put something in his mouth. A pencil?

"Okay, okay, whatever you say." She tossed her gun. "I'll

leave the phone for you. Right here." She set the phone next to Shadow on the woodpile and stepped back.

Her hand signal told Shadow to come to her side. He whined, wanted to run from the threat of fire. Told himself to stand brave and *wait. Wait* even though he hated the word. To be a good dog, he had to *wait*, even without September saying. He knew it, in his heart.

"Let Melinda go, and we'll leave, then you can collect the phone. You can escape. I sent everyone away. Nobody will interfere."

She gestured again at Shadow to *come-a-pup*.

The man pushed Melinda down before him, one fist still gripping her hair. "It's a trick. Nasty trick. Halloween tricks and treats and tricks and…" He blinked, staring side to side. His other forearm wiped his face.

The white pencil stuck out of his mouth. He brought his other hand up to the end of it… *Snick-shshsh.*

Fire.

Sometimes people didn't notice important things the way good dogs did. This time, September gasped, held out her hand in a warding-off gesture. The tiny flame sputtered when he lit the white pencil in his mouth. The man blew smoke.

Be brave despite the fire! Shadow grabbed the phone September had left on the stump. And began to climb the pile of wood toward the flame.

Chapter Fifty-Seven: SEPTEMBER

September stared, aghast at the wild man perched near the top of the bonfire, calmly smoking a cigarette.

Melinda crouched beside him, as he tugged and yanked her around, looking more angry than scared—*that's my girl!*—but any minute the killer could switch things up.

When Shadow ignored her silent command and began to climb, September gritted her teeth. Sometimes dogs knew better than people. But he could tip the crazy man into doing something even more lethal. Hell, the guy had a badge. Nothing worse than a crazy man with lethal training.

Shadow slowly, one paw-placement at a time, climbed

toward the killer. September held her breath, terrified a log slipping could snap his leg like a twig. He carried the phone the killer demanded but teeth could easily slip on the hard, slick surface. If the phone dropped into the twelve-foot tower of wood, nobody could reach it, at least not in time to ransom Melinda. The promise of the phone was the only thing to keep the girl safe.

She didn't see a gun but couldn't rule it out. He'd had a knife before. Savatch looked even more out of it than during the attack at Lia's kennels. His normal state of being? Or something worse… She remembered the smell of sickness on him while he throttled her.

His hands shook. A tremor. His head bobbled like a Pez dispenser. He'd chosen a spot near the witch effigy at the top. Granted, that gave him a good view but it also left him vulnerable to a gunshot. The better defensive location was the other side of the pile in case she had a backup gun.

She didn't, and wouldn't risk a shot if she did. A miscalculation could take out Melinda.

He stared with a blank expression following Shadow's slow ascension. Then his eyes focused.

His attention switched between her and Shadow. "Cute trick. Fed up with tricks. Here doggy doggy, bring it to me. Drop it or bite me and everyone's dead." He giggled. The cigarette fell from his lips, and he fumbled to replace it with another. The *snick-shshsh* ignited the lighter again. His shaking hand held the flame to the cigarette…

The bottom layer of the wood pile had been soaked with pungent accelerant-soaked straw, to ensure the bonfire caught quickly and didn't fizzle out. If Savatch dropped his lit cigarette, or the flaming lighter…

"Send Melinda down now." Panic and dread colored her words. She heard sirens drawing near. *Finally! Thank God.* "Hear that? The police are on the way. Just take the phone when the dog reaches you and get away while you can."

Chapter Fifty-Eight: MAGIC

Exhausted, Magic panted gasping breaths, constricted air making his chest heave. He couldn't loll his tongue to cool, or risked dropping Lia's cap. The scent on the cap kept him focused. *Timmy's-down-the-well,* find people, get help.

Sirens howled, all converging toward the big house, where dozens of cars lined the perimeter like coyotes around prey. At the notion, a chorus of plaintive howls joined the sirens' song.

He finally reached the gravel drive, a familiar place Magic often traveled when he and Lia ran in the early mornings on the weekends they stayed here. Black and white cars with flashing lights blocked his way. Slowing to a trot, Magic wove between the vehicles, noting the many people wearing uniforms with guns on their hips.

He'd been around such people while training. Guns didn't bother him, neither did strangers. Magic knew his job tonight had nothing to do with finding and holding bad guys, or sniffing out explosives, or any of the dozen tasks Lia had taught him. Tonight the fun game they played became the most important lesson he'd ever learned.

Bring help. Save Lia.

He whined deep in his chest and looked for the right person to approach. There. A woman, taller and heavier than Lia. Older. Scowl on her face. But her voice held command as she spoke to the others. He met her at the hospital.

Timmy's-down-the-well!

Magic wove between the cars, his black form melting into the shadows, only the white cap punctuating the darkness like a hovering ghost. He hurried, limping a bit. His paws ached from his bruising cross-country treks.

The uniforms split focus between the woman, a body on the ground between the cars, and a young man escorted toward them from the house. "Detective Brummitt, sorry." He hunched his shoulders, glancing back toward the house.

"What in the ever-lovin' wild world of sports are you doing here?" Brummitt glared at the boy. "Please tell me you didn't bring your little brother, too."

Magic drew closer. He whined. They didn't notice him. He raised a paw…

The boy shook his head, but his voice sounded defiant. "I found Uncle Ricky's phone. September's trying to swap it for Melinda at the bonfire. Once I figured out Mrs. Corazon asked for his help, I had to do something. If he hurts Melinda…" His voice broke.

She said nothing for a long moment, then turned to the officer. "One of you take Delaney in that golf cart back to our black and whites and put him in a car for safe keeping. You"—she pointed to two officers—"secure the body. The rest of y'all, with me." She turned away.

Before she could stride away, Magic pawed her leg. She whirled, startled, and hesitated for a moment. Recognition.

He wagged, slicking back his ears and offering the cap. Magic sat up, waving both paws in the air. *Timmy's-down-the-well…*

"Cadet Corazon's here, too? Shoulda known. Detective Savatch wanted to question her." She shook her head. "Time enough later." She broke into a trot, heading to the big house.

Magic debated running after the woman, but stopped at the boy's words. "That's Magic, Lia Corazon's police dog," he said to the appointed officer. "My little brother told me about him."

The officer held the boy's upper arm and pushed him toward the golf cart. "Just sit tight, like the detective says. She'll want to talk to you later."

Delaney pulled away. "You don't understand. Lia isn't here. And that scary guy who took Melinda, he's got a badge, too. Said he killed Lia!"

Magic hurried after the pair. He again posed, paws up, holding the white cap. Why didn't they understand?

"Say what?" The officer whirled Delaney around. "Don't talk trash, kid. Not funny."

Delaney wrenched his arm away, reached out and gingerly took the cap from Magic's mouth. "Good dog, Magic." He turned back to the officer. "He's a trained police dog.

And my brother said he does this cool trick to get people to follow him for help."

He looked at the cap and held it up for the man to see. "Look here: the word *help*. In blood. She needs help." He met Magic's eyes. "That right, boy? Lia sent you, right? *Timmy's-down-the-well?*"

Magic jumped up and barked with excitement. The boy understood.

Chapter Fifty-Nine: SHELLY

A weird buzzing sound filled his head. Shelly blinked, for a moment unsure of his surroundings. The girl beside him struggled a bit, and he reflexively yanked and shook her by the hair until she stopped.

Must've taken too much cold medicine. That made you woozy sometimes. *Focus, focus!* His eyes narrowed and stared down at the thin athletic woman below. September Day, Sorokin Glass, the Magpie. Three in one, an unholy trinity.

Tricks again, always tricks. She stood so far away, like at the wrong end of a telescope, a dozen miles away from his elevated perch.

Her dog crawled up the woodpile like a damn cat…

Hate cats. Cat, cats that claw, cat bite, dogs barking, biting, attacking he hated 'em hated them all so much. His gun. He'd aim at the black shepherd, big furry target, punch 'em full of bullets, that'd make the evil trinity scream for sure. He giggled again. And stared at the gun in his hand. Instead of the gun he saw the flame from his lighter.

How had his gun turned into flame? Tricks again.

No, couldn't shoot the mutt yet. That'd make the dog drop the thing. The stuff Savatch needed, on the thing. Phone, that's right, the phone. Stupid reporter got himself killed over those notes, evidence Savatch carefully protected all these years. He needed to figure out who talked to Molingo, so he could silence the remaining loose ends. Needed the phone for access to whatever files the man saved. He had to do the job right. He had a reputation, couldn't mess up now.

He'd already silenced that Corazon woman… women… both of 'em, the two bitches, got what they deserved. They made him do it, too. If they'd just left everything alone.

The dog slipped, then regained footing. Climbed another two feet upward. The girl whimpered. He shook her red hair.

Once he got the phone, he'd disappear. After he shot the dog. And the trinity-person below. Maybe he'd take this cutie with him, it'd be fun to teach her manners. Savatch licked his lips. He tasted snot and spat.

Too many had seen, could identify him, to return to his old life. But he'd easily access the funds squirreled away over the years. And wait for the next call. Those in charge of Wong Enterprises—the real movers and shakers—would reach out again when they needed him. Because he delivered. They always called him. He had a reputation.

Earthquake!

No, but dizzy vision spun his world for half a dozen breaths. Shelly braced himself, putting out his hand against the pillar of smaller branches above him.

His lighter fell. The flame flickered through the interweaving mosaic of limbs like a shooting star. It hit and bumped, a bright pinball, before landing somewhere far, far below…

BWHOOSH!

The sound startled the dog. His teeth clacked, snapping at something. And missed.

Savatch screamed as the phone with the evidence fell from the dog's mouth. He shoved Melinda aside, and dove with one outstretched hand for the phone. But it followed the lighter's path, bumping all the way down, to disappear into growing flames.

Shadow tucked his tail and slicked back his ears. He licked his lips, staring down between his braced front paws. The phone, he'd dropped it. And now fire whispered and shivered below, hungry, licking the nasty oil scent and biting into the wood. The choking cloud clogged a good dog's breath. He whined, looking frantically around.

His eyes met September's far below. He'd dropped the phone. His head dropped. *Bad dog!*

"Shadow, *guard* Melinda!" With the words, September scrambled onto the lowest stack of logs. She climbed awkwardly, holding the bo staff in one hand, clawing her way upward. "*Guard!*"

He knew what that command meant. Protect. Keep safe, prevent hurts.

Shadow couldn't stop the whimpers. To be a good dog, he must be brave. Even though fire scared him. He remembered fire, how it hurt, and made fur and flesh scream where it touched. He'd fought through fire twice before, once to save September, and another time to save himself.

So he'd do it again. Because September asked.

Searching for the right paw path, his head whipped side to side. No easy or fast way to escape, with fire below and bad guy above. And in between, Melinda screamed for help.

Chapter Sixty: SEPTEMBER

H ang on, Melinda! Can you come to me? Or move to Shadow." September lobbed a smaller limb at the killer, to keep him at bay.

But for some reason, he ignored them both. Instead, he scrambled down the pile in pursuit of the dropped phone like a spider stalking prey. Didn't he realize the fire had already rendered it to twisted plastic?

More importantly, September detected no weapon. Maybe the wood pile ate his gun or knife, too. She focused on Melinda, waiting for the girl to gather her courage and climb down to meet Shadow. Just touching the dog would lend the girl the courage she needed. "Come on, you can do it. Climb down."

"But I can't!" Melinda's voice climbed an octave, terror shivering in tremolos of anguish.

The smoke grew thicker. September's attention swiveled between Shadow, Melinda, and Savatch. The man muttered to himself, crab walking on hands and knees before disappearing around the other side of the wood pile.

"Melinda, focus on Shadow. Don't look anywhere else. He'll guide you down. And I'll come to you both." She scowled, alert and wary that the man's odd behavior hid an ulterior motive. She climbed, mimicking the man's posture, grabbing handholds with her left hand but still loath to abandon her staff.

The girl's tear-streaked face broke her heart. September understood how fear could freeze you in place, paralyze any ability to function. She'd lived that way for years. Then Shadow guided her back to the light. And Combs and the kids offered a reason to stay.

Melinda half-stood on her log perch and jerked in an odd rhythm before sinking back on her butt. "I'm stuck. My ankle, it's caught." Melinda put both hands on her calf, and tugged, then gave up. "A big old log shifted. I can't move it." Her lower lip trembled. "September, I'm scared. The fire's getting worse."

Shadow finally drew abreast of the girl. His hackles bristled, and September read his fear in the dog's shaking form. Yet despite wanting to run away, he bravely stood rock solid when Melinda braced an arm on his shoulders to again try pulling her leg free.

Second by second, the heat increased, a furnace blast from below. The base of the wood pile already boasted flickers of red-orange light with snake-tongue flames eeling their way through to lick and munch the accelerant-soaked wood.

"What do I do?" Melinda's eyes, saucer big in her pale face, filled with terror.

Without prompting, Shadow sniffed the girl's leg, following it down to where her ankle disappeared in the gap. He tentatively grasped one end of the log in his jaws and tugged.

Melinda screamed. "Ow-ow-ow, stop!"

He yelped, ears pressed flat, and tail whipping. Shadow's tug shifted the log, but in the wrong direction, increasing pressure on her ankle.

"Shadow, *wait*. Good dog." He'd tried to help. She couldn't fault the effort.

Smoke billowed. If they didn't get off the pile quickly, it would collapse with them riding the pyre to the ground. "Hang on, I'm almost there." September coughed, blinking hard as her eyes welled with the acrid smoke.

From the other side of the pile, the killer screamed, words and phrases making no sense. The beams above and to that side of the stack shifted. What the hell?

Gritting her teeth, Melinda grabbed at the log that captured her. "Hurry, hurry. He's tearing it down, September, he's gonna make everything fall apart. I don't wanna die, not like this!" She no longer acted fearful, but furious. "He went after the phone, he's digging for it. Crazy, menty-b guy, he's gonna burn us up."

He should run or Brummitt would arrest him. At the thought, September stared back at the house, willing the appearance of the cavalry.

The pile shifted again, in rhythm with the killer's hidden efforts. He grunted and screamed nonsense, something about an evil trinity of witches… or maybe bitches.

Shadow barked, then barked again. He pawed September's arm.

"Good boy, Shadow. You're such a good dog." She gave him the hand signal and reinforced with the command. "Go down. *Away*, Shadow, *go*." She couldn't bear for his bravery to end this way, burned alive like a grotesque witch burning, furry familiars and all. She couldn't leave Melinda. But Shadow must escape and live on.

Combs would care for him and Willie loved dogs. Shadow would help them recover as they mourned another tragedy.

But he ignored her, again pawing September's arm. Out of a desperate need to save him, if not herself and the girl, her voice turned harsh. She stripped the words of all affection. She needed him to run.

"*Go*, Shadow! *Go!* Get away from me." She hesitated, then squared her shoulders. "Bad dog, Shadow, *bad dog*. Go, get away from me. *Go!*"

He froze. Shadow slicked back his ears, tucked his tail, turned away. He scrambled back down the pile.

She choked back a sob. *Forgive me, baby dog…* It broke her heart that he'd remember her last words as harsh, unforgiving. But he'd live.

And September needed all her focus on getting Melinda loose. To help her daughter escape this fiery bier.

Chapter Sixty-One: MAGIC

Magic galloped ahead of the golf cart. He retraced his steps across the grassy field, returning fast as he could to Lia.

"Keep the flashlight on the dog, kid." The man in the police uniform shouted when the spotlight wavered. The small vehicle slowed, climbing down and back up a culvert before revving to ascend the hillside. Magic paused to wait for them to catch up.

"EMTs are on their way. Listen, Delaney, don't you dare tell Brummitt you rode along. But I may need extra hands if we find Ms. Corazon…"

"*When* we find her. Dogs don't lie."

Magic didn't understand the young man's words but read the emotion. When the cart started moving again, and the spotlight found him, he whirled and continued running ahead.

To Lia. *Timmy's-down-the-well*. Bringing help.

That was Magic's job.

Chapter Sixty-Two: SEPTEMBER

September's precarious climb finally brought her to Melinda's level. She dropped the bo staff, and it clattered three feet down the pile. She grabbed the wooden beam trapping the girl's ankle, bracing her feet to tug and pull. Nothing budged.

Heat grew more intense. Melinda coughed almost nonstop, holding her arm over her mouth and nose. She grabbed September's arm and squeezed. With no breath to speak, the girl gestured down, emphatic.

"No." September gasped, then looked around. She remembered the knife strapped at her ankle, unsheathed it.

Carefully, she cut Melinda's bound wrists, then reached between the logs. September found the girl's sandal and cut the straps, praying that it would offer enough wiggle room to pull loose.

Melinda pulled, face red and gasping, but still couldn't free her leg. She tried to speak. The roar of the blaze muffled spoken words, but September understood.

"I love you, too." They hugged.

Over the girl's shoulder, she spied the bo staff. She also saw Shadow had stayed near the pyre. Too close, he'd get burned. Her brow wrinkled, and she squinted through the smoke. Shadow ran toward the nearby water tank. He nosed the coiled hose.

Oh my heavens, please please God…yes!

Basic safety: before lighting the stack, they drenched the surrounding area. After the stack burned down, the water killed any remaining embers.

"Shadow, good dog!" She cleared her throat and spat. Her voice, already damaged from the throttling, didn't want to cooperate. September took a big breath and shouted as loud as she could. "Wanna play hose tag? *Fetch hose,* Shadow, *fetch!*"

She turned away, trusting him to do his best. A good wetting could give them the few extra minutes they needed to escape this deathtrap. September slid down the stack to retrieve her bo staff, then climbed back up to Melinda's side.

She inserted the staff between the pinching logs. Flames had climbed both inside the stack and a third of the way on the outside. "Get ready, okay?" Before long, the fire would block any escape.

Melinda nodded. The heat felt unbearable. Blisters rose on the girl's bare legs and the ends of her long hair singed.

Below, Shadow gripped the end of the heavy canvas fire

hose in his jaws. He backed away, playing *tug* to unroll the canvas tubing. He hopped up on the wooden pile, climbed steadily, weaved his way up toward them on a rapidly closing path between spitting embers and fire.

September heaved on the bo staff. And again. One more time… The log shifted.

Melinda yanked her foot free.

Shadow crawled to their level, panting so hard September feared he'd pass out. "Good boy, such a good brave dog!" She grabbed the hose from him, twisted the nozzle, praying for enough pressure. "Close your eyes, Melinda." She doused them all with the water, immediately feeling relief, before turning to the fire marching toward them.

Spraying flames barely dampened its progress. She aimed for the least damaged outside shell of the pile, intermittently spraying the three of them. "Shadow, down boy. Good dog, Go. Go!" He'd find the best path. And they'd follow, with the life-giving water leading the way.

A lifetime later, September stood on solid ground with the other two. Holding hands, she and Melinda limped away from the bonfire, which was now fully engulfed.

"Shadow, good dog! *Come-a-pup*, let's go." She looked back when he didn't lead the way. For a long moment, Shadow stood in front of the bonfire, a silhouette backlit by the radiant blaze.

The pile collapsed with all the world's hurts. Embers climbed toward the moon like a bespangled spirit filled with new hope.

Shadow whirled and ran to join his family.

Good dog.

FRIDAY,

November 1

Chapter Sixty-Three: SEPTEMBER

September topped off her cup of coffee, and leaned against the kitchen island, taking a moment before returning to the meeting in the dining room. Shadow pressed hard against her leg, and she bent down to caress his face. The scorched tips of his ears and singed area on his tail would heal. "Baby dog, I love you so very much."

He thumped his tail. He'd forgiven her harsh words at the bonfire. No matter how badly you treated them, dogs always forgave. At least, Shadow did.

"You okay?" Combs called from the other room.

"I'm fine."

But she wasn't. It'd take more than 24 hours to recover from the past week's revelations. She grabbed the coffee pot and walked back into the dining room. Combs and Teddy sat at the table, laptop humming and paper files spread out, comparing notes with Brianna Lockhart.

The woman smiled and held up her own cup. "Thanks, I'll take a refill."

Without a word, September sloshed strong brew into the cup. Both Combs and Teddy declined. Lips tight, she returned to the kitchen to return the coffee pot. And stood there, staring into space, for a long moment.

She needed time. Needed to figure out the shift in her feelings. At least the kids weren't here. Melinda remained in hospital, being treated for smoke inhalation, second degree burns, and a twisted ankle. Thank God her physical injuries weren't serious. Time would tell about the emotional scars.

Tonight, Willie had gone to the theater's Halloween party with high hopes of winning the costume contest. He decided to forgo his penchant for nefarious characters. Instead, he covered himself in aluminum foil as the Tin Man because he always acted brave despite creaky joints—just like his dad. She'd seen Combs surreptitiously wipe his eyes hearing that. They'd pick him up later tonight.

Melinda would be discharged in the morning. Lia's injury meant longer hospitalization. Magic wasn't happy about his incarceration at Doc Eugene's clinic. But now, they discussed the incarceration that started this week of mayhem.

"Need help?" Combs called again. If she didn't join them, he'd follow her and force a conversation she wasn't ready to have.

"I'm coming." Her voice still sounded rough.

Purple and yellow marks encircled her throat, but the bruises went far deeper.

Lockhart opened a file folder for all to see. "After multiple interviews with Wyatt Teves, my team compiled a list of contacts with connections to his conviction. Interestingly, Drummond's investigation only looked at Teves. No other suspects were considered or questioned."

Combs nodded. "Not unusual. You assign resources based on the evidence. No need to chase zebras when you've already lassoed the horse."

"Granted. But Teves always claimed they set him up. His public defender did nothing for him." Lockhart tapped the chart. "Lots of coincidences put Teves in the wrong place at the wrong time. He'd joined Wong's security team just six months before. Why'd he get team leader status with next to no experience? He was promised a pay bonus, but the big carrot was a free trip to Texas. He wanted to meet his daughter, Apikalia."

September frowned. "This happened, what, fifteen years ago? Lia only found out about Wyatt last year."

Lockhart adjusted her glasses. "He never got the chance to see Lia. Wong's murder happened two days after his arrival in Dallas." She shrugged. "I don't know all the details about what happened between Lia and her grandparents, but Mrs. Corazon decided she wanted to repair her relationship with Lia. She contacted me at the Innocence Project and advocated for Teves to get the ball rolling."

Cornelia Corazon turned out to be the big winner in all of this. Grammy had as good as moved into Lia's hospital room. September guessed she'd drive Lia—and her medical team— nuts.

"How'd she get the ball rolling?" Combs leaned forward.

"Takes more than a phone call, and claims of being framed."

Teddy took off and polished his wire rims. "She gave Ricky Molingo a juicy tip to investigate. I'm guessing she might have offered a financial one as well."

Lockhart nodded. "Teves had a list of people he suspected had a hand in framing him." She flipped a page in the file. "I passed that list on to Cornelia Corazon. Mr. Molingo proceeded to interview them, and possibly a few more." She pursed her lips. "Mrs. Corazon told me up front she didn't want Lia to know anything unless we had a reasonable chance to overturn the conviction. And based on our conversations, I think she'd be just as happy if the investigation confirmed his guilt." She shook her head ruefully. "I've not had much communication with Lia herself, nor with the other daughter, Pilikia Teves."

Combs nodded. He'd worked with Officer Tee Teves briefly a year or so ago. "She's openly skeptical of her father's claims." He shrugged. "Can't say I blame her, or Mrs. Corazon. The man was investigated, tried, and convicted. And y'all want to challenge that? Why? On what grounds?"

"Probably not much to go on, until now." Teddy squinted at his laptop. "I've got a copy of Molingo's phone documents. I'll leave the lawyering to you, Ms. Lockhart, but seems to me there's a good shot at getting Wyatt Teves a new trial, and maybe acquitted."

Lockhart's eyes widened. "You got Molingo's interviews? How?" She looked at September. "I thought his phone burned in the fire."

"Yep, along with Detective Sheldon Savatch. They found what was left of his body." September shuddered. A horrible way to die, but she took comfort knowing he couldn't hurt anyone else.

Teddy grinned. "Nothing digital ever goes away. A true writing pro, Molingo saved copies. Found it in the cloud." He glanced at Combs's frowning visage. "No worries, I sent it to Detective Brummitt. Just overlooked mentioning I kept a copy."

September smiled at Lockhart. "Teddy's got skills."

"So I see." She looked from the older man to Combs and September in turn. "Appears y'all got skills."

"I couldn't figure out why Savatch didn't run." September stroked Shadow's neck again. "At the bonfire, I mean. He had plenty of time to get away but acted, I don't know, sick? Deranged?"

"Typical of bad guys." Combs snorted. "As a species, they're not all that smart."

"More than that. I agree, a murderer has to be wired different." She struggled to put into words what she'd witnessed on the bonfire. "I told you about the bird die off when I tracked Lia's cat, and found Molingo, right? Doc Eugene suspected bird flu. The labs haven't come back yet." She hugged herself. "I worried about Macy getting sick. My cat got exposed, too," she added, for Lockhart's benefit.

At his name, Macy meowed from the kitchen. She'd need to feed him soon and give him the first dose of his new medication. "Luckily, he's fine." Maybe she'd get him another cat tree to help him with an extra boost to the elevations he loved.

"And that has relevance, because…?" Lockhart raised her eyebrows.

"Savatch also got exposed to avian flu when he killed Molingo. It's nasty." She shivered, remembering his red-eyed visage.

Teddy whistled. He quickly tapped the keys on the

computer. "How about that. Says avian flu is considered rare in people, but can cause life-threatening respiratory signs, and red inflamed eyes. Severe signs include neurological symptoms. The CDC lists seizures, even altered consciousness." He looked up from the screen. "The little boy you found out there, Peter? Also exposed, so probably should get him checked out, too."

Lockhart refocused on her notes. "Molingo talked to Clarence Walford and his wife a few days before they were killed."

"That's right. Walford worked at the Grand Chisholm Hotel when all this went down. Found Wong in the pool." Combs cracked his knuckles, something he always did when stressed.

"Yep." Teddy elaborated. "Walford identified Wyatt Teves as the last to see Wong alive. According to the deposition, Walford witnessed the two arguing over something. He didn't know what. He testified that Wong threatened to call police and have Teves arrested. That'd put a kibosh on seeing his daughter."

That didn't scan with what September knew about Wong. "Why would Henry Wong call the police? He had his own enforcement people." She raised her eyebrows. "Doesn't seem like the kind of threat he'd make."

"Right. Teves says he got vetted six ways to Sunday before getting hired, so that always seemed contrived to me as well. His defense never contested the testimony, or much of anything. Prosecution needed a motive, so they made one up." Lockhart tapped her fingers on the file. "Teves swears he never spoke to Wong. He got hired by Kaliko Wong, the man's wife. Now deceased."

September and Teddy shared a look.

"And before you ask, nope, there's no video evidence. Fifteen years ago, they relied on eyeballs, not recordings."

"How's any of that connected to today's situation?" Combs leaned forward, ticking off names on his fingers. "We've got Walford and his wife dead days after Molingo. Then Drummond's killed after threatening Lia. Sure, there's a tenuous connection to a fifteen-year-old crime, but—"

"Walford's wife got their killer on video." Teddy grinned at their surprise. "The Dallas PD tried to keep that quiet, but somebody leaked it. Sorry, Combs."

Teddy continued. "The killer, dressed as a clown, rang the doorbell like a trick-or-treat visit." Teddy tapped his keyboard, then swung it around for them to watch. "Detective Greer found the clown nose on Drummond's body. His partner Detective Savatch pointed it out. Convenient, eh?"

September shivered. "They already had Lia as a person of interest, with the video of Drummond at her room in the hotel. That, and Magic's bite marks on the man." She shivered. Similar play book, trying to frame the girl.

"Savatch volunteered to interview Lia." Combs turned to September. "He waited for her at the kennels but caught you instead." He grabbed her hand and squeezed it. "Detective Greer had his own suspicions about the man, I'm told. The bullets that killed Walford came from a.357 Magnum revolver, not Lia's semiautomatic. They found another victim in Dallas, killed with a knife around the same time as Drummond, still clutching the clown wig. Forensics isolated blond hair in the wig."

Her voice softened, speaking her thoughts aloud. "Lia wore a clown costume visiting kids at the hospital last Friday night. Oh my gosh!" Her eyes widened. "Savatch tried to frame Lia for Walford's murder, pushed Drummond to confront her, then killed him, too."

"Greer said the blond hair came from two different donors. One had frizzy blond hair like Lia," said Combs, "the other long straight strands like Savatch."

"Planting evidence, using Lia's own property to frame her." Lockhart sipped her coffee and set the cup down with care. "Just like he did with Teves. Maybe others. Savatch partnered with Drummond back in the day. They had access to records, evidence, and witnesses, probably bribe funds to influence those who resisted." She sat back in the chair. "I got a call from Detective Greer that set off alarms." She tapped her forehead. "I hadn't yet decided what to do when Lia called me. So I told her to run."

"If you hadn't warned her," September said, "Savatch would've killed Lia at the kennels when she *resisted arrest*." She put up air quotes around the last two words. "And I probably would've been the one to find her the next day." She shivered. "Instead, Lia ran and Savatch targeted me by mistake."

Or was it a mistake? Were the hoofbeats from horses or zebras? She needed to have another heart-to-heart with Jack, since he claimed to have a finger on the pulse of Wong Enterprises.

"Speculation." Combs rubbed his eyes. "Glad I'm not the one filing the reports."

September's shoulders stiffened. Yet something else to figure out.

Shadow pawed her leg when she felt her pulse rate increase. She finger-combed the silky thick fur behind his ears, careful to avoid the tender edges. Such a brave, good boy. He leaned into the sensation, moaning with pleasure.

The contact immediately helped calm her.

Combs hadn't wanted the Paladin Group's involvement. Neither had she, not at first. But would earlier engagement have saved lives or avoided injury? The dead kept their secrets, unless Molingo's notes worked in their favor.

Bottom line, someone wanted Henry Wong dead and made Wyatt Teves the fall guy. Kaliko Wong had the most to gain as his widow. She'd inherited Wong Enterprises, wielded all the power, commanded all the money. With her also dead, who benefited most to keep the secret buried?

Everything came back to Wong Enterprises. Or did it instead simply come down to Savatch and his crew protecting themselves? One could hope…

September drank the rest of her coffee in two gulps. "Why did Savatch take out Drummond? What soured the partnership?"

Combs added his own take. "Drummond only had a couple more years before he could retire fully vested. I'll take the bet he got paid off for looking the other way on the Teves case. The man was a jerk, but I can't see Drummond for murder. Savatch pulled all the strings, and when Drummond pushed back…" He shrugged. "Detective Greer said Savatch took a leave of absence for his mother's funeral. Then unexpectedly showed up at Drummond's murder scene."

Lockhart grinned. "That's when Greer called me. Said it had a whiff of something bad." She glanced at Teddy. "Savatch's mother died twenty years ago."

Teddy laughed. "Somebody else here got some skills."

So many names. Savatch. Walford. Drummond. And who else? Two were cops sworn to protect and serve, a north star she'd always trusted to guide her decisions.

Teddy pulled the laptop back toward him. "Here's what our facts seem to support. Molingo reached out to Savatch for an interview. The detective killed Molingo when he found out Walford pointed a finger at him, then took out Walford and his wife. He learns that a *Corazon woman*," Teddy used air quotes on the name, "started Molingo down the trail, so that's the next on the hit parade. He reaches out to one-time partner Drummond, who's already paranoid, and revs him up to go after Lia."

Lockhart scribbled more notes on the file. "So, we think Savatch pressured Walford to incriminate Wyatt and paid off his partner Drummond to make sure the investigation goes as planned, maybe paying off other witnesses, or influencing them in other ways. Most of the staff at the Grand Chisolm are gone after fifteen years. The public defender died six months after Wyatt's conviction." Lockhart shrugged. "Mugged, died of knife wounds."

"Molingo also talked to James Mann. And he reached out to Stanford Frisco." Teddy continued tapping the keyboard.

"Exactly." Lockhart made a few more notes. "James Mann prosecuted the case. Judge Frisco tried the case. Bet Savatch talked to them recently. Molingo, too. Easy enough for the police to find out."

Two detectives and maybe a prosecutor colluded to convict Wyatt Teves of Henry Wong's murder. While she'd always respected the police, and even fell head over heels for a detective, how could she continue to trust them?

"Did Savatch kill Henry Wong? And how'd he get the funds to pay off all these people?" September knew the answer. She just wanted confirmation. Evidence. She didn't know what to do with a world where bad guys made up the rules.

Lockhart shrugged. "Doesn't really matter from my perspective. We have more than enough to get Wyatt a new trial." She grinned. "Today's a great day for justice."

"Hey folks?" Teddy took off his glasses and rubbed his nose. "Just got a news alert. Funny you just mentioned the name Frisco."

"Why?" Lockhart leaned forward.

"They just found Stanford Frisco in his home. Murder-Suicide. He took out his wife first." He took off his glasses to polish on his shirt but couldn't seem to get them clean.

SATURDAY,

November 2

Chapter Sixty-Four: MELINDA

Melinda carefully climbed out of the hospital bed. She winced, stiffness and bruises only now announcing themselves. Her ankle, strapped and swollen, felt much better after overnight icing and a bandage wrap. She worried it could interfere with cheer practice. She missed the football game last night but planned to return to the squad by the next game. For sure.

Dad and September promised to pick her up after lunch today, any minute. She hoped they'd bring fresh clothes. The hospital gown sucked, but the fire and smoke had ruined the cute outfit she'd worn to the hayride. Her sandals burned.

Melinda limped into the bathroom and made a face in the mirror. No makeup, rats nest hair, a bruise purpling her chin. And—ohmygoshnonono—a bald spot?

She whimpered and fingered the sensitive area. That sonofapeachpit yanked out a hunk of her hair. She wanted to die…

Well, not really. Not after what she'd just survived.

But what the heck, would it grow back? What to do until then? What if it stayed bare? She could hear the catcalls already. *Hey baldy… all wigged out… naked wonder…* "Oh gawd!"

A hat. She'd make it a fashion statement. "You can do this." She finger-combed the part in her hair on the other side, flipping the long curly tresses to cover the spot.

Knock-knock. And again, *knock-knock-knock.*

Great. Time to go home. She wanted to curl up in her own bed with earbuds and her iPad and forget about the nightmare of yesterday.

"Just a minute." Dad and September wouldn't tease her, but Willie would. She wet her palm and smoothed the hair over the bare place, before heading back into the room. "About time. Can't wait to get a shower, and—"

Delaney stood in the open doorway. Dark circles under his brown eyes made him even more attractive. "Hey Melinda."

"Uh, oh hi. Uhm." Her cheeks warmed. She sidled back to the bed, keeping the gaping back of the gown away from him, and sat. "How're you doing? I mean, you got checked out by the docs okay and everything?"

He nodded, flipping long hair out of his eyes. "I wanted to thank you. For helping. I mean, you coulda got killed." He mumbled the last and knuckled his eyes. "Sure didn't want anyone to get hurt. Except for that… that…"

"Yeah. I get it. Glad you're okay, too." After all, Delaney wasn't used to all this mayhem stuff the way she was, after Dad working as a cop for years—and September being a magnet for bad guys. "I'm fine. My dad and September are coming to spring me any minute." She smiled. He really did have the most amazing eyes.

"I got you something."

She grinned. "Aw, you didn't have to—"

"Sorry, no. I mean, something came for you. Figured you could pass it over to September. Not a gift. Oh hell, guess I should have brought you a thank you gift. Sheesh, sometimes I'm clueless, ya know?" He had a small mailer in his hands, one of those next-day-delivery packages. Delaney shuffled forward and held it out. "It looked important."

She put the mailer on the bed. "Like I said, she'll be here any minute. Why'd it come to you?"

"Came to Uncle Ricky at the house." He shrugged. "I think he'd want September to have it, especially since we're leaving soon." Delaney wouldn't meet her eyes. "My aunt got here this morning. She's really upset about all this." He waved his hand, taking in the past week's trauma. "She lives in Kentucky. Wants to take me and Peter back there with her."

Melinda sucked in a breath and slowly let it out. "You're moving?"

"If it was just me, I'd stay for sure. It's my senior year and everything. But Peter, he's reeling from this. Oh, Lia said we can take Kai with us, the pup saved my life. And she really helps keep Peter calm. The kid's been through so much, and he's scared more bad people could still come after him." He smiled weakly. "Can't say he's wrong. That detective guy was off the chain."

"Okay." Her voice trembled on the whispered word. "But I'll miss you. Kinda." She swallowed hard. Wasn't like they were together, or anything. They weren't even in the same class. He was a senior. She wouldn't turn fifteen until her birthday in January. Delaney probably thought she was just a kid, like Peter. He only knew her from cheer team.

He reached out and took her hand, squeezed it and let go. "I'll miss you too. Maybe we'll see each other again sometime." He touched her bruised chin softly. "Feel better soon, Lindy." He turned to go.

"Wait. Why not wait for September?" She lifted the package, hoping to delay his departure.

Delaney shook his head. "I've been quizzed inside-out by the cops… the police, I mean. Any more questions and I might have a meltdown myself." He grinned, flipped his hair, and disappeared out the door.

She stared after him, sighed deeply, and cupped her hand to her chin where he'd touched her. Why'd he have to leave? Going to Kentucky, about a million miles away. She couldn't help a sniffle. Every time something cool happened, September's bad luck spilled over and ruined it.

Melinda fingered the mailer and flipped it to read the return address. If it came to Ricky Molingo, it probably had something to do with his investigation. Might even answer the questions that got Delaney's uncle killed.

The return address said *Judge Stanford Frisco, Fort Worth*. A judge. That meant lawyer stuff, she bet. And whatever was inside would just send September off on another dangerous *project*.

September's *projects* always stirred up trouble. That last *project* nearly got Willie hurt. The one before that almost killed Dad. This one ended up sending Delaney and his little brother away, clear across the country. And almost got Melinda herself burned to a crispy critter. The Paladin Group was supposed to keep them safe, but nothing had changed.

Dashing away tears, Melinda stuffed the envelope into the cloth bag containing her soiled clothes and waited for her ride home. She'd check out the contents before delivering the package.

If she delivered it.

Let other people chase bad guys for a change. Her dad—and September, too—deserved a break from all the *projects*.

Somebody had to protect them. It might as well be her.

FACT, FICTION, & ACKNOWLEDGMENTS

Thank you for reading TRICK OR TREAT, and I hope you enjoyed this ninth book in the September & Shadow thriller series. Thank you, too, for coming along with me on the adventure. There never would have been *Thrillers With Bite* without you, dear reader, adopting these books.

After publishing 35+ nonfiction pet books, research fuels my curiosity. While in fiction I get to make up *crappiocca*, as September would say, much of my inspiration comes from news stories, past and present—the weirder, the better. For me, and I hope for you, the story becomes more engaging when built not on "what if" but "it happened." So in each book, I like to include a Cliff's Notes version of what's real and what's made up.

As with the other books in the series, much of TRICK OR TREAT arises from science, especially dog and cat behavior and learning theory, and the benefits of service dogs. By definition, thrillers include murder and mayhem, but as an animal advocate professional, I make a conscious choice to not show a pet's death in any of my books. All bets are off with the human characters, though.

Before September can move forward with her life, she must address the past, including issues that affect her family and friends. Lia's story and resolving the relationship with her father Wyatt Teves (and Grammy!) opens future possibilities for collaboration with September's Paladin Group.

Because Lia and her animals played such a central role, TRICK OR TREAT had lots of extra furry characters…maybe a bit overwhelming? Let me know in your reviews. The animal viewpoints always make me smile, like brain candy for this author, so perhaps I went a bit overboard.

I rely on a vast number of veterinarians, behaviorists, consultants, trainers, pet-centric writers and readers, and rescue organizations that share their incredible resources and support to make my stories as believable as possible. Find out more information at IAABC.org, Dogwriters.org and CatWriters.com. For other expert advice, I rely on colleagues and research sources to keep stories as authentic and realistic as possible.

FACT: The *show me* game is real, created by trainer Kayce Cover as a vocabulary exercise to be used with a variety of animals, and which my own dog loves to play.

See https://synalia.com

FACT: Macy's diagnosis arose in the second book in the series, HIDE AND SEEK. All cats are at risk for hypertrophic cardiomyopathy (HCM), even that random-bred rescue beauty sleeping on your lap. Gene tests for the disease are available for some cat breeds including Maine Coon cats. Research funds are needed to make tests more widely available and ferret out the cause(s) of HCM and other cat-specific illnesses that take our cat friends from us far too early. As an added bonus, research into pet diseases often has applications and benefits to human health. The **Every Cat Health Foundation** (formerly Winn Feline Foundation) at Everycat.org is worthy of your support in this endeavor. Yes, it's a fact Macy's experimental medication has been released and still seeks feline participants in the ongoing study! Learn more at https://www.dvm360.com/view/first-drug-shown-to-reverse-feline-hcm-expected-to-receive-fda-conditional-approval and talk with your veterinarian to see if your cat would benefit to participate in the study, details in this link: https://www.hcmincats.com/halt

FICTION: Pet viewpoint chapters are pure speculation, although I would love to read dog and cat minds. However, I make every attempt to base animal characters' motivations and actions on canine and feline body language, scent discrimination, and the science behind the human-animal bond.

FACT: Yes, avian flu does wipe out susceptible birds, often waterfowl. Lately, though, back yard chickens and even some commercial poultry farmers have been affected by contamination crossing into some pet foods that use these sources. With virtually no treatment available for the birds, this can devastate flocks. And yes, cats that eat infected birds can become very sick (with dogs apparently more resistant). Learn more about avian flu and how it affects pets at these links: https://vcahospitals.com/press-center/vca-news/bird-flu-and-cats-frequently-asked-questions and https://catvets.com/clinical-resources/h5n1-in-cats

FACT & FICTION: Yes, avian flu can infect people! I've taken a bit of poetic license with Detective Savatch's illness, because frankly, I wanted him to suffer (he's a bad-bad man!). Here's the science: https://www.cdc.gov/bird-flu/signs-symptoms/index.html

FACT: Yes, many dogs (and likely other animals) may develop signs of PTSD. Shadow's traumatic experiences with fire set the stage for him to remember and do his best to avoid future encounters with such situations. Of course, that makes him that much more a hero when he overcomes his fear to save his special people. Learn more about canine PTSD here: https://vetmed.tamu.edu/news/pet-talk/caring-for-a-dog-with-ptsd/

FICTION…Kinda: While lots of Halloween events around the country include hayrides, bonfires, and cornfield mazes, I made all of mine up. And then…I must have been channeling the real deal, because I discovered Marble Falls, Texas has a Texas-shaped maze of 10-foot-tall grass. What fun! Should you want to visit, check it out here: https://sweetberryfarm.com/mazes.html

FACT: Real-life pets inspired some of the animal characters in TRICK OR TREAT. I've held a "Name That Dog/Name That Cat" contest for each of the novels in the series. For this most recent contest I limited nominations to my newsletter subscribers (join the list if you'd like to nominate your pet for a future book!).

I narrowed the nominations down to ten cat finalists, eleven dog finalists, and nine hero horse finalists. See pictures of the winners here.

Congratulations to **Carol Viescas** for nominating the winning hero dog, **Kai**! He received almost 51% of the votes, totaling over 11,000 votes. Wow!

"Our mixed breed Kai was found out in the desert by our vet techs. One of the techs fostered her until we adopted her. Kai, possibly a husky/shepherd and terrier mix, is 40 pounds of love, very protective but she does like to dig in the backyard."

Congratulations to **Ulrike Stein** for the winning cat nomination, a lovely longhaired gray and white boy named **Pippo.** He received 32% of the votes.

"Pippo is an 8-year-old male cat, dumped in a cardboard box at only five weeks of age. He is a food thief and therefore has learned to open bread boxes to chew on the bread, cabinets to take out treat bags, drawers just to look inside. He has dared to put his nose in the dog's dish and has lifted the cover of pans on the stove, to put his paw in the warm food. Ah, and if I am not quick enough, his paw will be inside my coffee mug! Sometimes it is practical because he does the dishes with his tongue and leaves the plates absolutely clean. He jumps on my face while I'm asleep ever since he was a kitten, I still have a scar over my nose between my eyes. In April he tried to reach the upper cupboard in the kitchen, missed it, hit his face and broke his upper canine tooth."

Congratulations to **Shari Lovelace** for the winning horse nomination, a gorgeous red pony with a dark mane and tail named **Sebastian.** He received 45% of the votes.

"Sebastian is a therapy pony that has helped my granddaughter through some issues and is a wonderful, gentle and a caring pony. He seems to actually care for my granddaughter and follows her and helps bring her out of her shell. She does ride him, bareback, so he can feel her close to him for bonding!" Since this is fiction, I fudged a bit on Sebastian's size. After all, small doesn't mean they aren't also brave and courageous!

THANK YOU to everyone who took part in the contest and to all the winners. I think they all deserve treats. Maybe even catnip, a carrot, and bacon!

FICTION: For purposes of the story, I changed the coat color of Lia's cat. In book #4 FIGHT OR FLIGHT, Gizmo the orange kitten grew up with Magic the dog. In TRICK OR TREAT, Lia has changed the cat's name to Pippo (one of the winning hero pets). Poor nutrition can turn black cat fur into a red color; Siamese and some other pointed cats are born white and develop color as they mature; and temperature also influences coat color. While kitten coat color can and does change, sometimes drastically, and a shorthair baby may develop into a longhair adult beauty, it's unlikely to change from even a pale orange to gray and white. I claim poetic license!

FACT: The Dallas Police Training Academy is real. Lia goes through the Basic Training Academy for 40 weeks of training with a total of 1400 hours of instruction. Different police academies in various parts of the country may use different terminology for instructors or have slightly different programs. In Dallas, Academy Instructors are experts in various aspects of policing and often rotate in and out teaching their specialty. After the training academy, new officers are assigned to one of the seven Patrol Divisions for 24 weeks of field training under the tutelage of experienced Field Training Officers (FTOs). This, of course, is a work of fiction so any errors in fact are simply in service to the story.

FACT: The Federal Bureau of Prisons has a site in Beaumont, Texas with an inmate population of people awaiting trial for violating federal laws or those who have already been convicted of committing a federal crime. The Innocence Project of Texas reviews cases of those that meet specific requirements:

- You must be claiming actual innocence. Either no crime occurred, or a crime did happen, but you did not have a role in it.

- Your conviction is a felony. They do not review misdemeanor cases.

- Your conviction took place in a Texas court.

- You have been convicted and have completed your direct appeals.

The average exoneree still spends 14+ years in prison, which makes Wyatt Teves 15 years imprisoned more believable. For the sake of the story, attorney Brianna Lockhart lives and works in Lubbock, Texas. In fact, the Texas Tech University School of Law in Lubbock provides legal representation to approved cases of those unable to afford an attorney. The school and students work with the Texas Innocence Project via their own Innocence Clinic. Learn more here: https://www.depts.ttu.edu/law/clinics-and-externships/clinics/innocence/index.php

FACT: This book would not have happened without an incredible support team of friends, family and accomplished colleagues. Special thanks to my editor, Nicola Aquino of Spit & Polish Editing, and first readers Kristi Brashier, Carol Shenold, Frank Steele, BJ Thompson, Marci Kladnik and

Andrea Neal for your eagle eyes, spot-on comments and unflagging encouragement and support. My ARC team (advanced reader copy team) also offered great help. Youse guyz rock!

I continue to be indebted to the International Thriller Writers organization, which launched my fiction career by welcoming me into the Debut Authors Program. Wow, just look, now I have nine books in a series! The authors, readers and industry mavens who make up this organization are some of the most generous and supportive people I have ever met. Long live the bunny slippers with teeth (and the rhinestone #1-Bitch Pin).

Finally, I am grateful to all the cats and dogs I've met over the years who have shared my heart and often my pillow. Shadow-Pup and Karma-Kat, and the new Trinity-Kitten inspire me daily. And the pets who live on in my heart continue to bring happy memories.

I never would have been a reader and now a writer if not for my fantastic parents, Phil and Mary Monteith, who instilled in me a love of the written word, and never looked askance when my stuffed animals and invisible wolf friend told fantastical stories. And of course, my deepest thanks to my husband Mahmoud, who continues to support my writing passion, even when he doesn't always understand it.

I love hearing from you! Please drop me a line at my blog https://AmyShojai.com or my website https://shojai.com and now my new Amy's Book Store where you can subscribe to my PET PEEVES newsletter, purchase discounted books (and maybe win some pet books!). Follow me on twitter @amyshojai and like me on Facebook: http://www.facebook.com/amyshojai.cabc.

ABOUT THE AUTHOR

Amy Shojai is a certified animal behavior consultant, and the award-winning author of more than <u>35 bestselling pet books</u> that cover furry babies to old fogies, first aid to natural healing, and behavior/training to Chicken Soupicity. She has been featured as an expert in hundreds of print venues including The Wall Street Journal, New York Times, Reader's Digest, and Family Circle, as well as television networks such as CNN, Fox News, and Animal Planet's DOGS 101 and CATS 101. Amy brings her unique pet-centric viewpoint to public appearances. She is also a playwright and co-author of STRAYS, THE MUSICAL and the author of the critically acclaimed <u>THRILLERS WITH BITE</u> pet-centric thriller series. Stay up to date with new books and appearances by visiting Shojai.com to subscribe to <u>Amy's Pets Peeves newsletter.</u>